IT DIES
WITH
YOU

IT DIES WITH YOU

A Novel

SCOTT BLACKBURN

CROOKED LANE

NEW YORK

Copyright © 2022 by Scott Blackburn

Published in the United States by Crooked Lane Books, an imprint of The Quick Brown Fox & Company LLC.

Crooked Lane Books and its logo are trademarks of The Quick Brown Fox & Company LLC.

Library of Congress Catalog-in-Publication data available upon request.

ISBN (hardcover): 978-1-64385-939-2
ISBN (ebook): 978-1-64385-940-8

Cover design by Nicole Lecht

Printed in the United States.

www.crookedlanebooks.com

Crooked Lane Books
34 West 27th St., 10th Floor
New York, NY 10001

First Edition: June 2022

10 9 8 7 6 5 4 3 2 1

To my wife, Tiffany, the best fighter I know.

CHAPTER ONE

I was bouncing at Red Door Taproom on a Friday night in January, which all but guaranteed that I'd be earning every last cent of my paycheck. My boss, Brent Thompson, had come up with this "genius" idea to kick up a little winter business: two-dollar drafts on Fridays. It was his weekly counterpunch to Shooters Pub across the street, which had bigger TVs and the best live music in town. For the most part, the lure of cheap beer worked. What that usually spelled for me was fireworks in some form or another.

That night, I was working the downstairs bar, a room the fire marshal claimed could safely hold one hundred and twenty people. But it felt more like three hundred bodies were packed together, separated only by clothing and sweat. Despite the crowd, things had been pretty uneventful for most of my shift, and I aimed to keep it that way. I hadn't been bouncing for long, but I prided myself on being able to spot potential trouble, redirect it before it grew into something bigger. Sometimes I could see it in people's eyes, their body language.

Around ten o'clock, a group came through the door that sent up all sorts of red flags. Four meatheads, drunk out of their minds, with various asshole calling cards: tight T-shirts despite the cold; shitty tribal tattoos; lats flared out like silverback gorillas. They shouldered through an ever-swelling horde, and when they passed by me, I offered a friendly nod to a couple of them. I hoped to establish a casual rapport, but neither nodded back. One of them even sized me up. It's something I'd grown used to. At six feet, a hundred and sixty-five pounds, I looked more like a tennis player than a boxer with fifteen professional bouts under his belt. Even the beard I'd recently grown didn't seem to score me any intimidation points.

I was keeping a close eye on the silverback crew, watching their endless parade of fist bumps and Fireball shots, when Sabrina, one of our bartenders, came by carrying an ice bucket jammed with Miller Lite bottles. She had a look on her face I knew all too well.

"You good?" I asked.

"Some prick just grabbed my ass."

"Which one?"

After a conga line of a bachelorette party stumbled by, Sabrina indicated a bald guy in jeans, a blue and white flannel. He had a couple inches on me, and at least fifty pounds of the corn-fed, country-boy variety.

"The dude dressed for a hoedown?"

She nodded.

I stayed cool. I maneuvered my way through a group of drunks, and when I reached the guy, I put my hand softly on his elbow and leaned close. "Think it's time you tabbed out and called it a night, sir."

He yanked his meaty arm away and took a step back, nearly knocking down a frat-boy type who was too shitfaced to notice. "The hell are you talking about? I just fucking got here."

The slight slur of his words assured me that Red Door hadn't been his first stop of the evening. "You can't put your hands on our staff," I told him. "That's the quickest ticket out the door. Now pay your tab and let's roll."

"Your staff?" He laughed. "You mean those skanks with shorts riding up their ass cracks, rubbing their titties up on everybody when they walk by? The hell out of here, bro."

"If this is the way you want to play things, fine by me. You had your chance." I whistled to get a bouncer's attention. Threw up a hand signal when he looked my way: pinky and pointer fingers up like bullhorns. *Time to wrangle a dickhead.*

Greg was born-to-be-a-bouncer big. Me and the ass grabber, put together, big. He parted the crowd with the grace of a juggernaut and made his way over.

"This gentleman giving you a problem, Hud?"

"He's just leaving. Can't seem to keep his hands to himself."

The man said, "That's cute, calling your boyfriend over here because you can't handle the job yourself. Hell, I thought maybe you were banging Daisy Dukes over there. Guess I was wrong."

Greg winked at me. "I got this one." He grabbed the man's arm, and he wasn't so gentle when he turned him toward the closest exit and began escorting him out. The guy tried to break free of Greg's grip a couple of times, like a bratty kid being dragged from the toy section at Walmart, but his attempts were fruitless.

He jerked his head back toward me. "Let me at least pay my tab, asshole. My card is at the bar!"

"I already gave you that chance. Twice. You can pick your card up tomorrow when you chill out."

Greg got him to the door and gave him a firm nudge to the sidewalk.

The man turned, angry as hell. He painted the air with middle fingers, started hurling insults at the both of us. I thought "Twiggy" and "Biggie" was pretty damn clever.

Greg blocked the door and crossed his arms, snarkily grinning at the temper tantrum. Not a good move on his part, a little too casual—a chink in his armor that the man took advantage of with a swift kick to his balls. Greg dropped to his knees. Quickly, I shielded him from another kick, which my left rib cage took the brunt of. I caught hold of the doorframe and pushed myself upright. The man took a few steps back onto the sidewalk and got into a fighting stance. His version of a fighting stance, anyway. His legs were barely spread apart, knees locked, hands too low.

"Come on, bitch!" He beckoned me with his lead left. "Your boyfriend can't save your ass now."

Just like that, we'd become a spectacle. Half a dozen awe-faced drunks were dammed in the entrance behind the mountain of Greg, who was still hunched over, searching for breath that was surely minutes away. College-aged kids walking the sidewalks with pizza slices and jumbo to-go cups stopped and stared. A group waiting to get into Shooters Pub jockeyed for a better view. At least a few people had their cell phones out, aimed our way.

"This is the last time I'm warning you," I told the man. "Best leave while you're ahead." While I was speaking, I'd raised my hands in feigned submission and slid my right foot back to steady my base.

The man shed his flannel and tossed it onto the hood of a nearby truck. He made a show of cracking his neck and his knuckles, then settled into his clunky stance. I'd learned early in my boxing career that even good fighters usually signal, inadvertently, that they're about to throw a punch. A twitch of the shoulder, a swivel of the hips. This guy may as well have been holding up a sign: "Here comes a haymaker!" His eyes got big, he stepped heavy, and he loaded a right hook that came like a telephone pole. I ducked under it, pushed him to create some distance. When he found his balance, he squared with me again and swung a looping left that I dodged as easily as the first.

"Are you done yet?" I asked. "This is getting embarrassing."

I shuffled back, but he charged, ducking his head in an attempt to tackle me. I shifted a quarter turn, parried the oncoming train with my arms, and let gravity do its thing. He slid across the pavement like he was stealing second.

I leaned over him just as he rolled himself onto his back. I noted the road rash on his forehead. "That's going to sting like a son of a bitch in the shower."

His bleary eyes seemed to focus. With what energy he could summon, he spit, catching the side of my neck. I shrugged, using my shoulder to wipe it away, then clinched his shirt with my left as my right fist tightened.

"Fucking chill, Hudson!" a voice came from behind me. My boss's voice.

I released the guy's shirt and stood.

Brent yelled to the onlookers: "Show's over! Everybody go home!"

One of our bartenders struggled to help a green-faced Greg to his feet. Brent led me around the building to a side entrance for employees. He told a young barback washing pint glasses to get lost when we got inside. Once we were alone: "The hell did you just do, Hud?"

"What do you mean 'the hell did you do'? That guy just assaulted three of your employees, Brent. He grabbed Sabrina's ass, kicked Greg's nuts through his throat, then kicked the shit out of me." The mention of the kick immediately registered the pain in my side that adrenaline had mostly warded off to that point. I held my hand against it and winced.

"So you decided to handle your business on the sidewalk? Damn, man. You know you can't do that shit outside our property. As soon as you step out that door, it becomes an issue for me. How many times did you hit that guy?"

"I didn't hit him."

Brent stared at me. "Dude was on the ground and had blood on his face. What do you mean you didn't hit him?"

"His drunk ass fell face-first on the sidewalk is what I mean. I didn't lay a hand on him."

Brent seemed to recalculate the scene in his head. He ran a hand through his slick black hair and then crossed his arms that were sleeved in a collage of colorful tattoos of koi fish and pinup girls. "Well, you were *about* to hit him. And you know how that shit would've ended."

"I wasn't going to hit that dude," I said, not entirely convinced that I wouldn't have, had he made the wrong move.

"I'm not going to debate this. I just need you to clock out and go on home, cool your jets."

"Come on, man. I've got two more hours on this shift. I need the money, and you need the bodies. Place is packed. I'm fine."

"Haven't your fists got you in enough trouble this year?"

I winced but tried to keep an even keel. "That's not fair, Brent."

"Maybe it is, maybe it isn't, but you need to go, Hud. *Now*."

I grabbed my jacket from the coat rack and made it to my '99 Cherokee in the back alley, then drove to my buddy Danny's shitbox apartment a few miles away. For months, I'd been sleeping on a pullout couch in what used to be Danny's office, pathetic as that sounds. I was months shy of thirty, working at a bar and couch surfing, thanks to a boxing suspension that had dried up a chunk of my income back in the summer.

Danny wasn't home—he was staying at his girlfriend's house in Walkertown, as usual. I liked Danny just fine, but I was glad to dodge the convo about why I was home so early. I went to the kitchen and dug a bag of frozen corn from the freezer, a bottle of Buffalo Trace from a cabinet. I sat at the kitchen bar, held the bag tight against my ribs, and poured myself four fingers of liquor. My ribs hurt like hell, but I'd taken enough body shots to know they weren't broken. I hoped a drink would take the edge off the pain and settle my nerves.

I took slow breaths while the liquor ripped hot trails down my throat. With every sip, the drunk man's *SportsCenter*-worthy skid across the pavement became increasingly hilarious. I laughed as I raided Danny's fridge, searching for something to soak up some of the liquor before calling it a night. I decided on some leftover lo mein noodles I'd gotten earlier from a strip mall joint called Golden Wok.

I was hardly two bites in when my phone vibrated in my pocket. Had a feeling it was Brent, calling to give me more shit. I laid my fork down and dug my phone out.

The caller ID read "Dad."

I refocused for a second—my dad hardly ever called me, and he certainly never called me late at night. I thought it must've been a mistake; maybe he was drinking too, had dialed the wrong number. Maybe even a butt dial. I ignored it and put my phone down, but as soon as the missed call notification popped up, the phone vibrated again.

Again, it was Dad.

I couldn't land on a single good reason why he'd be calling. I picked my phone up, considered answering, but decided against it. I didn't have the patience to deal with any more horseshit, especially from him. If it was something important, he'd leave a message or send me a text.

But no call or text ever came.

CHAPTER TWO

In the morning, another call awakened me.

I rolled over and crawled my fingers through the carpet, blindly feeling for my phone. Since it was early on a Saturday, I thought it might be one of those creepy-ass robocalls that had been harassing me for months. Always from a different city I'd never even visited, usually the same type of message: *Hello, Mr. Miller. This is so-and-so, just returning your call about that ten-thousand-dollar-a-month opportunity you inquired about* . . .

Robot or not, I was primed to tell the caller to shove that ten thousand a month up his or her prerecorded ass until I saw "Flint Creek Police Department" on the far too bright screen. Now I was curious, so I answered.

A man's voice asked if he was speaking to Hudson Lee Miller. I gave an affirmative grunt, wondered why the guy included my middle name.

"Mr. Miller, my name is Travis Watson, I'm an officer for the Flint Creek PD." The line went temporarily silent. Before I could muster a response, he said, "Typically we prefer to deliver this type of news in person, but seeing as you don't live around—"

"News?" I sat up on one elbow. "What are you talking about?"

"Your father was involved in a violent altercation this morning, Mr. Miller." The officer cleared his throat. "Maybe *altercation* isn't the right—"

"Is he okay?" I asked, remembering the unanswered calls from the night before.

"I'm afraid not," he said. "Your father was the victim of a shooting. Down at his salvage yard. He . . . uh . . . well, there was no pulse when the paramedics got there."

Now I was fully up, but the cop's words were snagged in the cobwebs of a slight hangover and early morning brain fog. I asked the officer to repeat himself.

"The fellow that works for your father, Charlie Shoaf, got to the salvage yard about a quarter till eight like he usually does and found your father near the front desk, facedown and unresponsive. Had blood coming from his head. Most certainly from a gunshot wound."

This time, the words took full effect and almost paralyzed me, like a left hook to the liver. "Somebody shot him," I managed. A statement. A question.

"Once. From behind as far as we can tell. And as far as the *why* of it all, could've been a robbery gone bad. Mr. Shoaf found the cash register wide open, empty as the Lord's tomb. Back door of the place was left open too."

I swallowed hard and closed my eyes and whispered *"Holy shit,"* and then I asked, weakly, if my stepmom, Tammy, knew yet.

"Reckon she does. Chief Coble headed out to her house just a little while ago." There was another voice in the background, muffled words like the receiver was covered. "You're still living out in Greensboro, correct?"

"Greensboro. Yeah."

"You might want to head on down to your father's house. As soon as you're feeling up to it, of course. The chief will try and clear up any questions you might have."

Jesus H. Christ and *I'll be there shortly, Officer,* were on the tip of my tongue, but I mumbled something that was neither of those things, and ended the call with a sudden realization: *I don't have a dad anymore.* I imagined Dad's body lying on blood-soaked concrete. An armed intruder, masked, emptying the register and bolting out the back door. Disappearing.

A murderer. Not the half-a-pack-a-day Marlboro Reds, the microwave diet, and bottom-shelf whiskey that I'd always expected to be the reaper at Dad's door.

I'd more than halfway been expecting a bad-news call of sorts. Not from my dad or the police, but from my stepmom, who had called six months before, and over a year ago before that, to tell me about the heart attacks Dad had suffered. It seemed inevitable that he would have another that would do him in for good. And why not? Far as I knew, he never pumped the brakes on all that smoking and drinking after the first two.

In light of the gunshot, none of that seemed to matter anymore.

But why did he call me last night?

I stood from the sleeper sofa, off-balance, feeling like shit, ribs throbbing. I found an Advil bottle on the floor, dumped four pills into my hand, and swallowed them dry. Four was the magic number I always took after my boxing matches, but they were barely down my throat when images of Dad's dead body flickered again. The concrete floor. Blood filling the cracks. I rushed for the trash bin next to the closet and purged a stomach's worth of liquor and lo mein.

In the bathroom, I swished mint Scope and turned my phone to silent. I brushed some beard whiskers off the counter, lay the phone facedown next to the sink. In a little town like Flint Creek, news spreads fast; with Facebook and the like, it'd be a miracle if half the state didn't know by noon. I wasn't ready for any calls of sympathy and shock and questions I couldn't or didn't know how to answer.

I showered hot, sat in the tub with my knees tucked in as water gathered in my hair, trickled down my cheekbones. I'd barely spoken to my father the last couple of years, had barely gotten along with him for most of my life, but I felt I should be crying. I almost willed myself to cry—scrunched my nose up, pinched my eyes shut—but there were no tears. Just shower water. I dug my thumbs into my temples and tried to knead the pulsing whiskey aches away. Maybe I was in too much shock to cry, maybe the tears would come later.

As I got out of the shower, the thought came again: *I don't have a dad anymore,* trailed by another thought: *I never had much of one anyway.* Shitty, to think a thing like that, but it didn't make it any less true. Even in my haze, it was easy to remember the last time I'd seen my dad—at one of our infrequent meetups that never served much purpose on my end of things but maybe soothed some sort of paternal guilt on his. We'd met two days before Thanksgiving, at a Greek-owned restaurant near Flint Creek called Zeto's. Subs and country cooking and everything between. A place we compromised on because I didn't want to eat at the gaudy diner where Dad knew every waitress by name and bust size.

Dad had been particularly negative that day. Bitching about my refusing to talk politics during our strained conversation; bitching about our waiter who was young, Middle Eastern, and overwhelmed with a holiday rush. He or a cook had messed up Dad's order—mushrooms on a cheesesteak that didn't belong—so Dad stiffed the kid on a tip. I called him out on it as we were getting ready to leave, told him it was an asshole thing to do. I tossed a five-dollar bill on the table that may as well have been boiling lava on Dad's head.

"That's what happens when you hire a damn foreigner."

That's the last thing I remember him saying that day, other than that he'd call me sometime soon. I didn't say anything, but I was thinking, *Don't waste your time.*

I thought about that as I dressed in a hurry. Jeans and a flannel. A pair of scuffed Vans. I threw a zip-up hoodie over my shoulder, didn't bother eating.

Outside, the sky looked like a slab of marble—smudges of grays and whites—and it was breezy and cold as I half filled my Jeep at a Tank 'n' Tummy near the highway. I bought a large cup of burnt coffee in the gas station, popped a few more Advil, hoping they'd stay down long enough to combat my lingering aches. I headed south on I-85, still salt covered for a snowstorm that was supposed to have shown up two days earlier but dropped half a foot in southern Virginia instead.

I was hardly five minutes into my thirty-five-minute drive when my stepmom called—in hysterics, almost unintelligible. *"Oh my Gods"* and *"Why, Hudson, whys?"* hemorrhaging through the phone. I said very little. Once she hung up, I made some calls of my own, starting with my roommate. I left a message but spared him the details of the situation. Then I called Brent.

"Shit, Hud. I'm so damn sorry. Take whatever time you need," he said. I hoped the time I needed would be as short as possible.

Those calls worked me up to my last one, my mom, Ann, who'd divorced my dad almost twenty years before.

"The cops just called me . . ." I told her, unsure how to say what I needed to. "From Flint Creek, Mom."

"Flint Creek?"

"About Dad."

"Did he do something?"

"No, Mom. The cops said that somebody . . ." I took a breath. "Somebody shot him at the salvage yard this morning."

"Is he—"

"He's dead, Mom."

A gasp on the other end. "No, Hudson. What are you say-ing? Tell me he's not. Tell me . . ."

"He is. I think they robbed the place."

"They?"

"I don't know who. The cops don't know. I'm headed to meet Frank Coble now."

She started crying, far more than I'd expected. For years, she'd resented my dad. But that didn't mean she hadn't once loved him or that the news didn't hurt. So I let her cry.

She finally collected herself. "Baby, I'm so sorry. I'm so, so sorry. Please let me know what I can do. I just pulled up for a women's breakfast at church, but I—"

"Drive on back home if you need to. Or stay at church. Whatever you think. Maybe going in will be good for you. Shit, I don't know."

"Don't worry about me, baby. I just want to be here for you. You'll let me know if I can do anything?"

I told her I would and that I loved her. She said she loved me too.

I put my phone away. Choked down the last sip of coffee and exited toward Flint Creek, a town with no grand entrance, just a dated, green sign announcing: "Flint Creek: Miles of Friendly Smiles."

I rolled my eyes at the cheesy welcome as the Advil and coffee crawled their way back up my throat.

CHAPTER THREE

Miles of friendly smiles . . . *but hardly a set of teeth between them.*

That had been the running joke for as far back as I could remember. One of the countless jokes I'd heard throughout my life about Flint Creek and its locals. The country-bumpkin wisecracks were mostly exaggeration, but there was no denying the town tended toward rural living. A town built mostly on agriculture. Fields of wheat, corn, and tobacco along the roadsides. Farms and produce stands scattered about. There was even a concrete plaque next to Town Hall that boasted Flint Creek was pumping out more beef and dairy cattle per square mile than anywhere in the Tar Heel state. Next to the plaque, a concrete pig in sunglasses. Outside of farming, most folks in town held down blue-collar jobs, owned little businesses, lived in modest houses in small neighborhoods or sparsely populated back roads, like my dad did.

His house was the last on the right on a gravel two-lane called Creekview Road. A long, ranch-style house from the seventies, with an attached garage and a front yard sloping into a ditch that met the road abruptly. In the yard, a concrete birdbath that I used to line with action figures before shooting them off with a pellet gun.

But that was a different lifetime. A different Hudson Miller. Over the last several years, I'd visited the house sparingly, and when I had, I preferred to sit outside, endure minimal small talk on the porch during my brief visits. My dad and Tammy had always smoked in the house, and it was all I could do not to have a coughing fit every time I stepped through the door.

I pulled up a little before ten. There was a black Dodge Charger parked crooked in the driveway. Definitely a cop's. I rang the doorbell, and Tammy's lapdogs, Cody and Stormin' Norman, started up like lit firecrackers, yipping and barking, scratching at the door until Frank Coble answered it. He was a sturdy man with a goatee so expertly trimmed and stark white that it looked to be painted on. He swept the dogs back with his foot and opened the door. "Come on in," Coble said.

When I stepped inside, he put his arms around me, gave a quick, manly hug. Two firm pats on the back that reverberated through my ribs. "Real sorry about your daddy."

Coble and my dad had been close for many years, but the embrace surprised me. Last time I'd stood so close to the man, I was fourteen years old, in a pair of handcuffs that he held the key to. "Appreciate it, Frank," I told him. "I'm sorry about it too."

"Tammy's in the dining room." Coble said, making eyes like *"prepare yourself for a shitshow."*

I took shallow breaths as I followed Coble through the living room, readying my lungs for the nicotine onslaught. The smell of smoke was even stronger than I remembered. Not for the first time, I imagined if I were to scrape my thumbnail across the wood-paneling walls of the house, the yellow tar from a million cigarettes would pile under the nail.

I could hear Tammy in the dining room before we reached her. Low sobs and sniffles, a conversation. She was on the phone when we came in, dabbing her eyes with a balled-up Kleenex. Tammy wasn't a hair over five feet tall, a hundred pounds at most, but her distress made her seem even smaller. When she ended her call, she squinted through tears and mouthed "Hey, Hudson," the kindest greeting she'd offered me in years. The usual welcome was "Leland, your son is here."

I slid out a seat across from her and sat. "I'm sorry, Tammy."

She nodded. Another low sob.

I looked at Coble, who was still standing. "Y'all have any idea who did this?"

"They ain't going to find who done this," Tammy said with a bubble in her throat. "Some drugged-up piece of shit probably."

Coble tapped his fingers on the back of an empty chair. "I've got my best detective at the scene right now. If there's anything to be found, he'll find it."

My brain fog didn't cloud my logic. "Did Dad have any security cameras?"

"Not a one," Coble said. "Guess he thought a padlock and that guard dog of his were all he needed. Some cameras could've helped us for sure. Even if there was just one at the front gate, to catch a suspicious car or license plate between six-ish, when your daddy went in, and whenever Charlie showed up."

My dad's salvage yard, Miller's Pull-a-Part, was in the middle of nowhere. The possibility of any witnesses seemed a long shot.

Tammy's hands moved toward a soft pack of menthol cigarettes but stopped. "What kind of monster would want to kill Leland?"

"Maybe nobody *wanted* to kill him, Tammy," the chief said.

"The hell do you mean?" She took a cigarette from its pack, tapped it on the table, and lit it with a plastic lighter. I scooted my chair back a few inches, rested my elbows on my knees and cupped my hands over my nose, kind of nonchalant. A makeshift filter.

"I mean, maybe they just wanted that money real bad," Coble said. "They were desperate, hit the first place they saw. Or they owed somebody. That's how these things happen sometimes."

I suggested the killer could've shot my dad just to cover their tracks. Sounded reasonable.

Coble said, "Exactly. Or something spooked them. Maybe they heard something outside—a car driving by, or that dog. Saw Leland's gun maybe."

"He would've shot their ass if he had his gun on him." Tammy's cigarette dangled from her lips, twirling with her words. "Leland never would've let them have that money. He didn't take shit from nobody."

"Of course he wouldn't have," Coble told her, "but the .38 was on his side, still snapped into its holster. Which makes me think somebody got the jump on him. That, and the fact he was facedown. He probably never saw the person, or at least not the gun they were carrying."

"Spineless coward," Tammy muttered.

"So where do y'all go from here?" I asked.

"Well, after we fully process the crime scene, we'll continue our investigation based on what we learn from the evidence at the scene and your dad's body."

"The body?" Tammy jammed a finger toward her face. "He's got a hole from the back of his head, out his goddamn eyeball. What the hell else do you need to know? Somebody fucking shot him."

The detail about the eyeball was something the cop on the phone hadn't told me. *Brutal.* But at least it meant Dad had died quickly. The fact it had happened that morning also meant Dad hadn't made those calls to me while bleeding out on his office floor. That would've been a difficult guilt to navigate.

With effort, I pulled my attention back to what Coble was saying.

"You're right, Tammy. But there are still procedures we—"

"Don't start with your cop-speak mumbo jumbo, Frank. This is my husband we're talking about. *Your* friend. So you need to go find the bastard that done this."

Coble interlocked his fingers across his belly. "I get that you want answers right now. So do I. I loved Leland like he was my own blood. I'm talking like a cop because the cop in me has to do what's best, what's *right*, to find out what happened." After a long sigh and a few clucks of his tongue, he said, "I really hate to tell you this, but that involves us sending the body off to Raleigh."

Tammy slammed her hand on the table, an ash from the cigarette falling, burning out next to a tissue. "I don't want my husband's body going nowhere."

"I understand that," Coble said. "But we need to know for sure whether there are any other injuries, signs of struggle and whatnot. Payne Regional don't have the means to do a full examination, so we'll have to send the body off to Raleigh."

"And how long until we get some answers?"

"Could be weeks," he said. "But they'll likely release the body in just a matter of days. Meantime, we'll continue doing what we can on our end." Coble walked over and squatted next to Tammy, placed a hand weighted by a bulky class ring on the table. "We're going to find out who done this, Tammy. And when we do, we'll throw the law at them. Bet your ass."

Tammy shook her head.

I cleared my throat to catch Coble's attention. "So what are the chances the examiner finds anything?"

He stood up straight, his knees popping. "May find nothing. Could be exactly what we said: a shooting from behind, and that's it. But it's always worth a closer look."

Tammy extinguished her cigarette in a near-empty cereal bowl, a sizzle in the sugary milk. "I got to pay for that?"

"The autopsy?"

She nodded.

"Won't cost you a red cent," Coble said.

"Bullshit it won't," Tammy grumbled.

He tapped his watch. "I best get back to the station, get to work on this. If you need anything in the world, Tammy, call me. I'm awful sorry about all this. Maybe Patti can send some fried chicken and mashed potatoes over this evening."

Patti. Coble's wife. I remembered her face and teased bangs, her high-pitched laugh. I thought about the fried chicken and mashed potatoes and wondered if they were to blame for the chief's belly that looked at least two belt loops thicker since I'd last seen him.

Tammy dismissed him with a wave of her hand. She turned in her chair and looked out the kitchen window, a gray light highlighting her tear-damp cheekbones.

Coble left, and part of me wished he could've stayed a few minutes longer, served as a buffer in the room where Tammy was still crying and I wasn't. I just didn't know what to say to a woman I'd known for years but had never been close to. Never wanted to be close to.

I was afraid she might mention Dad's late-night phone call—assuming she knew about it—but she didn't say a thing. She buried her face in her hands, silently trembled.

I looked around the room that was hazy with smoke. A lot had changed in the house since my childhood. The linoleum floors and curtains and appliances. All different now. But one thing caught my eye, as it always did: a magnet picture of myself on the refrigerator. I was probably eight, in a bright orange baseball cap, an orange T-shirt that didn't quite match. Number 9 for the Little League Astros. I hated those colors as much as I hated baseball. The mosquito bites in the outfield. Entire afternoons of little to no action except for parents shit-talking from opposing bleachers.

Maybe the picture stayed on the fridge because it depicted the ideal son, suited up for America's pastime.

Or it was one of Dad's few reminders in the house of how things were before he dismantled our family.

* * *

Rewind twenty years, and Tammy was just a neighbor of ours, renting a place two houses down with her boyfriend, Steve. They had moved from Cherryville and befriended my parents; for a short while they breathed some excitement into our household. Steve and Tammy were several years younger than Mom and Dad, had this exotic glow about them, partly from the tanning bed that eternally burned UV blue through their garage windows.

Not long after they moved in, they came by to introduce themselves. Soon enough, they started coming over on Saturday evenings for cookouts, most times carrying glass bottles and a deck of playing cards. On one or more of those nights, I remember my dad walking me to the basement door, saying something like *"I want you to stay down here tonight, Hot Rod, but you can stay up as long as you want, watch whatever you want to."*

Back then, whatever I wanted to watch was *The Goonies* and a box set of *Nightmare on Elm Street* tapes. But when I tired of Sloth and Krueger and my Legos and Nintendo games, I'd sneak up the basement stairs and through the living room, just far enough to see the dining room table and the four adults who carried on around it. There were always beer bottles on the table, fancy glasses filled with icy, lime-green drinks, and loud oldies like "Sugar Shack" and "Hang on Sloopy" blasting from Dad's cassette player.

I think everyone enjoyed those nights—except for Mom. She'd never been much of a drinker, and she was too damn nice to put her foot down when those parties carried on well past midnight. As for me, I was fine with the get-togethers. They were a welcome escape from the routines of the week and the nine-thirty bedtimes, but within a matter of months the exotic Saturday nights stopped like a plug was pulled on that Sony cassette player. Suddenly it was no longer four adults sitting around that table; it was just Dad and Tammy Jenkins.

The transition from normal family to my mom hiring a lawyer and moving into an apartment didn't happen in the blink of an eye, though. After the luster of those Saturday night shindigs wore off, there had been signs that things were headed south that I'd tried to ignore. Arguments and more arguments between my parents, the *I love yous* between them stopping altogether. Dad helping Tammy with car problems and sink and gutter problems while Steve worked late. Tammy's name becoming a part of the shouting matches at home.

"Maybe you'd be happier with Tammy, Leland."

"Let me guess. Tammy's car isn't working again?"

"I've seen the way you look at her."

"I've seen the way she looks at you."

* * *

So how was I supposed to feel, sitting across the table from the woman who was the driving wind of that shitstorm? Who'd caused her ex to sell their house and move back to Cherryville and added a layer of angst to my adolescence. A woman whose skin no longer held that tropical glow, but had aged to worn leather like her voice.

It made me wonder, now that my dad was dead, how quickly Tammy would completely wither away. Fucked up as the whole thing was, I knew she loved my dad—at least in some sense of the word. They were perfect for each other in the worst ways possible. Cancerously codependent. It's like Mom had kept Dad's worst qualities in check for years, and Tammy in short order unraveled and amplified them.

I pushed a box of Kleenex closer to her, certain I wouldn't need them.

CHAPTER FOUR

The rest of my afternoon passed in a fog of fitful napping at the apartment, icing my ribs, and ignoring texts and phone calls. My dad's death scene kept playing in my head, each time a little different. Sometimes the killer wore a ski mask, and another time it was a Ronald Reagan mask like one of the surfer-dude bank robbers wore in *Point Break*.

One thing remained constant: a gunshot ending.

I couldn't stop thinking about the phone calls Dad had made to me—I guess I'd never know what he had to say.

* * *

I slid on a Red Door Security shirt that evening and drove to my job in downtown Greensboro. Brent looked surprised when I walked through the door.

"Damn, Hud. Dave's already on his way. I asked him to cover your shift. Thought I told you to take some time."

"Guess he can turn around and go home." I handed my jacket to the new door girl Brent had hired a couple weeks before. Her name was Kirstin, or maybe Kristin. I couldn't remember. The way she open-mouth stared at me told me she'd heard the news about my dad.

"You sure about this, man?" Brent asked.

"I need to keep busy. I'll drive myself crazy."

"I get it. I did the same when my cousin passed last year in that car wreck. I couldn't sit around and mope when I found out. Got drunk and got a new tattoo instead."

"Drunk and a new tattoo? Sounds like an average week-end for you."

He grinned and slung a wiry arm around my shoulders. We walked between a couple of worn-out pool tables, stopping when we got to the main bar. "Listen," Brent said, his grin fading. "About that mess last night . . ."

"Anything happen after I left?"

"People were amped up for a little while. You know how they get. But there wasn't any more bullshit. Cops never came."

"I could've finished my shift. Just saying."

"I couldn't take any chances," he said. "I wasn't trying to be a hard-ass. You've been a good employee, Hud. I'll take you at your word that you weren't going to whip that guy's ass, but I've told you what happened a few years back."

"Yeah, I know the story," I said. I'd heard it at least a dozen times: A bouncer they called Aquaman rammed a guy's head into a parking meter right outside the bar. Months later, the guy filed charges. Brent nearly lost his job.

Brent said, "You just can't take any chances outside these doors, especially with half the world posting videos online. Can't fucking sneeze without everybody knowing it. And you know how that is."

I nodded.

"Anyhoo," he said, "doubt you'll have any issues tonight. I've got you working the private bar. Got a VIP party at nine o'clock. The Randleman Pin Pushers or some shit."

"A bowling team?"

"Got to be."

I gave him a thumbs-up.

He thanked me, and I turned and labored up the creaky stairwell to the upstairs bar.

I would spend my shift monotonously checking names on IDs, then marking names off a list. Bowler names like Wes, Kenny, and Dennis. Probably nobody who'd cause any trouble. It was mindless work that would hardly keep my brain occupied, but a temporary distraction wasn't the real reason I'd showed up that night; I was broke as hell.

My boxing career was on hiatus, if not over completely. My last match had been in June, when I co-headlined a fight card at the Greensboro Coliseum Annex, hoping to boost my professional record to twelve and three and earn myself a bigger fight come fall. I prepared with long runs and sparring sessions and by heeding my coach Rob's advice of no booze or sex while training.

I'd been ready. I'd made my cut to a hundred forty-seven pounds with ease, and I had a game plan: keep my much shorter opponent, a journeyman named Mickey Lomax, at the end of my rangy jabs all night. Use my length and stamina to win. It was a strategy that had won me many fights since my Golden Gloves days. But not that night. Lomax was a bulldog of a welterweight who could take the sting of my jabs and keep on trucking. Had a head like a fire hydrant.

Stayed up in my chest the whole fight, which made it near impossible for my long arms to pepper him with one-twos or unleash hooks with any dynamite behind them.

The bout went the distance. Six frustrating rounds.

After the announcer called the decision, a consensus four rounds to two, Lomax's corner celebrated like they'd hit the Powerball. That didn't anger me, nor the judges' decision—I knew I'd lost the fight. But before I left the ring, Lomax's cutman made some smartass comment, accused me of an intentional headbutt in the final round, which was total bullshit. I ignored him, but one of my cornermen, Jay, took offense, and that brought on a standoff in the middle of the ring.

Coach Rob and I tried to intervene, which meant more people stepped in and around the situation. Testosterone is magnetic like that. As the jawing got worse, bodies and egos crowded the ring, like a bunch of bumper cars at the fair, nudging and vying for a piece of the action. People started pushing and shoving. Even a few from ringside decided to join in.

I was never sure why, but I was the proud recipient of the first punch. Lomax's cutman landed a shot between my shoulder blades. Felt like a sledgehammer against my already battered and exhausted body. When I turned, instinct took over.

My gloves had been removed, but my hands were still tightly wrapped. My knuckles were like a cinder block on the man's chin when I launched a right cross, straight down the middle. The sweet spot. His eyes went vacant, his knees wobbly like Bambi on ice. The bitch of it was, when he finally fell, he went right through the ropes and over the ring apron, the back of his head connecting with the scorer's table. Messed him up good. The paramedics had to break out the stretcher. The whole shebang. That was the extent of my involvement— a single punch—but the ensuing anarchy brought more punches and shoves in and around the ring, metal chairs being tossed from the crowd. Several arrests.

For me, two things worsened the situation: the guy I'd laid out wasn't some twenty-something: he was fifty-six, and a bunch of people caught it on video. YouTube and Facebook blew up with video clips in no time, people sharing and commenting, tagging their friends. In some of the videos, the trainer's cheap shot to my spine wasn't visible. Made me look like a raging asshole. That's exactly what one YouTube commenter had called me: *"That raging asshole should never step in the ring again."* The dozen or so other people who'd joined the post-fight brawl seemed to be forgotten. I was a trained fighter, held to a different standard.

In the days after the fight, more dominoes started to fall. The Boxing Commission suspended my license and took my twelve-hundred-dollar purse. Along with losing that payout, I lost a chance at a bigger fight—possibly an eight rounder I could've got two-fifty a round for. And it cost me my day job, training kids and teenagers in the afternoon at Langley Rec Center. There was no way a city-funded facility was going to let YouTube's newest villain train a bunch of kids.

My only other job was at the bar. Since then, I'd added to my duties there to supplement my income: along with more bartending shifts, I started bouncing on weekends, a risky job I didn't dare take on when I was still boxing.

* * *

The night of the day Dad was murdered, things were low key at Red Door, and I was glad for it. The private party of mostly bowlers showed up and drank pitchers of light beer for two hours. They threw a few rounds of darts with no major injuries. One bowler, short and toupeed, winked at me and called me Slugger. I laughed it off, offered a lazy combo at an imaginary opponent—a sideshow for the drunks.

CHAPTER FIVE

The days that followed were a little less hazy, but my emotions were still in some sort of purgatory. Monday evening, Mom drove in from Wilmington to check on me, ignoring the fact I told her not to. She picked me up from Danny's place, gave me a long hug in her car, then pulled a Ruby Tuesday's BOGO coupon from her purse and smiled at me.

We talked for a long time at dinner. Most of it your typical mom-and-son type of talk.

"You seeing anyone, Hudson?" I wasn't.

"Looking for any other jobs?" I said I was, but I wasn't.

"Still training at the gym?" Nah, not really.

I asked her about work, about her new condo in Wilmington.

She said her place was nice and that she was pretty happy. Told me she'd broken up with this guy named Michael, whose name I'd forgotten until she mentioned it. To me, he was just another faceless guy in a series of failed relationships Mom had endured, including a three-week marriage to a guy named Chet, who later did time for starting a Ponzi scheme. Not that I had any room to judge her relationships. The two

I'd had in my twenties didn't last a year combined, my pre-occupation with boxing the common denominator to their ending.

I was the one who finally brought up Dad, then Mom spoke her piece as we shared an appetizer sampler.

"Your dad wasn't always the man he became, Hudson. Seemed with every year he became more like his own dad."

"I know that," I said, though distinguishing my childhood dad and the one who'd had the affair was difficult. Oftentimes, I've wondered just how much of his character I'd turned a blind eye to when I was too young to know any better.

"He was quite the charmer when he was your age. Sweet almost. Knew how to make me feel like a million bucks."

"I guess charmer and bullshitter overlap a little sometimes, huh?"

"More than a little," she said. "He used to call me 'Fancy Face.' I ever tell you that?"

I shook my head. "You've always been pretty, Mom. Too bad I got most of his genes."

She smiled. "Oh hush. You're a good-looking man and you know it. Just wish you'd shave that beard. Those things carry germs, you know?"

I winked at her and scratched at some hair under my chin. "Chicks love germs."

Mom's smile faded slowly. "I guess I was pretty once. Maybe that's what got me into trouble."

"Don't even think about giving him a pass. None of what happened was your fault."

"I know that. I'm just saying, your dad always liked the newest, shiniest thing on the block. Like that Chevy truck he had when you were little. The one he took to all those shows."

"You mean the Super Sport that broke down all the time because he refused to let anyone else work on it?"

"That's the one," she said. "I guess I was like that truck when he saw it in the Autotrader. Leland just had to have me. He told me as much."

I took a bite of a cheese stick. "You were the best thing he ever had and he screwed it up. And if you didn't know, Tammy was never the shiniest thing on the block. Just the newest for a while."

Her eyes got lost in her plate. "How's she handling things?"

I wiped my fingers on a napkin and said I didn't give a shit.

Mom said, "I'm still praying for her."

"That's sweet of you, but she's the worst. I think Jesus would agree."

Mom put her hand on my arm, smiled an endearing grin. "I'm glad you're not like your dad. And I'm glad you aren't like me. You've always stuck up for yourself. Always stuck up for me."

I shrugged. "Not so much when I was a kid."

"Nonsense," she said. "Other than having you around, I think what got me over all that was knowing, deep down, that Tammy did me a favor. Marrying your dad like she did. Kept him from trying to crawl back to me."

"What would you have done if he had?"

"I'd like to say I wouldn't have considered it, but I missed our little family sometimes," she said. "To be honest though, we weren't that happy. Your dad and me. At least not those last couple years. He was too worried about that God-forsaken junkyard all the time. When he wasn't there, he was at that stupid Boars Club."

I spotted our waitress walking toward us, carrying a water pitcher, and we dropped the topic of my dad. Mom asked the waitress what kind of margaritas they had. After she got the brief rundown of flavors, she calculated points on her Weight Watchers app, which I thought ridiculous given the fact she'd probably never been a pound overweight in her life. She ordered herself a skinny margarita, no salt on the rim. For me, she ordered an original on the rocks, even though I didn't really want one.

I ended up having two, and we didn't mention Dad the rest of the night.

CHAPTER SIX

Halfway through my Thursday shift, Randy the Regular stopped by the bar. Randy was a sixty-year-old retired software engineer with more time and money than he knew what to do with. His retirement plan seemed to amount to parking his ass on a barstool a few days a week, which I was more than fine with. He was a living, breathing encyclopedia of conspiracy theories. There were some theories he was so adamant about that by the time he tabbed out most days, I wasn't so sure that they didn't have some truth to them.

Randy wore a burgundy Member's Only jacket, loose-fitting jeans that nearly covered his white New Balances, the only outfit I ever saw him in.

Between sips of Pinot Grigio, he'd been telling me about this naval ship that disappeared back in the forties during a top-secret military experiment. "When the dern thing finally reappeared," he went on, "some of the crew was embedded into the metal of the ship. Fused together. Metal and man. Wildest thing you ever heard, Hud."

I laughed as I poured Randy a refill. "So you're telling me that those men died? Just ended up as part of the ship, then the military covered it up?"

"Look it up if you don't believe me," Randy said. He swirled his wine around the glass, sniffed it just to mess with me. "Go ahead, type in 'Philadelphia experiment.' See what comes up. It's as real as me sitting right here in front of you."

To humor him, I walked over to the coatrack, fished my phone out of my jacket pocket. I opened my home screen to a flood of notifications: four missed calls from Tammy, who'd also sent a text message.

Call me or Frank now.

I told Randy I'd be right back. I stepped outside and called Tammy.

"You need to get down here to the police station," she said when she picked up.

"There's no way the autopsy came back that quick," I said.

"This is something else. Some bullshit you need to hear in person."

"About Dad?"

"Who the hell else, Hudson? The ice-cream man?"

"Can it wait? I'm at work right now."

"No. It can't."

I said I'd be there as soon as I could, then found Brent in his office. He was on the phone but covered it when he saw me.

"Hate to do this to you, boss, but I got to roll out."

He checked the time on his computer screen. "Jesus Christ, Hud. You realize nobody's on the schedule for another four hours? Can you just—"

"The police called. About my dad."

His expression changed. "Go on," he said. "Just go on."

* * *

Tammy's Cadillac Eldorado was parked outside the police station when I got there. She was sitting on a bench in front of her car, looking all pissy and ridiculous in a sequined biker jacket. When I walked up to meet her, she said nothing. Just stood and stamped out a cigarette. I followed her into the police station with its stained wood walls like a log cabin, a fish mounted on the wall behind the front desk—a folksiness so deliberate it came off as phony.

I hadn't been in the station since the day I hurled a grapefruit-sized rock through the back glass of Dad's Mustang; it was his and Tammy's wedding day. Coble, just an officer back then, had taken me to the back of the station that afternoon and showed me a holding cell. I'd never seen one in person. Didn't know what to expect. I thought I might see some mean-mugging criminal locked up, gripping the bars. Somebody with tattoos and piercings, maybe long hair. But the man I saw wasn't like the bad guys in movies. He was older, with ratty clothes and dirt on his face. Looked like one of the roadside beggars I used to see near the mall in Greensboro. The man wasn't scary at all, just pitiful. Not that it mattered, really, because we never shared a cell. The whole thing was a scare tactic. After Coble gave me a speech about where my life was headed if I didn't shape up or seek Jesus, I found out Dad hadn't pressed any charges. This he'd held over my head for years afterward, like it made up for the reason I'd trashed his car in the first place.

Tammy and I reached the front desk, and a baby-faced guy in his twenties called for the chief. Coble appeared at his office door. He was eating a long stick of beef jerky, the wrapper splayed like a banana peel. He waved us back.

Another man was in his office, half sitting on the corner of Coble's desk. He was probably a few years older than me, with a military-style haircut and a clean-shaven face. Even his forearms appeared to be straight razored.

"Mrs. Miller?" The man slid off the desk.

Tammy looked at him like *duh*.

"Jeff Holden," he said, shaking her limp hand.

"*Detective* Holden," Coble added, his mouth full of jerky. "Joined us about a year ago."

Holden offered me the same greeting, said it was nice to meet us and that he was sorry about what had happened. The way he said *nice* let me know that he wasn't born and raised in Flint Creek. Probably from the North Carolina mountains somewhere.

I didn't take a seat, but Tammy did. Coble eased into his rolly chair behind a desk that was too large for the room. A desk well organized with notepads, sticky notes, a calendar, and a picture of his family in front of the Epcot Center in Disney World, Coble with his arm around his wife, Patti. I almost didn't recognize her because of the plastic surgery—facial and otherwise—she'd clearly gotten over the last decade. Coble's daughter, Leslie, was also in the picture; a curly-headed girl several years younger than me who I thought was kind of cute. They all wore mouse ears.

Tammy crossed her bony arms. "Go ahead, Frank," she said. "Ask him the shit you asked me on the phone."

Coble took out a notepad and a red pen, popped off the cap that had been chewed on like a dog toy. For a moment, I thought he might say that they'd reviewed Dad's phone records, then bring up the fact Dad had called me the night before his death. Instead: "Hudson, I know you haven't been around much over the past few years, but I'd like to ask you some questions about your daddy's business."

"Don't think I'll be much help, but I'll try."

"You used to hang around the salvage yard when you were younger, correct?"

"A little bit."

"A little bit," he repeated, scribbling something down. "So here's the deal. We've been down at the salvage yard almost all day, following up on some information Charlie Shoaf gave us this morning."

"Thought you said he didn't know anything."

"Maybe not, but Detective Holden here called him up. He asked Charlie to walk him through the crime scene again today, take him through the entire shop now that his mind is a bit clearer. As you can imagine, he was pretty shook up the morning it happened."

"Get to the damn point, Frank," Tammy barked.

Coble looked over at Holden, took a deep breath. He seemed to be teetering on telling Tammy to take it down a couple notches. "Anyways, the two of them were walking through all the rooms: the main office, the garage, even the bathroom. But when they got to the storage room, Charlie noticed something. So he hollered for Holden to come back there, showed him this." Coble picked up his phone, ran his sausage of an index finger across the screen a couple times, and then handed the phone to me.

There was a clear picture of the storage room on the screen. Something in the image struck me as peculiar: a piece of beige carpet lying crooked on the ground, a metal surface sticking out from beneath it.

"Swipe to the next picture," Coble told me.

In the next picture, the carpet had been pulled away. A metal door below it was lifted. Beneath, there were an array of guns: pistols, assault rifles, a big revolver with a tiny scope mounted on top.

"You ever seen any of this before? The guns? The cubby?"

I told him I hadn't. Curious as I was as a kid, I'd never found a secret door in the floor. That's something I would've remembered.

"Tammy told us the same thing."

I studied the screen. "I know he liked to collect guns. Always had some in his closet at home. Think he kept some at work too." As I spoke, I could only recall one instance of Dad ever shooting one of those guns. A silver, pearl-handled pistol, at a copperhead in the backyard.

"Mm-hmm," Coble agreed. "But this is something different. We counted seven guns total in that little bunker."

"Eight," Holden said.

"*Eight* guns in total," Coble said. "And here's the kicker: all of them had their serial numbers ground off."

The significance of the discovery was lost on me. "What's this got to do with everything else?"

"Well, that little door had a handle on the side. A place for a lock." Coble pointed at the phone, mimicked a swipe.

I swiped.

"See the lock?" Coble asked. "Or what a bolt cutter left of it?"

The words lined up with what I saw. I nodded and looked at Holden. "You found that in the storage room?"

"Up under one of the shelves," Coble answered for him. "So we're thinking there were more guns in that little cubby before last Saturday. Somebody probably took what they could get their hands on, left these behind, then got the hell out of there. Could explain why the back door was open. Wouldn't be surprised if the perpetrator had a driver back there waiting on them."

I laid the phone on the desk. "Charlie say anything about those guns?"

"Claims to know nothing about it."

"*Claims,*" Tammy made quotes with her fingers. "Probably because they're his damn guns. Not Leland's. Awfully convenient how he suddenly found them."

Coble said, "Of course Charlie could be involved, and it's something—"

"They think your dad was a gun dealer or some bullshit," Tammy said, her eyes on me, a shaky finger pointing at Coble.

"What makes y'all think that?" I asked.

"The guns were tagged," Holden said.

Coble brought up another picture and turned the screen toward me; the picture was clearer, a closer view of the guns. They were lying on a blanket, each tagged around the trigger guard, something I hadn't noticed in the previous pictures.

Coble stuffed the phone in his shirt pocket. "Based on some things we saw at Leland's desk, the numbers on those tags look a hell of a lot like his writing."

"Don't listen to this nonsense, Hudson," Tammy said. "I would've known if Leland was doing something like this. He didn't keep nothing from me."

"I knew him for forty-some years," Coble said. "Assuming it's true, he sure as hell kept it from me."

"Because you're a *cop*, Frank. Ain't quite the same, now is it?"

I worked my fingers through my beard, thinking that maybe there was someone Dad hadn't kept his secret from. Somebody dangerous. "You really think he was a gun dealer?"

Coble sat back in his chair, which made a cushiony sigh. "If so, he was probably just a middle man. Knew somebody that had a bunch of these guns, helped whoever it was sell them. A side hustle for some extra cash. A big-time gunrunner would have a much bigger stash than what we found."

"Who do you think he'd be selling to?"

"Could be any-old-body. It's no secret that Payne County is one of the most armed in the state, so I'd venture to guess that he's sold some stuff locally. People maybe wanting weapons at a bargain. Stuff the government can't track. Again, this is Flint Creek we're talking about. Doubt he'd be selling to any gang members or some hillbilly drug cartel."

"You sure do flap your gums a lot to know nothing, Frank," Tammy said. "How the hell are you sure of any of this?"

"Tammy, I'm not ruling a damn thing out. But I am trying to be logical. You know as well as I do that Leland wouldn't take a dime from somebody he didn't trust."

"He's *dead*, Frank. You think he trusted the person who shot him?"

She made a good point.

"What about his buddies?" I said. "Maybe somebody from that club he was in? One of them might know who he was dealing with."

"Both Detective Holden and I plan on speaking to folks close to your daddy, including members of The Boars Club, if that's what you're referring to. Those are some of the most upstanding men in town. They'll probably be as shocked by this as I was."

"Says the club president," Tammy said.

"Tammy, the club don't even have—"

"Listen," I said, hoping to cork the bickering, "I don't think I can be much more help today, but at least y'all have somewhere to start."

Coble let out a long breath and pushed himself up from his desk. "That's exactly what we have, Hudson. Somebody will know something before long. Only a matter of time."

"Hope you're right," I told him. "Wish I could be of more help, but I need to get back to work."

Holden kindly thanked me for my time.

As I reached the door, Tammy asked, "You actually believe all this? About your own daddy?"

I stopped and looked at her pleading eyes, but managed no more than a shrug as I walked out.

The news about the guns certainly added possibilities to what happened to Dad, though I wasn't entirely shocked by what the detective had found. A little surprised, maybe. But I knew that was the sort of thing people in small towns like Flint Creek got involved in. People like my dad, especially. A self-proclaimed red-blooded, working-class American.

A description that, at least in his case, came with a specific worldview attached to it. One that trickled down from Grandpa Miller, blossomed into that special brand of bullshit I came to know as Dad's everyday cynicism. A fair amount of his bitching and philosophizing started with, *"Like Pops always said . . ."* or *"Pops was right about one thing . . ."*

Dad was forever sounding off about something, and it got progressively worse once Mom was out of the picture. His favorite dead horse revolved around "the Man," and how he, she, or it was out to get hard-working Americans. And the Man came in many disguises: the banks; the IRS; big pharmacy; and of course, the government. Dad was convinced they'd take away anything that wasn't bolted to the damn ground—*especially* your guns, if they could.

I guess when you talk about shit like that enough, believe it enough, it starts to show itself in all sorts of ways. For the life of me, I couldn't remember Dad owning credit cards, but I remember him stuffing rolls of hundred-dollar bills into coffee tins and liquor bottles, hiding them in undisclosed locations in and around our house. He kept a hefty stash of batteries and flashlights, ammo cans packed with water jugs and nonperishables in the loft of his storage shed. It was like he was slowly preparing for some sort of fallout, like a bank crash, or Y2K, or a race war, or a war against whoever the hell might spring from the bushes to destroy the middle-class White man. If Dad was a veteran in any war, it was the one that news talk radio and the echoes of Grandpa Miller created in his head.

I knew that selling black-market guns meant the government couldn't track those guns and the money my dad made from them. If that didn't scream Leland Henry Miller, then nothing did. It's something he would've been proud of, arming like-minded folks against the evils of the world. Of all people, Tammy shouldn't have been surprised by it. If anyone knew the cynical, everybody-is-out-to-get-us attitude my dad had, it was her. In that regard, they were soulmates.

CHAPTER SEVEN

The next day was the funeral. Tammy had handled the arrangements, so other than a closed casket, I wasn't sure what to expect. I borrowed some dress clothes from my boss, then watched a YouTube video on how to tie a tie into a half-Windsor knot, trying several times before it finally didn't look too short or too long or like a chokehold around the collar. I hid a small flask in the inner pocket of my jacket; I snuck a swig in the funeral home parking lot before making my way inside.

Instead of my dad's body on display that afternoon, there were pictures on and around the casket, mostly of him and Tammy. Some were from holidays and trips they'd taken and NASCAR races they'd been to in Martinsville. There was even a shitty caricature of the two, something they'd had made at the Dixie Classic Fair. The artist had zeroed in on my dad's cleft chin and Tammy's big, outdated hairstyle. In the drawing, the two were sitting in a convertible version of what looked like the General Lee. Probably Dad's choice.

Around two thirty, the crowd for the visitation started to arrive, and things grew even more uncomfortable. Some people regarded me with surprise, like they forgot or never knew my dad had a grown son. The people I did recognize I hadn't seen in years, which was perfectly fine with me. Far as I was concerned, they were small-town cliquey types who considered me an outsider because I'd done my damnedest to put Flint Creek and my dad squarely in my rearview years before. A select few surely remembered the wedding incident and had gawked from the church foyer as Coble hauled me away in cuffs.

Maybe I shouldn't have done what I did, but what I despised about Flint Creek was that you could get a pass on being a shitty person—like my dad stepping out on his family—so long as you hobnobbed appropriately and showed up to church on Sunday mornings.

At least a hundred people showed up. A group of Dad's buddies congregated near the entrance, several of them wearing small, gold boar pins on their jackets—members of the circle jerk of a fraternal organization my dad belonged to, the one Mom had devoutly loathed: The Boars Club. I didn't even know it still existed. I never knew much about the club except it was for men only; they'd meet at a place in town called Flint Creek Lodge, where they'd play poker and watch ball games. Dad always came home late on club nights, reeking of cigar smoke and beer.

Among the Boar faction at the funeral was Frank Coble, a couple of local firemen, and the longtime mayor, Roger Segers, whose pompadour was in full spirits, as if he was out campaigning. I wouldn't have been shocked to see him handing out bumper stickers or flyers: *Segers: The Right Choice*.

I stood near the casket, shoulder to shoulder with Tammy on my left, some distant cousins I'd only met once on my right. It felt more like a punishment than an honor. Even more so when Dad's acquaintances passed through the receiving line, most shaking my hand half-heartedly, looking like *"I'm surprised you even showed up."* Undoubtedly the result of whatever narratives Dad and maybe Tammy had spun in the years following the divorce. Wouldn't have surprised me at all if some believed my mom had been the one in the wrong.

A few of the older, churchy types hugged my neck, my suit jacket becoming a pungent mixture of aftershaves and perfumes. Some of the passers-through stopped to heap praise upon Dad, talk about what a good man he was. I nodded and grinned, just to hurry the funeral guests down the line.

Tammy? Not so much. She indulged the stories, added her own details while she hugged and cried and bled mascara down her cheeks:

"Aww, Leland just adored you."

"Yep, that was Leland all right. Straight-shooter if I ever met one."

"They don't make them like Leland no more. He was good as gold."

Even more unbearable were the speculators and armchair detectives reminiscing about the crime that was public knowledge by that point. Tammy indulged that too. There was no mention of the gun stash, of course. Chatty as Tammy was, she only said one thing to me that day, in a not-so-quiet whisper: "That damn Charlie knows something." She'd pointed out a gangly, white-haired man in his seventies or thereabouts. He seemed to keep his distance from the crowd, and in that way I envied him.

I tired of the stories and theories, like I tired of the music that played a bit too loud through the funeral parlor's shitbox sound system. Conway Twitty and Willie Nelson songs. All treble. Guitars and twang from a tin can. Tammy had put only four songs on the dedication CD: two from Conway, two from Willie. By the time the visitation was over, "Blue Eyes Crying in the Rain" had played five times. I could almost swear Tammy's tears ramped up every time Willie belted out the chorus.

After the visitation, I sat on the front pew in the parlor's sanctuary. The pastor from Hope of God Baptist, Dean Peterson, led the sermon, the same sweaty-faced man who'd worked the pulpit when Dad dragged me to church as a kid. He started with a prayer, led the crowd in the singing of a hymn about the roll being called *up yonder*, then began his message. He spoke unnaturally slowly and squinted his eyes every time he said "Jesus," which he pronounced "Jay-zus," the *s* at the end like a snake hiss in the microphone. That unique voice that TV preachers seemed to share, as if their annunciations along with fancy suits and sweat beads were a magical elixir that granted access to the Holy Spirit.

Peterson got to one part in his sermon about living a Godly, blameless life, and I damn near laughed out loud. To my dad, Hope of God Baptist was no more than a social occasion filled with gossip and back patting and potluck socials. He'd even been a deacon at the church when I was a kid. On Sunday evenings, he'd make Mom and me stay late. While I made paper airplanes out of tithe envelopes, Dad would vote on church matters like the color of seats in the choir section or whether to serve pulled pork or baked chicken at the upcoming church picnic. To hell with the local food drive or the missionaries in Honduras.

The sermon ended with an altar call that nobody answered, and the funeral procession made its way to Pleasant Grove Cemetery, where Peterson was much shorter of wind. He only spoke a quick eulogy, and I was thankful for that. The afternoon was sunny and clear, but frigid. Especially when an occasional breeze would slide over the tombstones and the concrete mausoleums. It made everyone huddle a little too close together, like the casket was a campfire that might radiate heat.

After the final prayer, a man played "Taps" on a bugle while two funeral directors began folding an American flag into a tight triangle. It was a ceremony fit for a true hero, like my grandfather on Mom's side, Papaw Davis, who'd taken two bullets in Normandy before coming home and marrying my mamaw. Wounds that had earned him a Purple Heart had turned into plasticky scars on his leg and shoulder that he'd showed me one afternoon when we went fishing at the Yadkin River.

My dad didn't have any battle scars or war medals. He'd never seen action on the battlefield. He was stationed in Korea for a few months in the mid-eighties, and the only stories he'd ever told me were about fights he'd gotten into at bars, places he'd visited, food he'd tried. He taught me a couple of Korean cuss words too, like *gesekgi*, which means "son of a bitch."

Mom had other stories she'd told me a few years after the divorce. She'd gotten engaged to Dad a month before his departure, but a few months after he came home, he'd gotten drunk, told her he'd slept with a woman in Korea, then bawled his eyes out and asked for forgiveness, said he'd never cheat again in a million years. I saw novels of pain in Mom's eyes when she told that story: *"If I hadn't had you a couple years later, Hudson, forgiving that piece of shit would've been the biggest mistake of my life."*

After the flag was folded—thirteen times to be exact—a director presented it to Tammy. Her tears dripped onto the blue fabric and stars that lay in her lap.

The whole charade felt completely wrong, like all the praise during the visitation. Dad was none of the things that the service had made him out to be. I was almost angered by it. It was like the life he lived had robbed me of something, even if that something was genuine grief and sadness. There just wasn't much good that he'd brought to my world.

I wasn't glad he was gone. I just wished he'd been somebody different when he was alive.

CHAPTER EIGHT

The rest of my weekend was filled with texts and voicemails from Tammy, trying to convince me, or maybe herself, that Dad had nothing to do with all those guns. She even berated me for not calling the cops to echo her sentiments. Even if I had agreed with her, I figured the cops could uncover the truth quicker without one more person hounding their asses.

The one thing Tammy *should* have called about, but didn't, I found out when an unknown local number left a voicemail late Monday morning. I pressed "Play."

"This message is for Mr. Hudson Miller," it began. "This is Hank Biggs. I'm your . . . uh . . . I was your father's lawyer. Just making sure you're aware that I released his will to its executor, Tammy Jenkins Miller, early this morning. She assured me she'd give you your copy as soon as she saw you, since you're the other beneficiary. If you have any questions, feel free to reach out to my office. You take care now."

As the message ended, I stared at my phone like it was in on some sort of elaborate joke, the word *beneficiary* the punch line. My dad's will wasn't something I'd considered after his death. Not for a second. It was unimaginable that he would've left me a damn thing, but the lawyer had sure suggested otherwise.

I double-checked Tammy's barrage of texts, wondering if there was one I'd missed about the will, but I found none. So I rang her up, asked her about Hank Biggs's message.

"Oh, so now you give a damn?" she said. "Now you've got something to gain from it?"

"When the hell were you planning on telling me about this?"

"You got your call."

"From Dad's *lawyer*," I said. "So what's the big secret? Did Dad leave me a broken weed eater? A sack of marbles?"

"I'm not discussing this over the phone," she said, "so I suggest you come to the house to get your copy of the will."

"Christ, Tammy. Can you—" I stopped myself. I had a profusion of insults on deck, but I hung up. My bar shift was supposed to start at four o'clock. Wasting any time bickering on the phone was pointless.

Within minutes, I was in my Jeep, my mind all over the place as I made another drive to Flint Creek. Of course I was wondering what the hell Dad had left me in his will. Another part of me was curious about how much my old man was worth to begin with. I wasn't sure a mathematician could've formulated an equation fucked up enough to determine that, but it's something I'd pondered before. Dad had left Mom high and dry after their divorce.

At the time they'd split, Mom was working part-time at an insurance agency, and I was sure whatever child support or alimony the judge awarded her paled in comparison to what Dad actually had—she'd been busting her ass to make a decent living ever since. Among other dead-end ventures, she'd worked as a cosmetics retailer at the mall; a leasing agent at an apartment complex that went belly-up; and most recently, selling cable and internet packages for this company out near the coast that changed names and owners like the seasons. Those vultures even had her selling door-to-door for a while. The pay wasn't complete shit, but it wasn't the type of job I liked to see my fifty-seven-year-old mother doing.

Watching her struggle while my dad never wanted for a thing really bolstered my resentment for him. He didn't live a lavish life, but that was a personal choice. When it came to stuff outside of guns and cars and his membership dues to the Boars Club, he was tighter than two coats of paint.

* * *

Other than dogs barking and sniffing my leg, there was no greeting when I walked inside the house. Tammy just tapped her nails on a file folder and said, "Leland wrote this up after that first heart attack last year, so I already know what's in it. Ain't nothing changed."

Whatever was in it sure had her ruffled, and that was a gift within itself. I took a seat next to Tammy on the couch, but not too close. "Let's get to it," I said. "I have work this afternoon."

Tammy lifted her chin, leered through two tiny slits. "Your daddy always said that was just about the stupidest job anybody could do. Babysit a bunch of drunks for a living."

"Ask me if I give a damn," I said, feeling disgust for both her and Dad. I'd lost count of how many times Dad had bad-mouthed my boxing career—or anything else I did that wasn't a nine-to-fiver. In his eyes, anything outside of a traditional workday wasn't real work. I held out my hand. "I didn't drive my ass all the way out here to talk about my job."

Tammy huffed, pulled a paper out of the folder she was holding, gave it an icy glance, and then held a burgundy-speckled fingernail next to a section titled "Money and Personal Property."

I took the paper, read the lines below the heading.

I give all the money from my personal savings, my vehicles, and my tangible personal property at 1701 Creekview Rd., including all policies and proceeds of insurance covering such property, to my wife, Tammy Jenkins Miller. I give my three rental properties at 110, 111, and 112 Wynt Road, as well as my personal business, Miller's Pull-a-Part, the land on which it sits, along with all accounts and professional equipment belonging to the business, to my son, Hudson Lee Miller.

I read the last line again. And one more time, very carefully, to be sure. The truth of the words was confirmed when I looked up and saw the animosity in Tammy's glare.

"You've known about this for over a year?"

She searched her purse, only producing an empty pack of cigarettes. "Thought some of this might change," she said, pushing the purse away. "Never thought he had so little time left when he wrote it."

There was no doubt: she wanted the rental properties and the salvage yard for herself. She wanted everything.

"Guess you can sell all that shit off." Her words oozed bitterness. "Don't know who'd want that salvage yard. And those rental homes are more headache than they're worth. Leland should've got rid of them years ago."

I hadn't even known my dad still owned the rental properties, three modular homes no bigger than double-wides he'd bought when I was pretty young. They sat side by side on a piece of property Dad called The Ponderosa—though I never knew why. He probably thought it sounded fancy, but it was far from it. It was more like a mobile home park, except the homes weren't mobile.

"Somebody might want the salvage yard," I mumbled.

"Keep in mind, the Winnebago parked out there belongs to me." Tammy held up her copy of the will, pointed at the word *vehicles*.

I ignored her greed. My mind was reeling, trying to solve the biggest mystery of all: why Dad had left me those things. Beyond the fact that we weren't close and had never once discussed any of this, I didn't know shit about being a landlord and even less about running a salvage yard. Maybe, I considered, it was the macho side of my dad, making sure a man took over his businesses—and not just any man, but someone from the Miller bloodline. Or, possibly, my dad knew Tammy was too damn stupid to know what to do with all of it.

My personal bias aside, Tammy was as helpless a person as I'd ever met. After all the grief my dad gave me for boxing and bartending, it was a real mindblower that he gave her a pass. Her idea of a job, for years, was sitting her ass in the living room, smoking and drinking Diet Mountain Dew while she stuffed envelopes full of entry forms to every sweepstakes, prize drawing, and contest imaginable. Occasionally she'd even win, which I credited to sheer statistics, a numbers game, like a terrible boxer landing a lucky punch once in a blue moon. Sometimes Tammy would win a check, sometimes a gift card, one time this mini-fridge she sold in a garage sale within a week of winning it. Still, I was pretty damned sure she never broke even considering all the money she blew on postage.

Now, here she was, greedy as Don-fucking-King. She'd just *won* a house, a truck, an RV, and whatever cash Dad had tucked away over the years—that is, if she could ever find it all. She'd probably need a treasure map just to scratch the surface. That part tickled me, imagining Tammy crawling through Dad's backyard with a garden shovel, her knees and elbows mud-caked.

I got up from the couch. "I guess I'll have to sign some papers soon?"

I wasn't purposely salting her wounds with the comment, but I didn't regret its obvious effect when she cut me a dirty look.

"You know? It must be nice to get something you didn't earn," she said.

"Last I checked, my last name is Miller."

"You ain't been a Miller for years."

"The hell is that supposed to mean?"

"How much did you come around to see your daddy once you left town? Once a year? Twice?"

"You've got to be kidding me," I said, withholding words like *psycho*, *bitch*, and *nutjob* that swirled in my mind. "You think that's all my fault?"

"You barely even called after the heart attacks."

"Of all people, I don't owe you an explanation, Tammy."

I turned to walk away, but her words followed me to the door, along with her sniffling dogs: "I used to clean those rental units. Won't be doing that anymore."

I looked back with a squinty-eyed smile. "I think I can manage," I said. "And speaking of earning something. You know who really deserves everything Dad left you?"

She cocked her head.

"My mom," I told her.

* * *

I drove back to Greensboro in a silence as heavy with confusion as it was uncertainty. From the time I'd woken up, I'd gone from owning nothing but a Jeep with bald tires and shitty wiper blades to owning three rental houses and a salvage yard. All courtesy of a single sentence on a piece of legally binding paper.

Maybe that explained what Dad's call had been about. Perhaps he'd known something bad was going to happen, wanted me to know about the salvage yard. Of course, there's no way that question would ever be answered.

The news would've been a bombshell either way. It wasn't the sort of thing that came with a set of instructions explaining what to do next and how to feel about it, nor was it the kind of thing I could crumple into a ball, leave on Dad's headstone, tell him, "Thanks, but no thanks." All that stuff was mine now, a burden I hadn't signed up for. Whether that burden would be a blessing or a curse, it was too early to tell.

I called Mom when I got back to the apartment. She was preoccupied with berating midday traffic until I broke the news.

"You're yanking my chain," she said.

"I read it with my own eyes, Mom."

"Wow," she said, then laughed. "Just . . . wow."

"Guess I'm not the only one who's surprised."

I could hear a car horn through the phone; Mom called someone a *turkey butt* before she sighed heavily. "You know, Hudson, that's the first time that sorry bastard's given anyone a thing in his life other than a last name and a headache." She apologized for calling my dead dad a sorry bastard, though she probably knew I wasn't offended. "At least those rental homes could bring you some extra income. I know you could use it, honey. If you don't want to mess with all that, sell the blasted things."

She was right, and that part of the equation seemed pretty simple. It was Miller's Pull-a-Part that lurked in my mind like an angry heavyweight. When I asked her what I should do about it, she offered some advice that didn't push my sails one way or another: *Just do whatever makes you happy.*

I asked, "You read that on a bumper sticker?"

She laughed. "A fortune cookie."

"I don't know what kind of money I'll get out of all this, Mom, but when I get my head above water, I'm sending you some of it."

"I'm your mother, Hudson. Not a charity case."

"I know that, but you earned it for putting up with his ass all those years. Call it hazard pay."

I heard another honk, another expletive I assumed was directed toward Wilmington traffic. "That's sweet, honey. But I wouldn't take a damn thing that came from him."

CHAPTER NINE

My shift was slow that night. It had been freeze-your-ass-off cold that whole week, and there weren't any good college basketball games on TV to draw an early-week crowd, so I was the sole bartender. A few people lingered around one of the pool tables, but none looked interested in picking up a pool stick. At the end of the bar were a man and woman; the man was probably forty, at least a decade older than the woman. They both wore business attire and were drunk-flirting. He was on his third Guinness, and she was nursing her second rosé, working her finger around the rim of the glass, real suggestive. I figured them for out-of-towners. Either that or they had done a shit job at picking a bar. There were at least three nicer places for a drink within a block of Red Door.

I was hoping Randy the Regular might stop by so I could solicit some advice, but instead, I got a different visitor around ten thirty—my roommate, Danny. He came over and mounted a barstool. He turned his Atlanta Braves hat around backward, started shaking his head. I knew he was waiting on me to ask what was the matter, so I obliged.

"I don't understand women," he said.

I smiled and took a glass from the drying rack. Poured Danny's go-to, Fat Tire, and slid the full glass across the bar. "What did you do now?"

He looked insulted. "Didn't do anything, man. Told Lindsay I wasn't staying with her tonight and she pitched a fit."

"And you actually left?" I gave him a slow clap. "Look at you . . . finally growing a pair."

He took a big gulp, wiped his upper lip. "I have to work early tomorrow, and she's had this God-awful cough for about a week. Can't hardly sleep when she's laying there, hacking up her lungs all night long. It's torture."

"Oh, so you're being *insensitive*."

"Her exact words," he said. "It's always something."

"She just wants her big teddy bear to cuddle with," I said with the empathy of Mister Rogers. "Is that such a crime?"

"She's being dramatic."

"She's about to be a lawyer here soon," I said. "I wouldn't raise your white flag just yet. Those services could come in handy one day, especially with the way you drive."

"You got jokes, huh?"

"Trust me. I'm the only one that dealt with somebody crazy today."

Danny scrunched his eyebrows. "Jehovah's Witness?"

"If I were only so lucky," I said. "Had to meet with my stepmom. About my dad's will."

"Terrible T," Danny mumbled. His nickname for Tammy. He nodded slowly, tried to look sympathetic. "I'm sorry, man. Shit. How did that go?"

"Well, the old man made me a beneficiary."

"He left you something?"

"Yep."

"Lucky son of a gun. Was it a million bucks?"

"Not quite."

"A hundred?"

"Not a dime," I said. "You won't believe it."

"Try me."

"According to the will, I am now the proud owner of . . . can I get a drumroll?"

Danny drummed his fingers on the bar and his face brightened.

I deepened my voice: "Not one, not two, but *three* rental houses, and for my grand prize . . ." Danny's drumming stopped. "Flint Creek's premiere junk heap: Miller's Pull-a-Part!"

"The salvage yard?"

"Yes-siree."

"No fucking way, dude."

"Yes fucking way."

"Man, just like on *Sanford and Son*." He attempted a Fred Sanford impersonation: *"I'ma give you a five across the lips."*

I shrugged.

"Seriously, Hud. Props on the houses—I'm sure they're fit for royalty—but what in God's name are you going to do with a salvage yard?"

"Beats me," I said. "Closest I've come to owning a business was a Kool-Aid stand when I was seven."

"I bet it wasn't even real Kool-Aid either."

"Probably not. And my only customer was my mom."

"That's pretty sad," he said. "Know how much a place like Miller's-Yank-Yer-Part is going for these days?"

"More than the Kool-Aid stand, I'm sure."

"I'd figure that shit out pronto. Then sell that bad boy. It's not like you have any other choice."

"What do you mean?"

"You sure as hell couldn't keep that place running. Even if you could, imagine going back to Flint Creek, having to rub elbows with all those slack-jawed, Jerry Falwell wannabes." He jutted out his chin, turned his hat around, resting it atop his head. "Mr. Miller, my wife . . . er . . . my sister's looking for a chain-link steering wheel for her Trans Am. Y'all got any?"

"You're a special kind of dumbass, but you're probably right."

"Damn skippy. I'd sell that place quick as I could."

"Assuming it's even sellable," I said. "And then what?"

After another big gulp of beer, Danny belched impressively and said, "Correct me if I'm wrong, but I'm sure you're ready to move out of my lovely little guest room."

I smiled. "You trying to kick me out?"

"Nah, man. I like having you around. Makes me feel better about my life choices. But God knows that sofa sleeps like asphalt. I've had that thing since my one year in college."

"It's not exactly memory foam." I pretended to crack my neck. My current living situation wasn't ideal, but I'd appreciated Danny renting me a cheap room the last few months.

He took a long look around the bar, then at me. "If that salvage yard is worth enough money, and you can make some money off those houses, you could open your own bar. Something nicer than this. Have some live music and shit."

"A bar owner. My lifelong dream."

"Fine then. Move your ass out to Vegas instead. Give boxing another shot when your suspension is up."

I left that conversation alone and turned the tables. "Say you came into a little money. What would you do? Assuming your sugar mama wises up and finds another guy."

"What would I do?" Danny said, his voice trailing off. His eyes got lost in his beer glass for a moment; he used his thumb to wipe some condensation off the glass. "Let's see . . . I'm twenty-seven now, and I've been selling phones in a mall kiosk since I was nineteen, back when the flip phone was still cool. So I'd probably tell my boss to kiss my ass, then do some entrepreneur-type shit."

"The hell does that even mean?"

"I don't know, like flip some houses or something. My cousin—the one that drives the Hummer—gave me an audiobook that tells you exactly how to do it. Sounds pretty easy. Once I saved up enough money, I wouldn't do a damn thing for a while. Golf and drink myself fatter."

"I think you've got that last part down pat without the money."

"Such a smartass." Danny laughed, then looked serious. "Somebody told me you fucked some dude up the other night. Out on the sidewalk. How come you didn't tell me?"

"Fucked him up? That's not even halfway true."

"That's not what I—" he stopped mid-sentence when his phone rang. He picked it up but didn't answer. "Damn," he mumbled. "Sorry, dude. I got to catch this."

"Sugar mama?"

A nod. "I'll see you later on." He slapped some crumpled dollar bills onto the bar and was out the door in a breath, phone glued to his ear.

I poured out the last sip of his beer, checked with the couple at the end of the bar. The guy let me know they were doing just fine, so I sat down for a moment. I looked around the near-empty bar, took it in like Danny had. Imagined myself doing the same type of job a year from then, two years from now.

Becoming a career bartender or even owning a place like Red Door wasn't something I'd ever wanted. I started bartending because it fit my training schedule and didn't tire me out like the job I had when I first got my pro card, which was loading box trucks for a fabric company. Training was destroying my body enough as it was. I figured serving drinks wasn't as demanding as hoisting fabric rolls for eight-hour shifts.

I saw bartending as one of those jobs you do for a while to pay the bills; next thing you know, years have passed and you're still living that same lifestyle, hanging around the same kind of people, having the same conversations about what comes next. You get comfortable, complacent. But to be fair, the same could be said about a lot of jobs. And maybe that was true about my boxing career. Deep down, I knew I wasn't headed for boxing stardom. I'd enjoyed a solid run in the ring, just over seven years as a pro, but I'd never faced a real contender or fought on a Vegas undercard. I was a big fish in a small pond, living from one fight to the next.

My love for boxing was a double-edged sword. I loved the science of the sport. I loved the discipline of training as much as the ecstasy of victory, but somewhere along the way I'd fallen into a cycle: I would set a short-term goal, reach it, then bask in the afterglow.

Rinse. Repeat.

It's like I was slowly climbing a ladder that never reached high enough.

But if I had won my fight back in June, I could've moved on to a couple bigger fights before calling it quits, put the prize money away until I was ready to take a step forward in my life. One that didn't involve a future as a punch-drunk dude in his mid-thirties, still cutting weight and getting stitches on the reg. Maybe I could've used that money to open up a gym of my own. Something that I felt good about. Something bigger than myself.

In my twenty-nine years, the only true purpose I'd ever felt was back when I was still training youngsters at Langley Rec. Since the gym was city funded, it didn't cost but twenty bucks a year for a membership, so it served as an unofficial babysitter of sorts to a bunch of kids who didn't have a dime to their names or parents that gave two shits about them. I had my own problems growing up, but nothing like what some of those kids had gone through. I cared about them, and I think they knew that. That's what made it so hard when I had to hand over my coaching whistle. Felt like I'd let those kids down.

Since then, my only service to the community was helping folks drown their sorrows in beer and whiskey. Occasionally, I'd put a drunk in a full nelson to keep him or her from dishing out or taking an ass whipping. Not the type of thing that gives you the warm fuzzies when you lay your head down at night.

* * *

Soon, the pool table crew came over to pay their tabs. They left a tip of loose change in the oversized mason jar near the register, and more importantly, they snapped the drunk flirters out of their love trance at the end of the bar. Otherwise, I was fully prepared to play "Closing Time" by Semisonic in a few minutes to give them a clue.

The man checked his watch, came over, and closed out his debit card. He asked if I thought his date looked like Mila Kunis—loud enough so she heard the question. Other than her dark hair, she didn't look a thing like Mila Kunis.

"Total doppelganger," I told him, in hopes of a good tip.

He seemed confused by the word. After he staggered away with Fake Mila latched to his arm, I checked his thirty-two-dollar tab.

He'd left me a three-buck tip.

CHAPTER TEN

I more than slept on things. I daydreamed and drank on things. I weighed my options the best I could. Problem is, the things I was piling on the scales were equally murky and immeasurable; my current trajectory was as uncertain as being the heir to my dad's throne of rental houses and junk cars.

Meantime, life didn't offer a rest and a pep talk between rounds. I worked a double on Tuesday, the lunch shift on Wednesday. Made next to shit.

On Wednesday afternoon, my dad's lawyer carved out some time to meet with me at his strip mall office in Thomasville, a town just south of Flint Creek. I only knew Hank Biggs from low-budget commercials that used to air on local channels. Hank sporting a cowboy hat, acting real homespun, always ending his ads with *"If you want to get serious, you need to think Biggs."*

In person, he looked as I remembered, minus the cowboy hat. He was tall and husky with a white beard and flowing white hair reminiscent of a Kenny Rogers album cover Dad used to have in his garage. He welcomed me into his office and shook my hand with a grip that didn't complement his huge presence.

I thought he might offer a word of sympathy, but instead he said, "So you're the fighter, huh?" His Southern accent was slight. Nothing like the TV ads, where his drawl was better suited for *Hee Haw*.

I almost said "I used to be," but I just nodded as we both settled into a seat.

He beheld my stick arms and bird chest, probably thinking that those things didn't belong on a guy that got paid to beat the shit out of people. "Looked you up on the internet this morning," he said. "Found a couple matches of yours. Hell of a jab you got, kid. They ever give you a nickname?"

"Not that I'm aware of," I said. "And I always thought you'd have to be a real cheesedick to make up your own."

He looked out of his office window, into the parking lot, as if that's where he stored old memories, looked back at me and said, "They called me The Train. Back in my ring days."

"You boxed?"

Biggs inspected the knuckles on his right hand. They were burly, with deep lines in the skin like cracked earth. A thin scar between the last two knuckles was particularly telling; he'd probably punched a wall at some point and broken his hand. A boxer's fracture, doctors call it. More obvious than my only visible battle wound: an ever so slightly crooked nose, thanks to an illegal elbow.

"Used to do Toughman Contests in the eighties," Biggs said. "City Lake Gymnasium hosted them pretty regular. I even won a couple. Got a trophy and cash prize. Still got the trophy somewhere. Spent the cash."

I pegged him as one of those peaked-at-age-twenty guys who refused to let go of his glory days, wanted to brag about the shit he did before life dished out things like joint problems and responsibilities. "I was kind of like the White Larry Holmes," he told me twice before finishing his verbal pugilist memoirs.

"Good times," he finally said after a sigh. He scooted closer to his desk and then started sorting through some paperwork and offering mind-numbing legal explanations of the inheritance process. About the time he completely lost my attention, he opened a folder with Dad's most recent financial and tax statements. "You plan on being a landlord, Mr. Miller?"

"To be honest, Mr. Biggs, I didn't plan on any of this," I said. "Kind of just fell into my lap."

"There are plenty of things we don't plan for in this world. But life goes on, as they say. Wasn't there a TV show called that? *Life Goes On?*"

I said I thought there was and pointed at the folder Biggs was holding. "The whole landlord thing. Would it even be worth my time?"

"You ever owned a house before?"

I shook my head.

"I see," Biggs said. He sucked at his teeth, took a piece of paper out of the folder and studied it. "As it stands right now, two of those properties are under contract for the next six and eight months, respectively. The other was vacated back in December." His finger navigated the page and stopped. "The tenants are paying six hundred bucks, plus utilities, but any maintenance issues were coming out of your father's pocket. Busted water lines, broken A/C, mess like that."

"He wouldn't have toyed around with all that unless he was making some decent money though, right?"

A nod. "After taxes and all that fun stuff, he was probably pulling in over a grand a month, give or take, when all three places were tenanted. Not a bad supplement. Especially since he had those houses completely paid off almost fifteen years ago."

He handed a couple of the papers over, and I looked at them like I understood all the words and numbers, but a bigger issue was distracting me. "What do you know about the salvage yard?"

Biggs thumbed through some papers in a different folder. Told another unwanted story as he did, this one about how Dad once sold him a dual exhaust for an older model Plymouth Duster that he used to drag race at Caraway Speedway.

When he came to the right paper, he said, "First off, Leland kept his bills and taxes paid up. Never owed squat to anybody. That, my friend, is a damn good thing. I've seen folks leave their kids or spouses nothing but a pile of debt. Situations like that can get real ugly. So I'd say you're pretty lucky, Mr. Miller. Your father ran a solid business."

Solid business. I couldn't help but picture the treasure trove of illegal firearms.

Biggs pulled another page from the folder. "With all those vehicles, parts, equipment, and whatnot, it appears your father had about three hundred and seventy-five thousand dollars sitting on that property. At least that's what it says here. And he reported a profit last year of just over fifty-six grand. Not too shabby."

"Fifty-six grand," I whispered; it was far more than I'd ever made in a year's time. And I knew that number didn't include my dad's hustle of buying shitty cars, fixing them up at the yard, and selling them for cash. It's something he'd done when I was a kid. Something Grandpa Miller had taught him. "What about Charlie, the guy that worked for him? How much was he getting paid?"

Biggs had a good laugh at the question. "There aren't any stakeholders listed in these documents, if you catch my drift, son."

Understood. Dad had been paying Charlie Shoaf under the table.

Biggs went on: "As far as the property the business sits on, which has been in the Miller family for over forty years, there's some good news and bad."

"What's the good?"

"Like I said, the land has been in your family for nearly half a century. You own those four acres. Bad news is this: if you wanted to sell it off, you'd have a hell of a time doing it."

"It's in the middle of nowhere."

"That may be true, but that's not the reason," he said. "The salvage yard sits on what they call a brownfield property. Meaning, it's a piece of land that's had hazardous waste on it for a long damn time. Stuff that comes from those cars—gasoline and fluids and all that nasty junk. It's not good for the soil."

I dropped that into the shit-I-didn't-know bucket. "Meaning I'm stuck with it," I said.

"If you want to look at it that way, I suppose."

"How would you look at it?"

"Like somebody gave me an opportunity," he said. "There's something to be said for owning something, young man. Not having to answer to anyone about it." He spread his arms wide like he was Lord of creation. "That's why I opened my own firm. My old boss was a real prick. Now I'm the head asshole in charge."

He went into more legal explanations. There were more papers for me to sign. Luckily, no more bullshit stories.

As I gathered some documents, put the keys to the salvage yard and rental properties in my coat pocket, Biggs left me with one last sentiment: "I didn't know your father real well. He wasn't big on lawyers, which I can understand, but I can tell you this much: he wanted you to have that salvage yard and those houses."

I looked at him curiously.

"Wasn't a question about it," he said, nodding. "He never wavered on the fact."

"All this has thrown me for a loop, Mr. Biggs. Me and my dad weren't exactly tight these last few years. Everything that's happened feels like some sort of weird dream."

"I understand that." He stood to see me out. "That don't mean he didn't give a shit. Maybe he wanted you to have some responsibility. Something lined up for your future. Bet you didn't go to college, did you?"

"I could've," I said, a bit defensive. "Brawn without brains is a one-way ticket to the poor house. That's what my coach used to tell me. He used to leave books in my locker, made me show him my report cards every nine weeks. So, if you think I'm—"

"Hell, I didn't mean nothing by it, Mr. Miller. I'm just saying. Maybe Leland wanted something for you apart from all that boxing. Ever think of that?"

I hadn't thought of that. But the part about Dad giving a shit was laughable.

CHAPTER ELEVEN

I had plenty to contemplate after the meeting, more questions I needed answered, so I did some more homework that evening. I searched online, called up a couple of salvage yard operators in Payne County, hoping they'd let me pick their brains. Hoped even more they'd want to buy some inventory from Miller's Pull-a-Part.

I got hold of a couple guys: a fellow named Francis Wilkes who ran Triple-A Auto Salvage, and a guy named Sidney Creech who owned an outfit called Metal Junkeez. Both of them had heard about my dad's murder and sounded deeply sorry about it, but neither were interested in buying any inventory on a piece-by-piece basis. Creech told me I could crush the vehicles, sell them for scrap metal, liquidate the remaining inventory for dirt cheap. He also said I could make a shit ton more if I ran the salvage yard the way my dad had, especially since I already owned the land.

The extra money sounded good, but the know-how to run a yard? I didn't have a fucking clue. There was only one person that I could think of that did: Charlie Shoaf. If he could help me out, I'd at least try to keep the business afloat until I found a buyer.

I called him up. "This Charlie?"

"Who's asking?"

"Charlie, this is Leland Miller's son. Hudson."

"Listen, boy. I done told the cops I don't know nothing about none of them guns or who shot your daddy. Wish to hell I could be just left alone."

"This isn't about the investigation. I'm calling because I need some help."

"Don't believe there's anything I can help you with."

"I own the salvage yard now. Dad left it to me. Don't know if Tammy or Dad's lawyer told you or not."

"She didn't tell me nothing. And I sure as hell don't talk to no lawyers."

"Go figure," I said under my breath. "I know you worked for Dad for quite a—"

"Nine years," he said. "Nine years and three months."

"So you know his place like the back of your hand."

"What is it you're asking? You're interrupting my TV shows."

"I need some help down at the yard. At least for a little bit."

"Don't tell me you're thinking about keeping it open."

"I am for now," I said. "Can't let it just sit there. And I'm going to need some help running it."

After a wheezy laugh, Charlie said, "Ain't you some kind of barkeep? The salvage business ain't no—"

"Spare me the lecture," I said. "You don't know shit about me."

"Well, your daddy—"

"He didn't know me either," I said. "I'll figure this thing out one way or another. With or without you. Now, you can be an asshole like Tammy and laugh in my face, talk shit about what I do to pay my bills, *or* you can help me and make some money in the process."

There was silence on the other end that made me fearful my little rant had scared Charlie off.

He laughed again, less condescending. "She is a bit of a pill, ain't she?"

"Tammy? Hell, yeah," I said. "She doesn't think I can handle this, but I can and will. Even if it's just to prove her wrong."

"To be frank with you, boy, it ain't easy for me to drive by the salvage yard right now after what happened. Plus, when your daddy *was* alive, things were simple at the yard."

"Simple, how?"

"We had ourselves an arrangement."

"I already know," I said. "Dad paid you under the table."

"Ain't just that. He didn't breathe down my damn neck or hound me about shit so long as I was working hard. He even let me drink beer on Saturday afternoons. It was like my reward for the week. A bonus."

"Dad let you drink on the job?"

"As long as I didn't have too many or try and operate heavy machinery."

"Doesn't sound half bad. I've worked at a bar for years. My boss would can my ass if he caught me sneaking a drink on shift."

"Reckon I had it cushy."

"If you don't mind me asking, how much was Dad paying you?"

"Four hundred a week, exactly how I wanted it: seven fifties and fifty singles."

"Fifty ones?" I laughed, and then asked if those ones were for Rear Ends, Payne County's dumpiest strip club.

"Hell, no. You ever been in that joint? Ain't even got lunch specials. I spend that money on video poker down in Asheboro. This joint called Lucky 64. Cambodian fellow that owns it pays winners cash money."

"I don't give a damn what you do with your money," I said. "I'll pay you with four hundred singles if that'll make you happy."

He groaned again, so I tried a different tactic. "I'll keep whatever arrangement you had with Dad, and I'll raise him one."

"Go on . . ."

"What kind of beer do you drink?"

"The good stuff," Charlie said, like there was one universal truth to what that was. "Keystone."

Good if you're into drinking piss, I thought. "How about this: four hundred bucks a week, however you like it, and on Saturdays I'll bring you a case of Keystone."

He made a whistling sound. "I don't know about—"

"Listen, Charlie. I need money, and I'm sure you do too. Nobody in their right mind would hire an old-timer like you right now. And they definitely won't pay you in cash and beer."

"I ain't that old."

"The hell you aren't," I said. "I saw you getting into your car at the funeral. A damn champagne-colored Park Avenue. Has one of those fur steering wheel covers, I bet."

"What in the hell's that got to do with anything?"

"Do you want the job or not? I'll find somebody either way," I told him. "I'll post the job online. Probably find me somebody that isn't drawing Social Security."

A grunt, then, "I don't like no warm beer. Once that shit gets room temperature, it ain't ever the same again. Loses its—"

"You come work for me, I'll bring it in a cooler."

"God almighty, you're pushy."

"And you're unemployed," I said. "I don't mean that as an insult. You just strike me as a man that likes to keep himself busy. Plus, something's got to fund that video poker. You have to work hard to play hard. Am I right?"

A long pause. "I don't need you riding my ass about every little thing. Understood? I know how to do this job just fine on my own."

"I'm not much for ass riding," I said, "but I am ready to get this thing rolling."

"How soon are you talking?"

"This week sounds as good as any."

"What . . . like Saturday?"

"Just told you that Saturday is beer day. You'll have to earn that little bonus. How's Friday sound?"

Charlie mumbled some choice words, then said, "Meet me at seven in the morning."

"Don't know if you've checked a calendar, but tomorrow's Thursday."

"No shit," he said. "I need to show you just enough so you don't burn the place down come Friday."

CHAPTER TWELVE

I pulled up to the salvage yard just before seven Thursday morning. Unlocked the metal padlock and swung open the double gates to the lot. It had been a long time since I'd seen the place, but things weren't wildly different from my expectations. Though my perception of the place had changed, everything looked as I remembered it. Except back then, it was a rusted, metal wonderland. The place where Dad worked. A dad that still occupied that role of hero, who did interesting things at work all day that gave him that special brand of fatherly scent: motor oil and sweat, sometimes lingering aftershave. But that was over twenty years ago. Now, the salvage yard was mine, and so were the anxieties and uncertainties that came in a package deal with ownership.

In the center of the lot was "the shop," as Dad always called it. A white cinderblock building that housed the main office that was surely surrounded by police tape just weeks before. The other half of the building was a roomy, double-bay garage where Dad used to work on his black Chevy truck, changing spark plugs and oil, buffing its chrome wheels until they shone like mirrors. Before my dad took over the lot,

Grandpa Miller had run a full-service mechanic shop in the garage. He'd worked on so many clunkers that weren't worth fixing, he ended up buying some of them from customers, selling the parts from those cars. That's how Miller's Service and Lube became Miller's Pull-a-Part.

Stories like that, along with any fond memories I had of the place, had lost their luster over the years. The things that once wowed me as a kid were now intimidating. Rows of cars, trucks, and vans that had served as walls and top-secret hideouts when I would play imaginary football and war games were now just barriers between me and some semblance of a profit.

I moved my Jeep close to the shop, noting the monstrosity of a Winnebago parked just beside it. *Tammy's* Winnebago. Twenty-five feet long. A custom-painted eagle and American flag on the side. If I were as petty as Tammy, I'd have charged her to park the damn thing on the lot.

I walked to the shop entrance that had been left unlocked for whatever reason, and I opened the door to an igloo. Another memory: Dad rarely ran heat in the shop. A lousy way for him to save a buck. I turned the lights on, walked to the left side of the room, and turned on a small, ceramic heater in the corner. It groaned to life, pushing dusty, lukewarm air into my eyes.

I turned on another heater up front in the waiting area, which consisted of a few chairs and a faded leather couch huddled around a table fashioned out of old tires and a piece of acrylic-coated plywood, chipped away by years of use. Next to the furniture, a drip coffee maker and a seventies-style Coke machine with faux wood on the sides. A small bubble

gum machine was in the corner, courtesy of some unspeci-
fied Boars Club fundraiser; it was nearly full of the tasteless,
ten-cent pieces of gum that I used to chew by the jaw full
when I was a kid.

The rest of the room was occupied by a large, L-shaped
desk, the front covered in old license plates except for a spot
where two hand-painted signs were mounted:

"Body and electrical parts sold as is."

"The deadline for complaints was yesterday."

It was in front of this desk where the cops said Dad had
been shot and killed. I examined the floor, wondering if there
were any bloodstains on the bluish concrete, but I saw no
blood. I'd never knowingly stood in a spot where a murder
had taken place; there was an eeriness to it, so I kept moving.

I walked around the front desk to the hallway that ran
behind it. There was a tiny bathroom on the left. Beyond
it, a break room with a mini fridge and microwave, a cork
board covered with restaurant menus, business cards, some
Clinton-era political cartoons, and a vintage centerfold fea-
turing two topless blondes. A caption: "Everything is Bigger
in Texas."

A storage room was across the hall. When I looked inside,
the piece of carpet I'd seen in Coble's pictures was no longer
on the ground; someone had rolled it up, stood it in the corner. What it once covered, the no-longer secret cubby in the
floor, piqued my curiosity, but before I had time to inspect it
further, a bell jingled from the front of the shop.

When I reached the end of the hallway, Charlie Shoaf
was standing just inside the front door in a flannel jacket and
grease-smeared jeans. He had a dog leashed just behind him.

A brown and white pit bull—or something close to it—with a cartoonish underbite.

I said good morning, but Charlie barely made a sound.

"Bring-your-dog-to-work day?" I asked.

"This is Buster." A solemn tone. Strike one on me breaking the ice. "Our security system. I've been keeping him at my place since the . . . uh . . ."

"Probably didn't like all those police around, did he?"

"Buster likes most everybody as long as it's still light out. I suppose he looks the part, though."

I walked over to the dog and crouched down to give his head a rub. Buster didn't wag his tail, but he didn't pull away either. "Mr. Personality," I said, looking at an unenthused Charlie.

Strike two.

"Need to chain him up," Charlie said, and then he and Buster walked outside, neither with any pep in their step.

Already I wasn't thrilled about having to work with Mr. Stick-in-his-ass eight or more hours a day, but I didn't have much choice. When Charlie came back in, he slid off his safety-orange toboggan that briefly clung to a wisp of white hair that wasn't nearly as thick as the eyebrows that had free reign of his forehead. He sauntered to the waiting area and started making a pot of coffee. Put a filter in the machine, heaped a couple scoops of Maxwell House into the filter, and then poured some water from his own thermos into the machine. Didn't bother washing out the grimy pot.

While the coffee dripped, neither of us said a word. Just the sounds of Mr. Coffee laboring and breath whistling out of Charlie's bulbous nose. Once the coffee was done, Charlie refilled his thermos and took a few cautious sips before he sank into the leather couch. All his movements were slow and exaggerated, and I could tell it wasn't just because of his age. I'd inconvenienced his life in some way, and he wanted me to know it.

Charlie sat his thermos on a Mopar catalog that lay open on the table. He gave me a sideways glance. "I think you've bit off more than you can chew. Coming back here like you've done."

I asked him what was the worst thing that could happen, and immediately I wanted to reel those words back in. For Dad, the worst *had* happened. I tried again: "I'm broker than broke. Need the money. And nobody's lined up to buy this place."

"Well, those cars don't come through here with a load of cash stashed inside. Actual work has to be done."

"I don't need you to 'mansplain' the situation. I know that. Why do you think I offered you a job?"

"Just so we're crystal, the only reason I decided to come back was out of respect for your daddy. Don't need him rolling over in his grave because you've run Miller's Pull-a-Part into the damn ground." He leaned forward, elbows on his knees. "So for starters, if you don't know how, what, or why to do something, don't do it. You're liable to fuck things up."

"Fucking things up is what I do best, so I guess you'll really be earning that four hundred a week then," I said, wondering how the hell I would come up with the money. "The Keystone too."

The mention of beer seemed to soften Charlie's scowl for a moment, like the stick in his ass had momentarily shrunk.

He snatched his thermos from the table and rose from his seat. He walked out the front door, so I followed. After a few more coffee sips and a Camel he smoked to the filter, Charlie began his official tour of the yard. He started by explaining some of the equipment, including a Bobcat and the big yellow car crusher, which I had used to imagine turning into a Transformer. He told me I better keep the hell away from both, then went on a tangent about how they preferred Jetty Oliver's Towing instead of Big Buck's Towing Service because Buck Gibson was a good-for-nothing crook that would steal a dollar from his own mother.

Don't fuck with the equipment. Don't fuck with Buck.
Noted.

The tour moved to the garage, which was empty of cars but contained a large metal shelf organized by product: "Engine parts," "Transfer cases," "Transmissions," "Truck hitches."

Charlie told me that Dad usually paid customers around a hundred and fifty bucks a ton for their vehicles. Before he put those vehicles out in the yard, he'd drain and recycle their fluids—a process that came with a whole list of dos and don'ts and EPA regulations—then remove any unusable parts he could potentially refurbish. Once a car was picked near clean in the yard, he'd crush and sell its metal frame for scrap.

After he gave me a rundown on what they did with engines and transmissions and other bigger ticket items, we walked into the office, where he got another caffeine fix. This time, a Coke from the drink machine. "They only serve Pepsis at the police station," he said for something to say.

I bought myself a Coke too.

Charlie walked behind the front desk, set his drink down. He turned on a computer that looked like it belonged out in the yard next to some rusted mopeds. "Prices and inventory is something you're going to have to learn quick. Kid your age should know his way around the computer. Unless you've been hit too many times."

"I can handle it." I eyed the computer. "All the info I need on there?"

A nasally laugh. "Guess you didn't know your daddy too well, huh, Rocky Balboa?" Charlie reached under the desk and started pulling out thick spiral notebooks and plopped them on the counter. "Only thing on that computer is current part prices and metal market trends. And that's only because Tammy pestered him about it for so long." He placed his hand on one of the notebooks like he was taking an oath. "Details about the vehicles and where to find them in the yard is in these."

Each was labeled: "Chevy," "Ford," "Volkswagen," and so on.

I said, "Wouldn't it be easier if that info was in the computer?"

"Everybody's got their own system for doing things, I reckon. Your old man had his. He bought a vehicle? He put it in those books. Even the folks' names he bought them from. The date he bought the car. The VIN. All that. Once Leland wrote that shit down, he could just about memorize it."

Charlie opened the Ford notebook to a random page.

1996 Ford Aerostar (Eddie Bauer Edition). Purch. from Janet Edwards—5/21/2013 for 280 cash.

*Fan engine and power seat motors not working
Location: Row 6*

"That's a hell of a system," I said. I wondered if Dad had written down prices for those illegal guns in a notebook like these.

"His daddy—your granddaddy—didn't have the luxury of no computer. Leland did his best to keep things the way they were." He fanned through the pages of the notebook. "You know what they say about things if they ain't broke."

"We're at a salvage yard, Charlie. Everything around here's broke."

The hard front he'd put up all day finally cracked a little. I could've sworn a grin started to spread on his dry lips, but it quickly dissipated, like Charlie was angry at himself for breaking character. He turned his attention to the computer, clicked the mouse a few times—much harder than anyone should ever click a mouse. He tilted his head back to invite me behind the desk.

He brought up a program on the screen, and his explanation of how to search for a part may as well have been in Japanese; I knew I could figure it out much quicker on my own, dicking around with it for a while.

"Prices on here are up to date," Charlie said. "And your daddy was always fair with his dealings, so there wasn't no talking him down. That's how he stayed competitive with bigger yards. Don't mean he didn't bust a few peoples' asses now and then."

I gave a questioning look.

"There's etiquette to salvage yards. Rules."

"Enlighten me."

"Pull-a-part yards are self-service," Charlie said. "Folks are supposed to bring their own tools. We'll provide a wheelbarrow, even an A-frame if they need one, but the rest is up to the customer. That don't mean they can go out there all willy-nilly, yanking and breaking shit that don't need breaking to get the part they need. Need a piece of wire? Then don't fuck up the whole wiring harness. If you have some greasy ass part, don't lay it on a car seat. Somebody's sweet old granny might need that seat." He took his toboggan from his coat pocket and pulled it onto his head, all the way to his jungle of eyebrows. "Your daddy kept his eye out for things like that. If folks didn't show respect for the process, then their prices magically went up when they came lugging stuff up to the counter."

"Act like an asshole, we'll treat you like one."

"Mm-hmm. So my word of advice is to be alert. Even if you're dealing square with folks, like your daddy always did, they'll try to screw you. Won't even pay for dinner first."

I nodded, thinking less about the dinner and screwing, but more about how honest and fair Charlie claimed Dad was. And maybe it was the truth. Maybe Dad cared more about treating a customer right than he did about treating his own family right. Then again, money was involved, so it made sense.

Charlie zipped his coat. "If you got no other questions for me, I'd like to get back to the business of doing nothing for a little longer."

I thanked him for coming in, told him I'd call if I needed anything.

Charlie said he hoped I didn't. When he reached the door, he paused. "One more thing: Buster stays in here at night if it's supposed to get real cold. That means tonight. His food's in the storage room. Bowls too. He'll curl up on the couch in here, be happy as a pig in shit."

"So much for a security system." I looked at Buster, who'd wedged himself between the couch and coffee table.

"If anyone breaks in during the winter, reckon you just pray they break a leg when they're shimmying their ass over the fence," Charlie said as he left.

Once Charlie was gone, Buster laid his head down and closed his eyes, but I wasn't ready to close up shop. I grabbed a hand-drawn yard map from the counter, put a few of Dad's notebooks under my arm, and spent a good part of the morning walking through the yard. I checked some notes Dad had left in those notebooks, seeing if they matched up with what I saw. In every instance, the cars and their locations lined up exactly.

Much as I tried to cram a little last-minute knowledge about the yard before Friday, I knew any real knowledge would come with experience. Like anything else in life, it would be a learning process.

I thought of it like my first few weeks of boxing. Coach Rob didn't have me in the ring sparring from the get-go. He didn't even have me hitting the bag that first week. Instead, he had taped off a square in the back of the gym, five feet on each side, and explained that my first lesson would be all about footwork. Punching was the last thing I needed to worry about.

"*You want to move forward? Move that front foot first, drag the other behind it. Want to move right? Move that right foot first, then drag the left."* He showed me the steps, moving around the taped square without ever crossing his feet. Then it was my turn. I did those steps—walking the box, Coach Rob called it—for the better part of an afternoon, rigid and robotic, but hungry to learn. Two days later, I was adding an awkward, flimsy jab to my steps. The next day, a right cross behind that jab. Soon enough, I was moving around a heavy bag, throwing one-twos. More pop and precision as the days passed.

If I was going to make the salvage yard work, that's how I was going to have to approach it. As a process. One step, then another.

CHAPTER THIRTEEN

Wynt Road is a long stretch of mostly clapboard homes sprinkled among fields and farmland that had assumed a state of wintery brown. The rental homes—The Ponderosa— sit halfway down, just after a snaking curve in the road. Before I pulled up the long gravel drive, I rolled down my windows and let some air creep in, curious if I'd catch the infamous odor from Tar Heel Wastewater Treatment that was just a mile or so south, locally known as the Flint Creek Shit Plant. There was no stench, but come summer or a heavy breeze, I knew that'd change. I rolled my window up and dug in my console, checked the Pigeon Forge key fob attached to the key for the vacant unit: *112 Wynt* scrawled in black Sharpie.

Until then, I hadn't thought much about which unit was vacant. Didn't think it made a damn. But 112 was the unit on the far end of the property—robin egg blue the last time I saw it—and it was where Grandma Miller stayed for a few years after Grandpa died from heart disease. She'd sold their house off, moved into the rental not long after the funeral. I was never sure Dad didn't charge her rent, but I knew the house she and Grandpa lived in, an old, white farmhouse, had been far too big for one person.

I eased up the drive of the modest-sized property that was surrounded by dense woods on the back and sides. The three little homes were perched roughly twenty feet apart at the top of the hill, the drive running in front of each: first a pink house, next a yellow one, and then number 112, still that pale blue. Had Dad put an aboveground pool behind the trio, maybe a gazebo, he would've had himself a low-class resort.

In front of the pink house were empty flower pots and a picnic table with a child's sand bucket on top. The lights were off inside, and no vehicles were parked out front. The yellow house next to it was more of a spectacle. On the porch, a toilet had been repurposed into a flower pot. Various hunting decoys—geese and ducks—and a couple of ceramic deer kept a lazy watch in the yard. A moped leaned against the lone tree.

I parked in front of the last house and went inside with a ridiculous notion that things were like they used to be. But before I even turned on the lights, I noticed the smell of the place was off. Stale and unwelcoming, like a motel room, with a hint of Lysol covering accumulated mustiness. There was a coldness to the place, in more ways than one.

I flipped on the light. The living room was simple: a corduroy loveseat faced the front wall that was crowded by a hefty, mahogany entertainment center. A dining area sat behind the couch, a narrow bar top dividing it from a cramped kitchen. The two bedrooms were on opposite ends of the house; the master, Grandma's old room, was on my right.

But the place was a far cry from Grandma's. There weren't any paintings of Jesus and snowy log cabins, no centerpiece of fake flowers and seasonal mats on the dining room table that wasn't quite the same table. No delicious smells like black cat pie and apple cobbler pouring out of the kitchen.

I inspected the house, checking things like lights and faucets to make sure they were functioning. I tested the disposal and dishwasher. Everything seemed in working order, which made me hopeful the other rental houses weren't fit to be condemned.

In the master bedroom closet, I happened upon something familiar: a blue plastic storage container covered in holographic *Looney Tunes* stickers. I popped the lid and pulled it into the light. It held a stack of games that belonged to my grandma: Old Maid, Apples to Apples, Chinese checkers. A few, like a Harry Potter edition of Monopoly, must have been added to the collection by tenants over the years. Below the games were two shoeboxes, each filled with Grandma Miller's favorite thing of all: VHS tapes of shows she used to record. The tapes were labeled with her handwriting: *Adam-12*, *The Doris Day Show*, *Laverne & Shirley*. One shoebox alone was devoted to the show Grandma and I always watched together: *The Twilight Zone*. I smiled, recalling the afternoons we'd spend watching it. Usually, I'd have a paper plate on my lap holding saltine crackers with quarter-slices of Kraft cheese and mayonnaise between them—my favorite snack for no other reason than that my grandma had made them.

I closed the shoeboxes, put the games back, and scooted the container back into the closet, with my mind settled as ever about one point: Grandma Miller was as good a person as I'd ever known. She was gentle and kind. Never heard her speak ill of anyone but the devil himself. Even after my parents split, she'd still call Mom and check on her, tell her she loved her.

Sometimes, I thought Grandma's goodness was in spite of the rest of her family. A settling voice in a sea of egos and endless negativity. I wasn't sure if my dad or Grandpa ever appreciated that, but I did, and I still missed her.

I locked the front door as I left, and before I could reach my Jeep, the sound of someone violently clearing their throat grabbed my attention. I turned to see a short, skinny, middle-aged man standing on the neighboring porch some twenty feet away. He had a sandy-blond mullet, no shirt or shoes. His only protection from the cold was the mane of hair that spilled down his neck and a pair of Washington Redskins sweatpants.

"If you plan on renting that place, the owner's dead." The man pointed at a "For Rent" sign next to the gravel drive. "Number on there ain't no good no more."

"Dead, you say?"

"Yes siree." He made a pistol with his fingers, mimicked the recoil. "Somebody shot his head off."

"In that case, I better put *my* number on the sign."

He lowered his finger gun.

"Leland was my dad," I told him. "Which makes me your new landlord. Name's Hudson."

He took a couple steps forward, his eyes narrowing. "Reckon I can see the resemblance. Except for that beard you got. You rub tobacco oil in that thing?"

I told him it was all natural.

"It really sucks what happened to your pops, but don't get things twisted: I still support the Second Amendment." This time his make-believe item was a holster he patted on his side.

"You know my dad pretty well?"

"Knew how to spell his name at the first of the month when I wrote my check. He fixed a clogged bathtub in here once from when I gave myself a trim, but I didn't much know him outside of that. Only been here since September. I come down from Virginia. I was a . . . I'm a truck driver."

"What do you know about your neighbor down there?" I indicated the pink house.

He looked at the house and turned back beaming. "Single gal named Brenda. Had herself a baby, but she's still got a figure. Got one of them onion asses. You know . . . just the sight of it will bring tears to your eyes."

"She sounds lovely. You live here alone?"

He nodded, tugged his sweatpants higher on his hip bones. "Clyde Jesse."

"Well, Mr. Jesse, guess I'll be seeing you around."

"Yep," he said. "And if you run into Miss Brenda, you be sure to tell her those nice things I said about her."

"I'll do that."

He gave me a salute.

I got in my Jeep and cranked the ignition, but hesitated before driving off. I must've sat there for five minutes, flip-flopping on what I was about to do. The way I saw it, I had two options: commute thirty-plus minutes to and from the salvage yard six days a week while still bumming it in Danny's guest room, or swallow my pride and move to Flint Creek for the time being. I could stay in the vacant rental house rent free.

Fuck it, I mumbled. The almighty dollar didn't need long to plead its case. I'd already assumed one new title that day:

Junkyard King. Adding *Slumlord* to my resumé seemed a natural progression. For several months, life had been backing me into a corner. Maybe this was the first of many punches it would take to get myself out. I opened my door and walked over to the rental sign, started working it out of the hard ground.

Clyde Jesse called to me: "Where am I supposed to send my check, Mr. Landlord?" He was now blazing a joint, leaning against the porch railing.

Once I'd unearthed the sign: "Guess you can walk it next door."

CHAPTER FOURTEEN

All things considered, breaking the news of my move was a clean rip of the Band-Aid. I suppose it was a byproduct of living a life that was tethered to few people and even fewer obligations. Brent agreed to let me pick up a couple night shifts a week behind the bar, which I'd need to supplement my income, and Danny seemed almost excited about my moving. I had my guess as to why: it was an opportunity for him to convince his girlfriend to move in. And she would. I was sure of it. I was even more sure that their relationship would end as smoothly as a tequila binger on an empty stomach.

Mom must've been knocked sideways, but she hid any knee-jerk reactions well on the phone. Even managed some optimism. She knew there'd be no changing my mind about it. If there was one piece of Leland Miller that I got honest, it was that dogged stubbornness once my mind was made up about something.

Packing for the move was no more involved than a weekend beach trip. I'd condensed so much when I moved into Danny's, there was no need for a U-Haul. I crammed my Jeep to the windows with clothes and other personal effects, a few odds and ends I could never seem to get rid of, among them an original Nintendo, a NutriBullet blender, and a couple boxes full of my boxing trophies and medals.

Danny saw me off Thursday night. We shared a good-luck whiskey shot before I rolled out. He left me with a final vote of confidence, as if I were trying cliff diving for the first time: "Can't believe you're actually doing this shit, Hud."

I could hardly believe it myself. The week had been a whirlwind, but it wasn't until I pulled out of Danny's apartment complex did it truly sink in—I was moving back to Flint Creek.

I reasoned that at least I was moving with my eyes wide open. I knew exactly where I was going. As a ten-year-old moving *out* of Flint Creek, I hadn't had that luxury. I was sad and scared, but I knew that I'd be living with Mom most of the time and that any sacrifice would be worth it. The home I'd grown up in, the life that I'd grown used to, had been poisoned. After the divorce, my parents had left the decision of living arrangements to me, probably the only thing they'd agreed on in a year. I wrestled with that decision for nearly a week. I was a child, and I'd yet to fully grasp what Dad had done. I just knew I'd never seen my mom so hurt. It was Mom who begged and pleaded for me to come with her. Not Dad. Not the one who should've been on his knees apologizing, offering promises that everything would be okay, that everything didn't have to be so painful and so confusing. But he didn't. And it was that far too casual apathy Dad showed in the situation that would define my view of him from that moment forward. In a way, he made my decision easy.

I'd traded my spacious backyard for the asphalt of an apartment complex, the smell of freshly ploughed fields for the stink of a dumpster next to our unit. The sounds of grunting tree frogs and buzzing cicadas from my bedroom window were now the voices and bustling of neighbors. Stars became fewer in the sky. But I never questioned my decision.

Not even when I faced my biggest adjustment of all: being the new kid in a school where the general population didn't look and dress like I did. It's the one thing Dad seemed to take issue with. I remember the day Mom told him what school I'd be going to, how he'd pulled me aside and said *"Stick with your kind, and you'll be all right."* I'm glad as hell I didn't heed that advice.

It would take a while to get acclimated, to stretch and to grow into my new world, like a new pair of sparring gloves getting broken in. It would take fistfights and new friendships to make me realize that shitheads came in all shapes, sizes, and colors. And so did good people.

So now, I was reversing course, so to speak. A move of twenty-some miles that felt like a million. I was leaving behind one of the biggest cities in the state, a place with a busy downtown and college campuses, shopping centers and museums, and one of the largest waterparks on the East Coast. A city where there's stuff to do and things to see. A far cry from Flint Creek, where conveniences were few and far in between. Where "downtown" is a small strip on Sunset Avenue, speckled with mom-and-pop businesses that have about the same charm as a tuxedo T-shirt.

* * *

Despite my upgraded digs, I slept like hell that night. I lay wide-eyed in bed. If there was a bad-case scenario concerning the salvage yard, my mind latched onto it and played it on repeat. And it wasn't so much the thoughts of me screwing something up or getting ripped off on account of my ignorance that troubled me most. It was the fear of Miller's Pull-a-Part becoming a ghost town for weeks on end. Just me, Charlie, and all those vehicles. Not a dime in the register and not a damn clue what to do about it. Maybe I was being ridiculous, maybe not. Either way, I'd been a prisoner to anxiety before.

In my early boxing career, I'd have dreams about fight night. The bell would ring and suddenly I'd forget every lesson Coach Rob had ever taught me. I'd just be a human punching bag, unable to raise my trembling arms for protection and too wobbly-legged to run away. Of course that never happened.

As far as the salvage yard goes, the jury was still out. I just hoped if I got my ass kicked, I'd at least have my guard up.

CHAPTER FIFTEEN

I pieced together what sleep I could and woke well before my alarm clock. I got to work early. Had the space heaters rolling and the computer running before the sun even showed its face. When Charlie came in around eight, I tasked him with putting out word that Miller's Pull-a-Part was open again: he called the towing service, then some local garages and body shops. He took a big piece of cardboard and spray-painted "Grand Reopening" in bright green, propped it next to the front gate.

His phone calls and ad campaign didn't conjure up any business, which made the day pass painfully slowly. Charlie intermittently nodded off on the couch while I watched the long hand on a Pennzoil clock drag by. The only activity we saw was a couple folks browsing the yard that afternoon before leaving empty-handed. Neither of us mentioned what a failure the day was.

The yard found a pulse on Saturday—a slow one. Our first sale. A transaction that Charlie handled while I shadowed and took mental notes. A man had pulled an airbag from a Toyota Celica. Charlie found the price list on the computer, took thirty-five bucks from the customer, and that was that. Wasn't any more complicated than taking a cocktail order.

Later that day, Charlie was helping a guy out in the yard while I manned the desk. The customer, a red-faced man with a comb-over, finally came in with this long, skinny metal part that he laid on the counter.

"Ring this gentleman up," Charlie told me, standing just behind the guy. "Pulled that from an '01 Ranger."

I didn't know what the hell kind of part I was looking at, and to make matters worse, the customer and Charlie appeared to be in cahoots; they both grinned and crossed their arms while I studied the contraption. I felt as stumped as I did when I was seventeen, learning to drive a stick shift for the first time.

"God bless, boy. Don't you know a torsion rod when you see one?" Charlie finally asked.

"I do now," I said. I clicked through the computer database until I found the part. "Bet your ass can't even spell *torsion*, Charlie."

His grin went away, but the customer thought it was funny. He paid me twenty-five bucks, which I was tempted to frame and hang on the wall. When the guy left, I found the Ranger in Dad's Ford notebook, and proudly wrote *Sold: torsion rod*.

Charlie disappeared to the break room, returning with two of the beers I'd brought him that morning in a Styrofoam cooler. "Reckon this calls for a celebration," he said, cracking one open.

"Damn right it does, but I'm not much of a Keystone guy myself. Maybe I'll just run a victory lap in the yard."

Charlie took a sip from the opened can, looked at the other can, sort of puzzled. "I wasn't offering, hoss."

"Maybe you shouldn't be pounding those out here in the shop in front of God and the public," I said. "Just my two cents."

Charlie muttered something. He headed toward the break room, turning on his heel before he reached the hall. "Want *my* two cents?"

"Not exactly, but I have a feeling you're going to offer it anyways, so shoot."

"If you want to see any real business around here, you need to start showing your face around town."

"I've barely been here two days."

"Sure, but I bet it's felt like two weeks, ain't it?"

"Two *years*."

"Exactly my point. You don't want to be here. It's written all over your face. Plain as day. May as well hang a 'Vacancy' sign around your neck."

"You're right, Charlie. I don't want to be here, so what should I do? Put a big smile on my face? Get myself an 'I heart Flint Creek T-shirt'? Wasn't like my dad was Mr. Sunny Disposition."

"He sure as hell wasn't," he said, "but people knew him."

"Yeah? And?"

"They don't know you from Adam, and if there's one thing about this town I'm sure about, it's this: locals ain't going to support somebody they don't know."

I don't know how loaded that word was to Charlie, but for me, *locals* meant folks with pasts that intersected with my dad's. Every nod, smile, or sneer I'd get in town would have some reason behind it, whether I knew the reason or not. There was nothing casual at all about just showing my face. "Problem is, Charlie, people around here think they know me. Half these people probably still see me as the teenage boy with a shitty attitude, eyeing the nearest exit out of here. That, or I'm just Leland Miller's boy. The one who pissed away his twenties in a boxing ring instead of starting a family like a good, God-fearing fellow should."

"Get over yourself," Charlie said. "You should hear what they say about me."

"And what's that?"

He shrugged. "Probably just call me a crotchety asshole and leave it at that. I pretty well keep to myself most the time. Ain't much Flint Creek has to offer I can't find on the TV. To be honest, I don't much give a shit what folks think."

"Guess we have that in common."

"That's all fine and dandy, but there's a big difference between me and you: I'm not the face of this operation. Just a cog in the machine. So while you might not give a shit what people think now, you will when you can't pay your goddamn bills."

CHAPTER SIXTEEN

It pained me to admit it, but Charlie was right. Enough to make me reconsider my original plan of living like a hermit at the rental house, leaving only for work and basic necessities. So Sunday morning I dragged myself out of the house, made my first official appearance in town as a newly reenlisted local.

I ventured out a little before lunchtime, with no particular destination in mind, and was quickly reminded how dead Flint Creek was on the Sabbath. It was like the biblical Rapture that Grandma used to talk about had occurred, and I was one of the few sinners left to fend off the ensuing plagues. The other sinners amounted to a Jetta full of vaping teens I passed when I turned onto Sunset Avenue, Flint Creek's crown jewel.

The first building I passed on Sunset was a standalone post office that faced an equally official building: a North Carolina license plate agency. Further down, the road was bracketed on each side by brick, two-story buildings that probably popped up when my grandparents were young, maybe before that. The end of the building on my left displayed a hand-painted Pepsi-Cola logo, the words "Say Pepsi, Please" scarcely visible, courtesy of the thousands of blazing suns and rainstorms it had weathered over the years. As I drove down the road, I noticed there were a handful of vacancies in those buildings. The largest of those vacancies used to house Flint Creek General Store; it was the only spot downtown I gave a damn about growing up because they sold glass-bottle Coke and had a self-serve popcorn machine in the back. The general store, like the other vacancies, must've raised a white flag because of increased rent or the convenience of Amazon. I could almost hear Dad's voice: *"If I've said it once, I've said it a thousand times. Computers will be the downfall of mankind."*

Some of the businesses that remained were Joe Stylez Barber Shop, Cleanworld Dry-Cleaning, and a taxidermy shop called Deer Tracks, all closed for the day, as was Sunset's sole restaurant, Sassy Sally's BBQ. The latter didn't surprise me because pig-killing and Jesus-loving folks are typically one and the same in the South. And since half the restaurants in Flint Creek were barbecue restaurants, I could only think of one decent lunch option a couple miles away: Captain Tim's Fish House.

On the way, I passed some local landmarks, most of which were tinged with some memory of Dad. There was the vacant field off Mackey, formerly a spot for the Central Carolina Drive-In Theatre, where he only took me once because he thought a six-dollar double feature was a rip-off. Nearby, the blacktop at Flint Creek Elementary that had seemed so vast in my childhood, where Dad taught me to ride my Huffy bike without training wheels. Then, off Russell Street, was the Big Star Grocery parking lot, where there was a classic car meetup every other Tuesday. If there was a place on earth where Dad seemed happier than that car show, it was a mystery to me.

I'd accepted the fact, years earlier, that Flint Creek wasn't home. I think Mom always felt that way too. Flint Creek, with all of its goods and bads and in-betweens, was Dad's town. I was convinced, no matter how many years he lay in his grave, it would always feel that way. That his long shadow was forever cast over that small, northwest portion of Payne County.

* * *

Around noon, I walked inside Captain Tim's, where the fluorescent lights burned too bright, casting heavenly brilliance on the corny decor—fishing nets hanging on the walls, wooden heads of haggard sea captains, plastic crabs, pictures of boats tossed on waves, a saltwater aquarium near the register.

There were enough patrons to occupy a few tables: two older couples, and a dad and his young son and daughter.

A stumpy hostess with dimples, wearing black Crocs came over. "You ordering to-go, hon?"

Since the restaurant was nearly vacant, I decided I'd dine in. "No, ma'am. I'm eating here."

"You waiting on someone?"

I shook my head.

"Just the one of ya," she said with a wink. She took a menu from a stand and led me to a tiny table in the corner. She said Gina would be with me in a sec.

And she was. Gina was young, maybe twenty. A brunette—save for a single clump of bright pink hair—with squinty eyes and a friendly smile. She tucked the pink strand behind her ear before taking my drink order.

"Water is fine."

"Lemon?"

I told her no, thank you, and she started reciting the daily specials.

I stopped her after her description of the crab-stuffed mushrooms, which she assured me weren't made with imitation crab. "I'll just have the chicken tender plate," I said, remembering the time I got a tiny flounder bone lodged between my bottom front teeth as a kid.

"Baked potato or fries?"

"Fries'll do."

She wrote down the order. Her hair had fallen back into her face. She tried, unsuccessfully, to blow it away before walking to the kitchen.

A minute later, it was another waitress who brought me my water. Seemed less like she was assisting Gina and more like she was on a mission to figure out if my dark, deep-set eyes and the face half-concealed under my beard looked anything like Leland Miller's. I must've confirmed her suspicions when I said thank you. Dad's voice and my own were unmistakably similar, though mine had lost some of its twang over the years.

I'd barely downed half my water when the lunch rush arrived. Families. Couples. A loner, an older man with a wooden cane. All unfamiliar faces. I'd actually started to feel pretty comfortable until a group of well-dressed folks came in, laughing as if they were on the tail end of a joke. They were regulars from Hope of God Baptist; the pastor himself, Dean Peterson, rounded out the group. His wife was with him. As they began making their rounds to various tables to greet nearby lunch-goers, I was reminded of restaurant outings as a kid, how Dad did the same type of schmoozing. He'd spend minutes shooting the shit with fellow windbags before finally making his way to a table where Mom and I waited impatiently, ready to place our order.

I purposely kept my head down, scrolled aimlessly on my phone, but to no avail. Out of the corner of my eye, I saw Dean Peterson looking at me. Once he noticed me, so did others in his group, with varying degrees of nonchalance.

I didn't lift my eyes until the pastor walked over to my table.

"Hudson?" he said as he neared.

I tried to act surprised to see him. "Yessir."

"Nice to see you, brother." He removed his wool gloves and offered a toasty handshake. "Certainly under better circumstances than last time we met."

"Yessir, it is."

"Just remember what the Good Book says: there's a season for all things."

I nodded.

"You waiting on Mrs. Tammy?" he asked.

"No," I told him, and it came out more direct than I'd planned, but being fake is hardly in my skill set.

"Oh, all righty."

"I'm living here now."

"Living here?"

"Down off Wynt Road. I'm running the salvage yard."

I'm not sure what was going through his head those next few seconds of lips moving and words failing to materialize, but he finally settled on, "Well, we've got a spot down at the end of the table if you'd like to break bread with us. Be more than happy to have you, young man."

Now, the whole table seemed to be looking. Some folks I recognized. The church's music director, Elmer something-or-another—Francis . . . or Frazier. A man named Jerry Popkin, who'd served on the deacon board with Dad. His poofy-haired wife and a teenage son with bulky headphones on.

"Appreciate the offer, Mr. Peterson, but I'm just getting something for the road."

He eyed my cup, the tightly wrapped silverware Gina had left me. His face scrunched into a smile. "Best cooking in three counties. But you best not tell my wife I said that, you hear?"

I laughed spiritlessly.

"If you change your mind, please join us," he said. "The whole church has been thinking about y'all."

Another handshake and his Baptist duty for the day was complete.

When he returned to his table, the glances from the church crew began to subside. I'd been movie-of-the-week for a moment, but the group returned their attention to their immediate company. I hoped their convos would follow suit: the women gossiping about whose daughter wore a skirt too short at service that morning; the men gabbing about the upcoming NASCAR season.

I flagged down Gina as quickly as I could and asked her to change my order to carry-out.

CHAPTER SEVENTEEN

The Ponderosa tenants didn't owe me rent until the first of February, over a week away, and I had barely over fifty bucks in cash from Saturday's sales. As for Dad's business account, he'd hardly left enough to cover the bills that were on the way. His whole cash-heavy way of life may have been good for him, but it left me with another obstacle of keeping the salvage yard afloat. Had someone brought a wrecked car in, wanting a cash offer, I'd have been left scratching my ass. Turns out, I didn't have to fork out any money our first Monday in business, nor did any customers for that matter. But we did have a visitor that afternoon.

I was at the front desk, researching the metal markets. I'd made up my mind that we needed to strip and crush a few cars, sell them for scrap to get a little cash flow going. Meanwhile, Charlie had just demolished a pack of Nekot cookies and was half-dozing on the love seat. He sprang to attention when the door opened.

It was Frank Coble. He let the door close slowly behind him, the icy breeze canceling out an hour's worth of our space heaters' best efforts. The chief had a toothpick hanging from the side of his mouth.

He split his attention between Charlie and me. "I'll be damned," he said. "It's true."

I eased off my stool while Charlie brushed some crumbs off his jacket.

"Heard I might find y'all down here."

"Live and in person," I said, wondering if my appearance at Captain Tim's had kicked up the rumor mill. "Monday's a business day last I checked."

"So it is," Coble mumbled. "Just didn't think this place was *in* business."

"Thought I'd give it a whirl."

"A *whirl* . . . even after what happened to your daddy, huh?"

I shrugged. "Thought all that was tied to those guns—like y'all said at the station. There aren't any guns around here now, so I guess that makes this as safe a place as any. Unless there's something else we should be worried about."

Coble's stern gaze didn't soften. "What's Tammy think about all this?"

Charlie worked himself up from the couch. "This place don't belong to Tammy, Chief."

"God knows you didn't buy it from her, Charlie." Then to me: "And I wasn't aware you had money like that."

"You don't need any money to inherit a pile of shitbox cars," I said.

It was a revelation to Coble. He took the toothpick out of his mouth and dropped it in his shirt pocket.

"We opened back up last week," Charlie said. "On Friday, wasn't it?"

"Sure was," I said. It seemed some embellishment was in order, so I added that we'd already made some big sales.

"You don't say," Coble said.

"Mr. Hudson here's a natural salesman."

It was the first time I'd ever heard Charlie say my actual name; I could've hugged him for the fabricated compliment.

"So what brings you out, Frank?" I asked. "Doubt it's a new transmission."

"For starters, we got the autopsy report from Raleigh this morning."

Charlie, who'd moseyed over to the drink machine, turned around.

"Findings were about what we expected," Coble went on. "A single bullet wound to the head. No signs of a struggle or defensive wounds. Leland had some bruising around his face and left shoulder from the fall that came after the gunshot." He clapped the meaty part of his palms to mimic flesh meeting concrete.

"So y'all are still at square one, huh?" I said.

"Wouldn't put it that way."

"Square-fucking-one," Charlie grumbled.

Coble cut his eyes. "Matter of fact, Charlie, we ain't. Over the weekend, we recovered a couple of those black-market guns."

"Recovered?" I said.

"Mm-hmm. Detective Holden and I started interviewing some acquaintances of your daddy's last week, and I reckon word got around town that—"

"Guys from the Boars Club?"

"How's that?"

"You said 'acquaintances.' Figured you meant the guys from Dad's little club."

"Your daddy had acquaintances of all sorts, Mr. Miller," Coble said, "This particular fellow came to the station himself, surrendered a couple of the pistols he bought. Revolvers like the ones we found in that bunker."

"And this guy's not a suspect?"

"Doesn't appear to be."

"Then how does that help y'all with the case?"

His face couldn't hide his annoyance, but since he'd grilled me about my job, I figured I'd fire a jab in return.

"Helps us establish a time line," he said. "When the guy fessed up, he told us what month it was he purchased those weapons, almost down to the day. Even confirmed another suspicion: Leland was doing that mess after business hours."

"A guy just handed the guns over?" Charlie laughed to himself. "What a damn saint."

"If by 'saint,' you mean somebody who actually helped us out, then yeah, Shoaf, I guess he was."

Charlie smugly grinned and faced the drink machine, straightened a dollar bill on the side of it. He looked over his shoulder when the machine accepted the bill. "Guess your saint got full immunity too, huh? Probably a shiny plaque to go on the wall."

"I don't think those particulars are any of your business," Coble said, "but if you know somebody that's got something they want to get off their chest, or something they've suddenly remembered, it's best if they come clean now."

Charlie pulled a Coke from the machine. He looked to be on the verge of taking Coble's bait, but I interjected. "Charlie doesn't know anything, Frank."

"So he says," Coble said. There was a tense silence, and then he finally took his eyes off a stone-faced Charlie, who seemed to thank me with a slight head nod.

"I need to get to the station," Coble said. "My word of advice to you two is to keep your heads on a swivel if you insist on keeping this place open."

"We're staying open," I said. "Except for Sundays. The good Lord wouldn't think it right."

"Uh-huh. Y'all best have an eye out for anything suspicious. Folks just lurking around and whatnot."

"Yes sir," I said with a tone worthy of a salute.

Charlie echoed me as he popped the tab on his Coke.

After taking one last look around, like a clue might suddenly appear, Coble said, "I'd have got rid of this place if I was you, Mr. Miller."

With that sentiment, he backed his ass into the door and was gone.

Charlie took a swig of his Coke. "What a dickhole," he said.

"He don't like you too much, does he?"

"Not that I give a damn if he does or don't, but we ain't ever had no problem until your daddy passed." He returned to his indention in the loveseat and sipped his Coke. "Bastard's just mad that I can't solve his case. I bet he tried to squeeze some bullshit out of his little confidante too."

"Yeah, you must've paid whoever it is off with all that money I'm giving you."

"Probably what Coble thinks. He'll pin it on me if he can figure out how. String me up in front of the police station, have his picture made next to me for the newspaper."

"Doubt he's that desperate," I said, "but I wish like hell you could remember something." As soon as the words left my lips, I realized how they might've come off.

Charlie's expression assured me it wasn't how I intended. "If I never hear another word about this murder shit again, it'll be too soon. Everybody thinks just because—"

"That's not what I meant, Charlie. Honest. I was just—"

"You want me to paint a picture for you?" he said, slamming his drink on the table. He was on his feet. "We've danced around this elephant long enough, so I'll fucking tell you." He moved to the door quicker than I thought he was capable. "It's early that morning, and Satan's barely squeezed the sun out of his big red asshole. And all I'm thinking when I walk through the door is that it's Saturday, and I need me a couple cups of coffee. Need to get some lead in my pencil so I can make it to six o'clock, get my week's pay. Then I could take my ass to Lucky 64 so I could blow that money on Deuces Wild poker and do it all over again come Monday. But guess-fucking-what?"

I was too stunned to ask what, or even shrug.

Charlie walked toward the desk and stopped. He got down on one knee, touched a finger to the ground. "I never had that cup of coffee. I was too busy wondering if my boss was lying dead on the goddamn floor. Too afraid to step in all that blood or touch him to see if his heart was still beating. Even more afraid that whoever shot him was still in here somewhere, ready to put a bullet through my head next." Now, Charlie's palm was spread flat on the floor. His chin sunk to his chest, and I could see the rise and fall of his back through his jacket. "I ain't been that scared since I was laying next to my platoon leader in Khe Sanh after a mine ripped his fucking leg off." He straightened up slowly and looked at me. "I shouldn't . . ." He kneaded the bridge of his nose. "Fuck . . . I'm—"

"It's all right, Charlie," I told him. "I'm sorry too. About all of it."

After Charlie got his bearings, he went back to get his Coke. He took a few audible gulps and said, "I never even got paid that week." A chuckle hoarsely broke off. "The son of a bitch they're looking for owes me that four hundo. Think they'll let him know when they catch him?"

"Doubt it," I said. "If I had it to give, I would."

"Ain't yours to give," he said, propping one of his feet up on the table, a clod of dirt falling on a copy of *JEGS*. "You should be more worried about keeping the lights on around here." He let out a long sigh, then shut his eyes.

I went back to my stool, hoping the room would soon clear of the funky energy left in the wake of Coble's visit and Charlie's out-of-body moment. Figured I wouldn't bother Charlie about stripping any cars for a little bit.

Just when I thought he'd dozed off again, he asked, "Remember what you told Coble? About there not being guns around here anymore?"

"Yeah . . ."

"That ain't exactly true."

I peeked my head around the computer monitor. "What are you talking about?"

Charlie still had his eyes shut, but he opened his jacket, tapped his hand on an inside pocket. I couldn't see any gun, but the dull thud assured me he had one. "Don't get your britches in a twist," he said. "I got a permit for it."

CHAPTER EIGHTEEN

Learning to take a punch is one of the toughest things about becoming a boxer. It never gets easy, but after a while, a fist connecting with your face or body becomes a little less shocking. Your mind adapts. You get used to it.

I hoped that's how living in Flint Creek would be, a little less painful as the days went on, and I suppose it was for the most part. I wasn't exactly rubbing elbows with the locals, but I'd show my face in town every couple days. If I got hungry, I'd grab a bite at one of the barbecue restaurants, or this newer dive called Cross Tie Meat Co. that served hot dogs and burgers out of an old train car near downtown. If I needed gas or a cup of coffee, I chose the Marathon Station that I used to ride my bike to as a kid. The guy that used to own the place, Jim Fields, was still running it, and he remembered me. I'd been buddies with his grandson, Garett, in elementary school. Jim asked about my boxing, about how my mom was doing. He had to be pushing eighty, but he was sharp as hell. By my third visit, he was making small talk when I came in for a cup of dark roast. *"You ain't much like your dad,"* he'd told me on one of my visits. He didn't elaborate, but I took it as a compliment.

As for my neighbors, they'd pretty well kept to themselves. Clyde Jesse, whose moped was certainly the result of a DUI, had brought his rent on time, as did my other neighbor, Brenda, who I'd encountered only once. I wasn't smitten by her like Mr. Jesse was, but she was plenty nice. Struck me as one of those people that life had blindsided in more ways than one, left them eternally exhausted. Her little girl's name was Chloe. She was about to turn two years old. Brenda never mentioned who or where the father was, and I didn't ask. Didn't tell her that our mutual neighbor was a big fan of her ass either.

Then there was Charlie, who I'd spent most of my waking hours with. He'd warmed up to me just enough that I'd finally started piecing together what I could about him. After serving in Vietnam, he'd lived in six different cities in the Southeast, and if there was a job that involved inhaling toxic fumes or jacking up his L5 vertebra, he'd worked it. I hadn't learned much in the way of his personal affairs other than his parents had both passed within a two-month span in 2008—though he didn't say how—and he'd been divorced at least twice, with no kids to show for it. None that he was aware of, anyways. As far as our relationship was concerned, it had found a tolerable balance between wisecracks and shop talk. And by the end of the second full week at the salvage yard, the first Thursday in February, Charlie had taught me enough to at least bullshit my way through a conversation with a customer.

Business had graduated from a crawl to a slow stagger. Our biggest hiccup had been this fuckstick who brought a claw hammer to the yard, started busting out the taillights on a couple of Hondas so he could get to the bulbs. I was inclined to introduce him to my right hook, but I just chewed his ass out and charged him triple instead.

Even with the slight uptick, I worried like hell that I wouldn't have enough money to pay Charlie and cover all the bills that awaited me just a few weeks away. Stuff like property taxes and the power bill, disposal fees I never knew existed a month before. Of course there was the Keystone too.

I was at the desk that Thursday afternoon, punching some financial numbers into my phone calculator, when Buster started barking outside. It was a little after six o'clock—the time we always closed—and I was sure Charlie had shut the front gate and let Buster off his chain so he could dart around the yard like a crazy dog, get his energy out. What was strange, Buster usually didn't make so much as a whimper unless Charlie was running heavy machinery, but that wasn't the case that evening. I assumed an animal had wandered in and put Buster on edge.

I tried to block out the racket, enter a couple more numbers into my phone when Charlie came through the front door, out of breath and sweat glazed. He was holding Buster's leash.

"You piss Buster off, or what?" I asked.

Charlie shook his head and coughed into the crook of his arm. He pointed at a small storage cabinet that was flush against the wall behind me. "Grab that big flashlight in there. Buster's found something."

There was a seriousness in his tone that prompted me to action. Inside the storage cabinet, I found a lantern-style LED light. I turned it on to test it; it lit up brighter than expected. I pinched my eyes shut, tried to blink away the blue Pac-Man ghost that lingered, then clicked the light off and met Charlie at the door.

"The hell's he found?"

Charlie didn't answer, just leaned into the front door and led me outside, where the frigid air made me regret not grabbing my jacket. Also made me wonder how the light drizzle that was falling wasn't in the form of ice or snow.

We followed Buster's bellyaching to the backside of the lot, our muddy walk illuminated by the lantern and what little pink light the setting sun was eking out.

"Ain't ever seen him act the way he is, Hudson," Charlie said as Buster came into view. "Lost his damn mind."

Buster was against the back fence line, half of his body under an old, stripped-down Dodge Caravan. The kind I pictured a pissed-off dad taking on a trip to Florida, wife and whiny-ass kids in tow.

Buster was digging furiously below the Dodge. To what end, I couldn't tell. Both of us yelled at the dog, tried to calm him down, but our commands were in vain.

"See if you can leash him," I told Charlie. "You're the only one he likes. Squirrelly bastard hates me."

Charlie looked reluctant to do so. He handed me the lantern and walked over to the caravan, squatted down like he was about to change a tire.

After a moment of fruitless wrestling with the almost pit bull, Charlie said, "Dammit, Buster!" A few more vile words and yanks, and Charlie finally hooked the leash, pulled Buster from under the van.

The mutt gave me a crazed look. He was filthy, like a Wrangler that had gone mudding and got its front tires stuck in a puddle. He was panting as hard as Charlie.

"I'm going to chain his ass up," Charlie said, tugging the leash.

I did my best to contain a laugh as the two walked away, then I moved closer to Buster's dig site. It was more than a trench of brown mud. There was something under the clawed-up mess.

I knelt next to the caravan, let the lantern do its work. I reached for the deepest rut, toward what looked like dull, red metal. My fingertips confirmed that it was. It didn't take a leap of logic to figure out that it was some type of vehicle. We were in a salvage yard, after all. The real question was, why the hell was it buried?

Charlie seemed as confused as I was when he came back.

"You know anything about this?" I asked.

He crouched beside me and angled his head a little. "I ain't even sure what we're looking at."

"Got to be a car or a truck. What else would it be?"

"Bossman, we don't bury cars around here."

"Somebody did. Don't think it was Buster."

Charlie snickered, mumbled, "Ol' Buster." He took a Camel pack from his shirt pocket, shook a cigarette loose, tapped it on his knee. "Why would he get all tore up about finding a car? He's seen thousands of them over the years. Don't add up."

"Maybe he smells something."

"Maybe it's Jimmy Hoffa under there."

"Think we can still collect a reward for that?"

Charlie lit his cigarette. "Reckon so. We'd have to split it with Buster, though. Suppose he'd probably leave us for greener pastures."

Out of quips, I stood up. "I want to know what's under there, Charlie."

Charlie checked his watch and looked up at me, adjusting his toboggan until it covered his ears. "Can't we mess with this tomorrow, boy?"

"You ain't got shit else to do. *Andy Griffith* will be halfway over by the time you get home anyway."

"Yeah, but—"

"You can still make it in time for *Wheel of Fortune* if you get moving," I said. "You know I can't drive that forklift, but I'll give it my best if you leave me by my lonesome. I want to know what's under there, damn it."

"You'll fuck that thing up something awful."

"Yeah, that'd be a real shame. Expensive piece of equipment, I'm guessing?"

Charlie locked his eyes on the buried vehicle and slowly shook his head. "I do this, you owe me a twelve-pack."

"The usual?"

"No sir. I want top shelf for this job," he said. "High Life."

"Deal." I patted him on the shoulder. "Let's get to it. I'm going to grab my jacket."

Inside, I enjoyed a last few seconds of warmth and slid on my jacket. In the storage room, I found a pair of large work gloves that belonged to my dad, whose hands were big and bony like my own. The gloves weren't made for warming fingers, but they were better than nothing.

Once we'd set up a couple work lights, it didn't take long for Charlie to position the forklift, haul the caravan away from the fence. He set it in a bare spot nearby, and then he disappeared around the front of the storage shelter. Buster offered a few half-hearted barks; he'd blown his load during his earlier tantrum.

Moments later, the Bobcat excavator crept into the misty light. It was well past its prime, but the machine was still badass. Made me a little jealous I hadn't learned to operate the thing yet.

Charlie narrowly missed the tripods that held the work lights, which surely would've been a costly little mishap, and then he got to tearing into the spongy earth. He lowered the Bobcat's shovel several feet from Buster's dig spot, pulled up muddy clumps bit by bit until he hit the outer edge of the vehicle. Possibly the roof above one of the side windows.

I pulled my jacket hoodie up and hunkered down to keep warm. I watched Charlie work, impressed by how efficiently he navigated the digging. He was concentrating so hard, he didn't even bother ashing his latest cigarette, just let the wind take care of it. The smoke pouring from the Bobcat's cockpit made it look like a tiny locomotive chugging back and forth.

Once Charlie outlined the vehicle's side, he began scraping away the ground above it, which looked only about six inches deep. What I could make out of the vehicle confirmed two things: it was a small car of some sort, probably a two-door, and it had definitely paid a visit to the crusher.

Charlie made a few more shallow digs before climbing out of the Bobcat to appraise the job he'd done. I walked over and stood next to him.

"Don't look like much of a treasure," Charlie said.

I said it didn't look much like Jimmy Hoffa either.

Charlie flicked his cigarette at the car. "Sure glad I worked overtime for this."

"You worked overtime for the High Life."

He met my eyes. "Reckon we should dig a little more and pull the thing out? Doubt there's anything worth salvaging except the metal, but it's better than nothing."

"Works for me. Still don't make any sense, though, does it? That shit's buried for a reason."

"Reckon so. Cars don't just crawl into the ground and hide," Charlie said, curiosity in his voice. He took a couple steps closer to the front of the car and leaned down, brushed his hand over a piece of the jaunty metal. "That's mighty peculiar."

"What is?"

"Looks like the engine's still in it."

Even I knew that Charlie never crushed cars until we'd pulled the engine and drained the fluids.

Charlie said, "And check this . . ."

I looked closer and saw what Charlie saw: a cracked, blue Chevy bowtie emblem. "I guess our ship's finally come in," I said. "How much you think we could get for it?"

"Not enough for that twelve-pack." Charlie wiped his muddy hands on his knees, and then rubbed his hands together. "Speaking of which . . ."

"You want that *now*?"

"Of course I want it now. You bring that into work in the morning, I'm liable to start drinking by noon. Won't get anything done if that's the case. Probably call up one of my exes."

Considering I'd made Charlie stay overtime in that shitty weather, I didn't have a leg to stand on.

"Fine." I propped my foot on the Chevy like it was some gigantic beast I'd conquered. "Go ahead and do whatever you're going to do with this beautiful piece of machinery. I'll be back in a few."

"I can handle that. Just don't go cracking one of my beers."

"If I wanted to drink piss, I'd just find the nearest toilet."

Charlie chuckled into a smoker's cough as I headed for my Jeep.

CHAPTER NINETEEN

Mac's #2 was two miles away. A mini-mart that once had working gas pumps. The store was empty but for a woman at the counter in a Jeff Gordon jacket. She was in the ball-park of fifty, skinny like an addict, with dark roots and bottle-blonde hair. She called me "sugar" when she asked if I needed help.

"Y'all carry High Life?"

"The beer?"

"Uh-huh."

She pointed to the cooler along the left wall. "And if you're feeling lucky today, twenty-three's been a big winner."

"Twenty-three?"

She tapped a display case of scratch-off tickets.

I thanked her for her advice and walked to the snack aisle. I grabbed a bag of Hot & Spicy Chex Mix to hold me over until whatever drive-through dinner my future held.

On my way to the beer cooler, my phone vibrated in my coat pocket; it was Charlie calling.

I answered: "Hold your tits, Grandpa. I just got to the store."

"Forget the damn beer, Hudson." Charlie's voice was shaky.

"Everything okay?"

"I just need you to get back here quick as you can."

"I can still get the—"

"Right fucking now, Hudson." He hung up.

My nerves kick-started; suddenly I was aware of the smell of hot dogs and beef taquitos that twirled on a nearby warming rack. Instant nausea.

I made for the door, and when I reached it, I remembered the Chex Mix that was in my hand; I tossed it onto a stack of *Boat and RV Trader* magazines, then I was in my Jeep, hauling ass out of the parking lot.

My mind didn't land on any theories about why Charlie called and why he sounded like he did, but I knew it couldn't be good. I pinned the gas pedal, praying my tires wouldn't break traction on the slick back roads that led to the salvage yard.

When I got there, I sped past a snoozing Buster, toward the lights at the back of the lot. The Bobcat had been moved closer to the car, and its shovel had the front of the Chevy lifted. Charlie was squatting next to the car, rocking. His hands were cupped over his nose.

I hopped out of my Jeep, called Charlie's name as I approached.

No response.

"The hell's the matter?" I asked.

Charlie exhaled loud and long into his hands then looked up, his pale face amplified in the artificial light. Eyes like a scared child. He took his hands away from his mouth, pointed toward the back of the car.

"Tell me what the fuck that is, Hudson."

"The fuck *what* is?" A light breeze blew, and I was smacked with a rank odor that I hadn't smelled earlier.

Charlie picked up a pocketknife from the ground, used it to point toward the back of the car. My eyes followed, but I didn't see anything that would warrant his behavior. The car, only a couple feet thick in its current state, had almost been unearthed. What once served as a trunk jutted above the rest of the wreckage because it was slightly pried open, like a failed attempt on a soup can.

I looked over my shoulder at Charlie.

"In the goddamn trunk," he said.

I crouched down on all fours, almost on my belly; I maneuvered myself to not cast a shadow on whatever it was I was looking for. The pungent stink grew stronger, and then I saw it. The reason why Charlie called me and why a seventy-one-year-old war vet was scared shitless. There was a black canvas bag of some sort, and through a slit in the bag, I saw a mangled hand, in some mash-up color of gray and blue and green. The color of decay.

I moved back as if whoever that hand belonged to might rise out of the wreckage, come after me for disturbing their grave. The tumbling in my gut returned, and I was sure my face looked every bit as ghostly as Charlie's. I nearly puked, but a hard swallow kept me from heaving. I closed my eyes, hoping a moment of darkness would rid my mind of what I'd just seen. But the image was branded there. It wasn't like the conjured image of my dad's bloody body three feet from his desk. This was as real as the smell of death in the air.

"Charlie," I whispered, my eyes still closed, "call the fucking cops."

*　*　*

After Charlie called 911, we waited inside with barely a word spoken between us. Ten or so minutes had passed. There'd been no sign of the cops, who I figured would've already arrived.

Charlie had dragged the largest of the shop's space heaters to the waiting area where we were seated. He stayed huddled up, and I held my hands toward the heater, certain that they shook more from nerves than from the cold we'd come out of.

"Buster knew," Charlie finally mumbled. "He knew something was back there."

"He's never acted like that before."

Charlie shook his head. "Used to never let him run loose, though. Your daddy always walked him on a leash when he was around. He always thought Buster'd dig his way out of here. Like that prison movie with that guy with the big forehead in it."

"Damn dog is smarter than I thought," I said.

"He's a smart boy," Charlie said. "Leland used to walk him over next to the crusher. Where we got a couple old Pontiacs. I always thought that was kind of funny."

"Why's that?"

A forced, unnatural snicker. "Figured there was no better place to take a big shit than next to a Pontiac."

I rose from the couch when blue lights flashed against the wall. Thought I would've heard a siren first, but there was none. I nudged Charlie, who was in too much of a daze to notice. We walked to the door, where I reached the handle almost the same time as Frank Coble. I let the chief inside, Detective Holden right behind him.

Coble looked past me. "Where'd you find that body, Shoaf?"

Charlie's voice was soft. "Out back. Where the lights are."

"And it was *you* that found it?"

He said it was.

Coble gave Holden a quick, knowing glance, and then he looked at me. "Y'all ain't mentioned this to nobody else, have you?"

I told him we hadn't.

"That's good. Don't need no hearsay running rampant before we figure out what it is we're dealing with here."

"Looks like somebody bagged that body before they buried it," Charlie said. "Seen it before on—"

"We'll handle the theorizing," Coble said.

Charlie weakly raised his hands in submission.

"Goes for you too, Mr. Miller."

I nodded.

"I'll show you the spot," Charlie said.

Coble pulled his service belt up with his thumbs, but his belly forced it back down. "We better get to it. Could be a long night."

Charlie took the lead and we all headed outside, where it had begun lightly snowing. Tiny flakes mixed with a cold mist.

Before we turned the corner toward the back of the lot, Coble stopped and looked at me. "Reckon you should go on. We'll find you if we need you."

I didn't protest. Seeing any more of that body didn't inter-est me, and I was tired enough as it was. Like the adrenaline dumps I used to get after a boxing match, my anxiety had drained what energy I had.

"Holler if you need me, Charlie," I said, digging my keys from my pocket.

Charlie looked my way wearily. He said nothing as the chief nudged him toward the nightmare.

* * *

I'd gone without dinner and I'd paced my bedroom for hours, waiting on Charlie to call. And I kept waiting.

At eleven o'clock I tried his phone, and it went straight to voicemail.

I was tired, but I did my best to put distance between myself and sleep. I feared the image of that zombie-like hand would give way to darker dreams in the event I did doze off. This wasn't like *Nightmare on Elm Street* when I was a kid. I couldn't watch two hours of Nickelodeon and wash those images from my mind. So I paced and I checked my phone and I paced some more.

Well after midnight, I tired of the endless pacing, so I tried an active meditation tactic an old sparring partner had taught me. I slid a coffee table aside in the near-dark living room. I calmed my breathing—three seconds in, three seconds out. I began lightly bouncing in a boxing stance, then eased into a fighter's rhythm, nearly in cadence with my heartbeat. I started throwing gentle punches in the air, the rust in my joints breaking away with every jab and cross. I shuffled my feet, maneuvered within my confined space, launching single shots faster and faster. Then two-punch combos. Three-, four-, five-punch combos. I bobbed and weaved. I focused and breathed. I boxed shadows, real and imagined. Fought away fears and flickering images of that hand and mud and metal and Charlie's eyes. The punches became more and the flickers less, and in fleeting moments, I felt like Hudson Miller the boxer again. Not the failing salvage yard operator who was lost and terrified, but a cocksure welterweight. No longer a name written in another man's last will and testament, but a name that was my own, stitched on a pair of red satin trunks.

Before long, my heart was pounding double time, and my skin was lacquered in a sweat that blew cool under the ceiling fan. It may have been ten minutes, maybe longer, without a rest, before I rang the final bell and toweled myself off. I collapsed on the couch and closed my eyes, where those terrible thoughts awaited me in full. There was no escaping them.

As my breath steadied and slowed, I wondered if that was how Dad's last night alive had been. A dark night of the soul, where he faced down some awful reality or wrestled with an insufferable guilt.

If I had answered one of his calls that night, maybe he would've told me.

CHAPTER TWENTY

I tried Charlie's phone again just as day broke. This time the line rang; still no answer. I brought up the number for Flint Creek PD, but I never made the call. I was too curious about the car and body to be railroaded by some secretary or rookie cop who was just as clueless as I was.

It was no longer snowing, but there was a dusting from an overnight flurry. Just enough to leave icy patches on the road, probably shut schools down for the day. It took me only about five minutes to get to the salvage yard, where the front gate was closed but not locked. I got out to push it open, and I noticed a silver Crown Vic parked in front of a garage bay. None of the official Flint Creek cruisers were there. I pulled beside the car that was blasting white smoke from its tailpipe. Through the car's tinted windows I could see Detective Holden. He exited his vehicle before I could get out of my own. I rolled down my window.

"Mr. Miller, I'm afraid you can't be around here today."

"I own the place, Detective."

"This *place* is a crime scene currently," he said. "And the chief will be back any second. Went to grab us a bite to eat so we can get to work again."

"Y'all find something else?"

"I can't discuss the nature of this investigation, but trust me when I say we're going to do a thorough job. We'll have the place locked down for the time being."

"I'm sure you'll have some visitors. Friday is All-You-Can-Carry Day."

The detective cocked his head.

"Sixty bucks. All the parts you can carry."

"Won't be any part-carrying today. We'll lock up the gate. Your associate left us a key."

Associate. The word sounded too fancy to pin on Charlie.

Holden said, "We'll make up a sign to hang out there if need be . . . 'Closed for repairs.'"

"Repairs?"

He shrugged. "We'll think of something. Don't need any citizens out here snapping pictures and such. You know how folks get curious."

"Y'all have any idea who's buried in that trunk?"

He looked at me for a moment, expressionless. "You best get on back, Mr. Miller. We'll call if we need you." His way of shooing me away had a lot less oomph than Coble's tone the night before.

I wished him luck and backed out, but I swung my Jeep wide so I could snatch a peek of the back of the lot. It looked exactly like Holden had described: a crime scene. Yellow tape was spread around, the work lights and fence line holding it up. Then there was the flattened Chevy, just as it was when I left the night before. From my vantage point, about fifty feet away, I couldn't tell if the canvas bag and body were still there, but there were a handful of tiny yellow flags stuck in the snow-and-mush ground. I'd watched enough *First 48* and *Dateline* to know those were evidence markers. Maybe it was a morbid thought, but the craziness that had happened at Miller's Pull-a-Part in the last month alone would've made one hell of an episode on one of those investigation shows. I could see Tammy fixing her hair up real big for the cameras, whipping up her best tears in an interview.

*　*　*

Charlie lived on one of those streets in town where every house looked like it was built at the same time by the same builder fifty or sixty years ago. Small, square Monopoly houses that showed the wear of time, though they'd probably been nice starter homes for young couples at some point. The white paint on Charlie's place seemed fresher than that of his neighbors' houses. I followed his sidewalk to a tiny Astro-Turf-covered porch that was shaded by a sun-bleached, blue awning.

I rang the doorbell, waited several seconds before I heard some movement inside. Charlie unlocked the door, opened it just enough so half his face was visible. He leaned his head against the door frame.

"Can't a man get some rest on his day off?"

"I tried calling."

"You should've taken a hint when I didn't answer."

"I got the hint, but I'm pretty damn stubborn," I said. "Aren't you going to invite me in? Cold as balls out here."

"Christ, Hudson. I'm going on three hours of sleep at the most. I'll give you a holler later on."

"Bullshit. If you wanted to talk to me, you would've already called," I said, and then I softened my voice. "Nightmares keep you up?"

"The cops did."

"They didn't run you off?"

An exhausted sigh. "You ain't going to leave me alone, are you?"

"Hell, no. I've got the day off too."

Charlie nudged the door open a little more. In the full light, the bags under his eyes made him look eighty years old. He turned to walk away. His version of an invitation.

I entered the warm house and was immediately in a living room that had two recliners angled at a TV that was no bigger than thirty inches. The room, like the walls, was bare, but it was tidy. The thick carpet—full of browns and beiges like a calico cat—made the house somehow cozy and welcoming.

"I'd offer you some coffee, but that would involve me making it," Charlie said. He motioned toward one of the matching blue recliners. "Sit if you want."

I sat on the edge of the seat.

Charlie settled in and yanked the lever on his recliner, leaned it back as far as it would go. Buster entered the room from a hallway and took a seat near Charlie's feet. I assumed Charlie hadn't wanted to leave him at the lot the night before.

The TV was muted, playing a commercial for a local company: Anderson's Plumbing, Heating, and Air. It was at the part of the commercial where the dipshit owner, "Crazy" Kevin Anderson says, "A good flush sure beats a full house."

"Dumbass," Charlie said under his breath, giving life to my thoughts.

"So what's the deal?" I asked. "They tell you anything?"

Charlie shook his head.

"Then why did they keep you there so long?"

"They didn't."

"But you told me—"

"They took me to the station after a bit," he said. "Well, Coble did. Other fellow stayed at the yard."

"He think you know something about it?"

"Of course he does. And of course I goddamn don't. Can't tell if he believed me or not, but that didn't stop him from drilling my ass with a bazillion questions. Surprised he didn't try the Chinese water torture."

"What kind of questions was he asking?"

Charlie reached for the remote that sat on a small table between us, a table that also held a lamp and two books, both romance novels as thick as the Bible. A likeness of Fabio on one of the covers. In chaps, shirtless.

"Asking me about everything." Charlie clicked through some channels. "About your daddy. About those guns. About the Chevy."

"Like they're all linked?"

"Something like that. Like your daddy or me was connected to whoever's body was stashed in that trunk."

It was a perfectly rational connection for Coble to make. Only two people had worked at the salvage yard the last several years: Dad and Charlie. The car Buster found sure as hell didn't exist when Grandpa Miller owned the yard. One of them had to have known something.

"What do you think, Charlie . . . about Dad . . ."

He looked down at his hands, dug dirt from under his right thumbnail. "You live long enough in this world, stuff stops surprising you. People stop surprising you. Once had a first cousin named Gary who moonlighted as a woman."

"People are dead," I said.

"Gary's dead too."

"Jesus Christ, Charlie. Can you—"

"The only thing I know for sure is that I don't know a damn thing about any of this mess. Maybe your daddy and that gun business is connected with all of it. His death, the dead fellow in the Chevy. Maybe he fucked somebody over or got tangled up in something real bad, but I can't say one way or the other. I was just the hired help that said 'yessir' and 'no sir' and minded my own damn business."

"You said *fellow*."

"What's that?"

"You said 'the dead fellow in the Chevy.'" From what little I'd seen the night before, the rotting hand, I couldn't tell if it belonged to a man or woman.

"Uh-huh. Coble kept saying *he* last night."

"They know who it is?"

"I'm thinking they do," Charlie said. "That Chevy had a VIN number. I helped that detective find it before I went to the station. Had to do a little cutting to get to it." He made a pair of scissors with his fingers, snipped the air. "Owner was a man, apparently. Reckon that was his body."

"Shit, Charlie," I said. "Somebody local?"

"You think they'd tell me that? Speaking of which, I probably shouldn't be telling you any of this."

"Somebody killed my dad," I said. "And his salvage yard, *my* salvage yard, is currently being hijacked by the cops. Got a damn made-for-TV movie playing out as we speak, so yeah, I think you should be telling me."

He seemed to appraise my sincerity for a moment. His eyes moved to Buster who was licking his paws. "Told you what I know. Now, if you could leave a man in peace, I'd much appreciate it."

Satisfied with the nuggets he had to offer, I told him to get some rest, and I walked to the door. "Guess I'll see you tomorrow. Or whenever they let us back in there."

Charlie chewed on his lip. He wouldn't look at me. "Yeah," he said. "I guess so." But something in his voice, the tired droop of his face, made me think he wasn't so sure about it.

"Charlie?"

He finally looked.

"Dad called me the night before he died."

The words I'd held prisoner were free, but Charlie's response wasn't what I'd expected: "People call people."

"Dad hardly ever called me," I said. "And I didn't answer that night when he did."

"So?"

"So what if he was calling to tell me something important?"

"You already said you didn't answer, so there ain't nothing you can do about it now," he said. "You know what they say about *ifs* and *buts*."

I nodded. "I never told the cops. Sort of feel guilty about that."

"Told them about a convo that never happened? Big deal."

"Then aim that logic at yourself. You shouldn't feel guilty about not knowing anything about that body."

"Thanks for the advice, Dr. Phil." He raised the volume on the TV.

"One more thing, Charlie."

He kept his eyes on an infomercial.

"You can keep Buster here anytime you want."

He reached down to rub Buster's head, and I pulled the door shut.

CHAPTER TWENTY-ONE

Back at the rental house, I was again left to my thoughts. My brain was working overtime, trying to solve a puzzle it didn't have all the pieces for, so I tried my damnedest to keep busy. I did some laundry and cleaned the house in the morning, though it hardly needed it. Around noon, I walked down to Brenda's place to change out an air filter and unclog a sink drain. When I got back, I dug the shoebox of *Twilight Zone* VHS tapes out of the bedroom closet. I hooked up the VCR in the living room and plowed through several episodes, one called "Nick of Time" being the most memorable. It had been my grandma's favorite because she thought William Shatner was a "real looker." In that episode, Shatner played a guy named Don who was obsessed with this penny-operated, tabletop machine called the Mystic Seer that could tell his fortune. Like the other episodes, it closed with the usual *Twilight Zone* ending with a twist, which always made Grandma look over at me, to see if I understood or liked it as much as she did.

Amid my TV marathon, I talked to Mom—who was beside herself over the news, and I called the police station twice. Both times, a cop told me that Coble or Detective Holden would be in touch if need be. Before the second call ended, I told the man on the line it'd be a shame if the local papers showed up at the salvage yard with their questions and cameras. I wasn't so sure the local news would even do that, but the suggestion changed the guy's tone. He promised me that Coble would be in touch.

The afternoon brought no calls, and by nighttime I'd grown stir-crazy. I found myself behind the house with a pack of kitchen matches and what was left of a Maker's Mark bottle my boss had given me as part of a sorry-your-dad's-dead care package. I dumped the remnants of the previous night's precipitation out of a fifty-gallon barrel that sat near the back steps, then sifted through a trash tote, where I found a good haul of paper and cardboard that I added to the barrel. Those scraps alone couldn't warm a tick's ass, so I snuck over to the shittily built lean-to behind Clyde Jesse's place and grabbed an armful of firewood I'd heard him stacking a couple days before. I figured with the buzz that had crept in, a little shotgun spray to my backside wouldn't hurt so bad if Jesse caught me stealing. I lit a couple matches and got the makeshift kindling burning pretty good, and then I dumped in the wood.

I wiped off and sat in a rusted glider that was probably older than I was, swiped through my phone until I found a Pearl Jam playlist. I turned the volume high as it would go, which still wasn't real loud on my Samsung that had been dying a slow death since I'd dropped it in a toilet at Red Door the previous spring.

Within half an hour, the liquor was running so low it barely covered the bottom of the bottle. I held the bottle up in front of the fire, tilted it different ways, and watched the fire dance through the leather-tinted bourbon, a drunk's lava lamp. I popped the top one last time and was just about to take a sip when I heard a vehicle pull up in front of the trailer. I lowered the volume on a tune called "Given to Fly."

I thought it might be Clyde Jesse I heard, that he might just stroll into the backyard and grill me with his eyes, take careful inventory of his woodpile. But the footfalls in the darkness didn't belong to Clyde Jesse. They belonged to Frank Coble, which surprised me since he'd never returned my call.

I offered him a seat, pointed to a stack of damp pallets, but the chief said he wouldn't need long. His car was still running, so that gave me hope that he was telling the truth.

"Looks like somebody got my message," I said.

My casual tone seemed to land like a flick to the nuts. I'm sure he could tell I was halfway to drunk.

"First off, you ain't going to say a word to any news outlet."

I held a grin in check.

Coble said, "Anything I tell you don't go beyond this shit-hole trailer park. Got it?"

I made a zipping motion across my lips, feeling no guilt at all for telling my mom earlier.

"Your old man was a dear friend of mine," Coble said. "Somebody I would never speak ill of."

"Which means that's what you're about to do."

Coble inched closer to the barrel that separated us; when he crossed his arms, the heat waves and liquor vision made it look like he was some beige-clad genie floating in front of me. The goatee and fat gut perfected the illusion. "Nothing's been proven one way or the other in this investigation."

"What exactly is there to prove?"

"Obviously somebody's deceased, Hudson."

"Two somebodies."

"This visit ain't about Leland's murder."

"You want to tell me who exactly it's about?"

Coble tapped a shoe against the barrel. Embers rose and popped. "After we ran the VIN number on that Cavalier, it didn't take us too long to come up with a theory of who that person was. Mind you, none of that information will be known to the public until it's a hundred percent confirmed."

I laid the near empty bottle in the grass next to me and sat up a little. "So I guess I'm part of 'the public.'"

"You are. Same goes for Charlie. Same goes for Tammy whenever we tell her."

"Tell her what exactly?"

"That your daddy may have been involved."

Of all the negative things I'd labeled my dad over the years—*cheater, asshole, redneck*—murder suspect was never one of them. "But you don't know for sure?"

"What y'all didn't see was the rest of that body. It was all crushed up and liquefying, so it's hard to tell what we will figure out for sure. Evidence might be scant as gold dust. Unless, of course, somebody owns up to something. Thing about it is, the only folks that we know who had full access to the salvage yard were—"

"Dad and Charlie."

"That's correct. And had you been working there much longer, you'd be on that list too. I'd probably have you in an interrogation room right now."

There it was: the smugness I'd been waiting for.

"So this is all tied in together. What happened to Dad, the guns—all of it?"

"Very well could be." Coble dropped his gaze to the fire. "If you're willing to hide one skeleton, like that illegal gun business, no telling what others you might be hiding."

Skeleton seemed a poor choice of words. "A murderer, Frank? Do you honestly think Dad would actually kill somebody? And believe me; I think he was a grade-A shithead, but a murderer?"

Coble's hands rose to a defensive position, palms glowing yellow. "*Murderer* is the last thing on Earth I'd want to call Leland, especially since he ain't here to defend himself. But who the hell knows? Could be that Charlie's involved. Beyond those two, any other suspect would be a stretch. At least at this point."

"A stretch. But not impossible."

"He ever say anything off-kilter?"

"Charlie?"

A nod.

Off-kilter. I couldn't think of anything that fit that description, but days earlier, Charlie had said it was cold enough to freeze the tit off a frog. I drunk-giggled at the thought. "Nah," I said. "Hasn't said shit."

"Something funny about all this?"

"Not a damn thing," I said.

"What's your stock in Charlie anyhow? You afraid you might lose your only employee?"

I scooted forward in the glider. "He's dragging his ass to a cold junkyard six days a week, working for chump change. If he did something illegal to get some money or personal gain out of it, he sure did a shitty job."

"Mm-hmm," Coble grumbled. "I'd keep a bead on that fellow. All I'm saying."

"And all I'm saying is y'all have a lot to figure out before you start pointing fingers."

Coble scoffed, like he was annoyed that of all people, a tipsy Hudson Miller was playing devil's advocate. Truth of it was, I genuinely hoped neither my dad nor Charlie had anything to do with the dead body.

"We'll figure out who killed the guy and why," Coble said. "No doubt in my mind."

Ten-four, Chief, I thought. *Like you figured out who killed my dad.*

"I'm sure you will," I said.

With that vote of confidence, Coble said, "Remember what I said, Hudson. Not a word about this. Not to your mama or one of your buddies. No one." Coble hocked and spat in the barrel, then turned to leave.

"How about the salvage yard?"

He turned around.

"I need to work," I said. "Can't keep up a palace like this if I'm not making money."

"You won't be making any tomorrow. Maybe Monday either, for that matter." Coble's words were a cloud of cold smoke against a light shining from atop Clyde Jesse's flagpole.

"You fucking serious?"

He kept walking until I heard a car door shut. His taillights trailed toward the road.

CHAPTER TWENTY-TWO

As expected, I heard jack shit from the cops over the weekend, and Monday was no different. Luckily, Brent called me, asked if I could cover an afternoon bar shift. I jumped at the opportunity. I barely made enough in tips to cover my round trip to Greensboro, but it beat the hell out of sitting idle.

Tuesday, around noon, I'd resorted to push-ups and ab crunches on the living room floor, something to keep a little blood moving. A sobering reminder that a year ago my core had been rock hard, and I could run three miles with ease.

My phone rang halfway through my third set of crunches. I rocked myself to my feet, swiped the phone off the couch, and answered.

It was Charlie: "Tell me you're near a television, Hudson."

"I'm two feet from a real shitty one. Why?"

"Flip it to channel eight news." His voice was serious.

I told him to give me a second. I hurried to the television and pressed the "Power" button, waited for the picture to clear. I pressed the "Channel Up" button until an eight appeared at the top of the screen, and I stepped back to see a familiar image: the outer gate of Miller's Pull-a-Part. Below it, a caption: *Remains Identified in Flint Creek Junkyard*

A woman's excited voice narrated: ". . . local authorities have been working around the clock since the discovery."

The broadcast cut to a picture of a man who looked to be in his twenties. He had dark hair, dark eyes, possibly Latino. There was a black and gray tattoo on the side of his neck. He was straight-faced and wearing a plain, white T-shirt that was stretched at the neck. The picture looked like a mugshot.

The woman continued: "Early this morning, FCPD Chief Frank Coble confirmed that the body was that of Marco Reyes, a twenty-two-year-old Flint Creek man who has been missing since October of last year. Reyes's family was notified this morning, and understandably, they have chosen not to comment at this difficult time."

Neither Charlie nor I said a word over the phone as the anchor spoke.

A shot of police tape.

Marco Reyes's face again. This time, I could decipher his neck tattoo: a growling lion.

Finally, Detective Holden came on the screen, standing in front of the police station. "This is certainly a tragic situation for the Reyes family. Not the sort of news you like to deliver as a cop, but, as we told the family this morning, our department will be working nonstop until we figure this thing out. As always, justice is our top priority."

The female reporter, middle aged with layers of makeup, was shown at the news desk: "If you are thinking the name Miller's Pull-a-Part sounds familiar, you may recall a story we ran in early January—"

I turned the TV off. "Did Coble tell you about this, Charlie?" Through the phone line, I could still hear the reporter's voice. "Charlie?"

"No," he said softly. "No, he didn't."

"Do you know who that guy is?"

"The guy," he mumbled.

"Marco Reyes."

He repeated the name back twice. "I swear I don't think I've ever seen him."

"Shit, Charlie. You've lived in this town for a long time. The news said he's been missing for months."

"Didn't know about anybody missing. I watch the news damn near every night. Get the local paper every week."

Charlie sounded tired, broken, so I eased up on the inquisition. "It's bullshit that we're finding out this way," I told him. "I'm taking my ass down to the police station."

He offered a quiet "Okay" before I hung up.

I was in sweatpants and a T-shirt, so I grabbed a jacket and slid my feet into a pair of sneakers before I left the house.

My phone rang on the way to the station. Of course, it was Mom. And of course I didn't want to talk about the news, although I could imagine she was worried about me. I sent the call to voicemail. I tossed the phone into the passenger seat and hammered my fist into the center console. "Fucking assholes," I seethed. I took another shot at the console, imagining Frank Coble as I did so.

The rest of the drive was a series of rolling stops and pep talks to remind myself that I absolutely wouldn't leave the police station without speaking to Coble about why I'd been left in the dark.

When I got to the station, I spotted Coble's and Holden's cars along with a white channel 8 news van. I parked in a space reserved for one of the officers and got out. On my way inside, I noticed a gel-haired news anchor sitting in the van; he took a rip from an e-cig while a cameraman at the back of the van wound some cords around his elbow. They both noticed me, but neither seemed to realize who I was or what fireworks my visit could ignite.

Coble was near the front desk when I opened the station door. He was standing with some other meathead of a cop that I didn't know. Dude had biceps the size of Igloo coolers.

"What the fuck, Frank?" I asked, not sorry that my anger hadn't subsided a bit.

Coble shot me this "oh shit" look before he told Cooler Arms that he'd handle things. He lifted a hand toward me. "Can you take it down a notch, Hudson?"

"You're joking, right? I have every right to turn my volume to fucking ten if I feel like it."

His face grew red as he stepped closer to me. Through gritted teeth, he said, "Damn it, boy." He looked over his shoulder, then back at me. "The victim's mother and little sister aren't but ten feet away in my office right now. The only people that I owe anything to right now are those two."

My eyes moved past Coble; a girl was standing in the doorway of his office. She was tall and broad at the shoulders, but young, probably not a day over sixteen, sipping a Dr. Pepper through a neon-green straw as she watched us. Her complexion and dark hair were like those of the man I'd seen on the news. His sister, I thought. I could only imagine the grief she was going through. If the look in her eyes was any indication, it was far beyond the grief I'd felt after Dad's murder. Suddenly, I was calmer—reality was whispering to me: *Somebody on this planet is having a shittier day than you are, asshole.*

I brought my face closer to Coble's, expecting to feel the heat from it. "Just thought I'd find out before the rest of the world, Frank. Same goes for Charlie. That poor bastard is beside himself."

The chief wiped some sweat—possibly spit—from his upper lip. "I fed you more information than I should've the other night, Hudson. Didn't have to pay you a visit at all or tell you a damn thing. You understand that?"

The words registered, but none of it mattered in the moment because the young girl haunted my periphery; she was still watching us. "Whatever you say. So damn generous of you."

He placed a hand on my shoulder, trying for sincere. "Now get on out of here so I can deal with this family. They deserve every second I can give them."

"Chief," a woman at the front desk called. She held up a phone and mouthed, "Newspaper."

"You heard what I said," he told me before he hustled to the desk, his keys and cuffs jingling.

Now that I was standing alone, no portly cop serving as a barrier, I consciously kept my eyes away from the girl. I made a quick exit just as the news van was pulling out of the lot. I thought that maybe I could come back, properly show my ass when things settled down a bit.

I fired up my Jeep but hadn't even made a move for the gearshift when the girl spilled out of the front of the police station. She scanned the parking lot until our eyes met, and then made a beeline in my direction. Coble and another cop came out of the door like bumbling dipshits, just a few strides behind her.

"What do you know about my brother?" the girl shouted loud enough to best the sound of my engine and my heat blowing full blast. When she got to the front of my Jeep, she slammed both of her fists down, a volcano from her soda can fizzling all over her arms and my hood.

My hands stayed on the wheel. I was sure the girl was about to bash my hood again, but Coble closed in and grabbed one of her arms.

"Easy, Lucy!" he shouted.

She broke free of his grip with ease, yelled, "Get your freaking hands off of me!"

Surprisingly, Coble stepped back and made a gesture like *"Let's all take a deep breath."*

Lucy declined the request, reminded Coble and the other cop they had no right to lay a finger on her. She didn't settle until a woman, fortyish and in scrubs—her mother, I assumed—came out of the station and made an apparent plea for calm that I couldn't quite hear. Whatever she said worked. Lucy looked around Coble and gave me one last stare, cold as the morning air; she shook her head as if I was as detestable a person as had ever lived. The cops led her back inside, but carefully.

I took a couple breaths and wrung my hands on the steering wheel. Before I backed out of my parking place, I leaned up to assess the damage to my hood. The Dr. Pepper had settled itself nicely into one of the fist-sized dents. My Jeep wasn't fit for a showroom by any means, but it was the one decent piece of property that I'd paid off myself.

Still, a dent in my hood felt trivial in the moment. I could give the girl a pass. It's not every day you find out that somebody's buried your brother in a big fucking hole in the ground in a cemetery meant for machines, not people.

CHAPTER TWENTY-THREE

It was Lucy Reyes who'd last seen her brother on Saturday, October 27. He'd just washed his car and was "heading out for the evening," though he'd never told Lucy where. Channel 8 news had published those details in an online article in early November. It was the only missing persons article I could find when I googled *Marco Reyes, Flint Creek*. In the final paragraph, it gave his physical description—five feet ten, a hundred and seventy-six pounds, with dark brown hair and brown eyes, a tattoo on his neck and forearm. Below it, a more flattering picture than the TV news had shown: a smiling Marco leaning against his car, wearing a blue button-up tucked into baggy jeans.

Of course my internet search brought up a slew of articles about the discovery of his body, but something else: three arrest reports for Marco Reyes on the Payne County mugshot database, from 2015 to 2018. Two for possession of marijuana, one for resisting arrest. The mugshot from the resisting charge, from last May, was the one from the news.

I contemplated, but not for long, why Charlie had never heard of Reyes going missing. Sure, Charlie checked most of the boxes for a man just over seventy: he was slow moving, stubborn, and a professional wiseass at times, but his memory seemed sharp. He would have remembered a news story or a conversation about a missing local. It had only been four months ago. But Marco Reyes wasn't a child; he was a grown man with a criminal record—a Latino man to boot. Not the type of person a community, as self-righteous as it was bigoted, would call a volunteer search party for.

*　*　*

It was Thursday before I got the green light to reopen the salvage yard, and it wasn't because the cops had stayed in touch. I'd bugged the piss out of them until Coble finally said they'd finished collecting and hauling away evidence from the burial site. Mom did her best to talk me out of reopening, even suggesting I move to Wilmington and stay with her awhile, find work at the coast. It was a sincere, simple offer, but I declined. Moving felt like the easy way out—a wiser man probably would have taken it.

Charlie actually beat me to work Thursday morning. He was out behind the shop, surveying the crime scene that was now just a muddy hole in the ground. No Chevy, no police tape, or evidence markers.

"Let's get inside," I called to him.

His face looked hollow in the early morning light. I wondered how much he'd slept in the past week, if at all. When I held up a brown, grease-soaked paper bag, he nodded and followed me into the shop.

Charlie hadn't been keen on the idea of coming into work, at least not yet, so I figured buying him breakfast was the least I could do. And not just any breakfast, but a fried tenderloin biscuit from Sassy Sally's BBQ, with a slab of pork so big, the biscuit could barely contain half of it.

We ate in the waiting area. I squeezed a couple of packets of Texas Pete onto my biscuit, but Charlie declined the hot sauce. Something about an ulcer flaring up.

Halfway through my biscuit, I said, "Can I ask you something, Charlie?"

"No, I won't be your Valentine," he said, brushing some crumbs off his lips.

I hadn't even realized it was the fourteenth. "I want to know what my dad was like."

He popped the lid on his tea, shook some ice into his mouth, and crunched it for a moment. "He was your old man for . . . how old are you? Eleven? Twelve?"

"Twenty-nine."

"Twenty-nine years. Which means you should know better than me."

"I don't want to know about Leland Miller, the half-ass dad and womanizer," I said. "I've got that part of the story memorized pretty good. Could probably write a damn book about it. Who was he to you?"

"Leland was my boss."

I rolled my eyes.

"God-a-mighty," Charlie mumbled as he sat back, crossed one leg over the other, painfully. "Your daddy was an all right guy. Had his faults like any other, but he never done me wrong. Butted heads a few times, but that sort of thing happens when you're around somebody all the damn time."

"Butted heads about what?"

"Hell, I don't know, kid. Stupid shit. Stuff guys argue about. About whether Corvettes or Mustangs were better, or whether Jamie Lee Curtis was hot back in the seventies or not. Argued about politics from time to time."

"Jamie Lee Curtis?"

"Damn right," he said. "She was a solid nine back in her younger days. Your daddy thought she was a seven at best. He was more into those *Baywatch* types." He held his hands about a foot away from his chest, cupped them like he was supporting a pair of double D's.

I laughed a little, but there was something I was curious about: "If you had known Dad was fucking around with that gun business, would you have ratted him out?"

Charlie sat forward. "Your daddy was my boss, like I told you before. My *boss*. He wasn't my bosom buddy. He didn't invite me over for cookouts or write me a Christmas card, and we didn't get matching tattoos on our ass cheeks. Did we get along? Sure. Most times. He liked how I worked, and I liked getting paid at the end of the week, but that don't mean I knew everything about him or what went on this yard twenty-four seven."

"But if you did know something . . ."

He pondered for a second. "First off, I want you to understand this: nine times out of ten, your daddy closed this place up. And sometimes he'd stay out here late as hell. He was a workaholic." He tapped the armrest on the couch. "Some mornings, I'd get to work and he'd be passed out on this couch."

"Drunk?"

"Maybe a couple times, but usually he was here because he'd had it out with that battle-ax Tammy. Reckon this cold shop beat the hell out of a cold house, if you catch my meaning."

I hadn't heard a peep from Tammy in a while. Unless she was coming by to move that damn Winnebago that was still parked beside the shop, I didn't care to. "I'd rather slam my dick in a steel door than deal with somebody like her."

Charlie nodded. "And you should also understand this: I worked my hours and went home. No telling how many extra hours your daddy spent here over the years. Would've been easy for him to run guns in and out of this place without a soul except the buyer knowing. Buster could've known too, of course. But he ain't much of a talker."

"So Dad could've kept that shit secret pretty easy."

"Could've? He *did*."

"Probably didn't want you mixed up in it."

"I wouldn't have given a damn either way, so *no*, I wouldn't have ratted him out." Charlie stood up slowly, looking down at me. "And I don't think he would've hurt anybody intentionally. If we're talking self-defense, that wouldn't surprise me, but I doubt he would've buried a fucking body out back in the trunk of a Chevy Cavalier. That's the move of a damn coward."

"You sound pretty sure about all that."

He started to walk away, and I wondered if I'd come on too strong. I asked him where he was going.

"The only thing I'm sure about is them biscuits tend to run right through me. Last time I had one of those I could've shit through a coffee filter for two straight days."

* * *

Around three, the wrecker service gave us a call, to see if we were open. A flatbed came by shortly after, hauling a 2001

Honda CRV that had been rolled in a wreck. I was surprised the driver had even lived, but he showed up wearing a cast on his left arm, his nose purple and his eyes black underneath. Considering the state of the CRV, he'd been pretty lucky.

Charlie and I walked outside and inspected the vehicle. While the driver was giving Jeremy from the tow service all the details about the wreck, which involved a guard rail and a mountain road, something caught the corner of my eye. Just inside the front gate, somebody was riding toward me on a bicycle. A couple of things about it threw me for a loop: one, it wasn't bike weather, being no better than forty degrees out; and two, I recognized the person as the bike got closer—Lucy Reyes, her hair pulled into a wind-frazzled bun.

"Can you handle this, Charlie?" I asked, motioning to the CRV.

He saw Lucy, but there wasn't a sign of recognition on his face. "Yeah, I can handle it."

I half jogged toward the front gate, and in seconds, the dead man's sister was bearing down on me, her front tire stopping just inches from my leg. "Got nowhere to run now, do you?"

"Lucy?" I asked, calmly as I could.

"Don't act like you know me, asshole."

We were about twenty feet from Charlie and the others, but I was certain they'd heard her.

"I'm not trying to run," I said. "Can we talk inside?"

She got off the bike that was at least three years too small for her, and dumped it in the dirt, a handlebar sticking in the mushy ground like a yard dart. She swept an arm through the air as if to say *"After you, dickhead."*

She breathed down my neck on the way to the shop, then slammed the door behind us.

"If you came to pound the hell out of my Jeep again, I parked it out front. Have at it."

"I came for some answers," she said, tightening a fist and holding it up. "You're lucky you're a boxer or whatever, or I would—"

I raised my hands in a conciliatory gesture. "There's no reason to be pissed at me. You probably know more about everything that's happened than I do. You realize I lost a family member too, don't you?"

"If he did something to my brother, then your *family member* deserved what happened."

I waited a beat or two before replying. "I'd feel the same way you do if I were in your shoes. Can we just talk about this without you waving your fists around?"

"Or what? You going to sock me in the jaw like you did that old man in that boxing video?"

"Christ. You know about that?"

"Everybody knows about that."

I shook my head. *Fucking YouTube.*

"Shows what kind of people your family is," she said scornfully.

I didn't bother defending my dignity. "If it makes you feel any better, I think a majority of the Flint Creek PD are a bunch of dipshits. They don't tell me anything that's worth a damn. They'll barely answer my calls, give me the company line when they do. What about you? Cops told you anything?"

"They think your dad killed my brother."

"They said that?" I was shocked, and it showed.

She shrugged. "Kind of. They mentioned his name a bunch and said he was tied up with some shady stuff. Selling guns or something."

"So they never actually said he did it?"

She turned the question over for a moment and then shook her head.

"I want you to know I'm sorry as hell about your brother," I said. "Another thing you should know is that my dad and I weren't close, so I can't vouch for what he did or didn't do. I don't really have a dog in this fight."

"He was your dad. Y'all worked together. How are you going to say you and him weren't close?"

It baffled me that the cops hadn't filled her in after she'd Donkey-Konged the shit out of my Jeep. No wonder she was so riled up at me. "Worked together? He left this place to me when he died. Probably because I was his only kid. I'd hardly spoken to him in the past year. I just moved back here a few weeks ago to keep this place afloat and see if I could make some money."

She took a breath, relaxed her posture. "Cops didn't tell me that."

"Of course they didn't," I said. I could tell she was still angry, but not, I thought, so much at me anymore. "By the way, I'm Hudson." I extended my hand, but she didn't take it. I dropped it to my side.

She asked, "So that old guy outside is who found him?"

I nodded. "Charlie. He's the one who found my dad too."

"Then I've got some questions for him," she insisted.

"Fair enough."

"And I want to see where my brother was."

"It's nothing but a hole in the ground now, and—"

"I want to see it."

Letting a teenager see the hole in the ground her brother had been dug out of felt all sorts of wrong, but I thought she deserved to see it. I also knew Lucy wasn't going to take no for an answer. I told her to follow me. When we stepped out the back door of the shop, she immediately eyed the burial spot. I stopped, but she kept walking toward it, not even pausing to steel herself over. She slowed as she neared the spot, and she squatted down. She stayed like that for about a minute, not moving or saying a word, so I walked over to her. I couldn't see any tears in her eyes or on her cheeks, but pain and anger resonated beneath the surface.

"Were you and Marco close?" I asked quietly.

"Mo," she whispered. "I called him Mo. He was seven years older than me, but we were always close. Fought a bunch, but we were close. Had to be. Never had a dad around . . . he probably doesn't even know his son's dead."

"Can't imagine what you're dealing with," I said. And I couldn't.

She squinted against the sun. "How could somebody do something like this and think it's okay?"

She was right: it was incomprehensible. "I don't know, Lucy. I don't know why a lot of people in this world do what they do. Whoever shot my dad. Whoever did this."

She turned toward me, belligerent again. "Like you give a crap. Mo is just another criminal off the street to people like you, but not to me. That's my blood. I had to love him, no matter if he did stupid stuff or not."

"I do give a crap," I told her, thinking I'd done some stupid shit in my teenage years. "You don't have to know somebody to want to see justice in a situation like this. Even if I find out that my dad is a hundred percent to blame, I'm in the same boat as you. I want to know the truth. About all of it."

"Justice," she said, standing up. "A family like mine getting justice in this town? That's a good one." She slid her phone out of her back pocket, took a few slow steps back. She took several pictures of the hole in the ground and then turned to snap one of me. I wasn't sure why, but I wasn't about to give her shit for it. She had plenty to be upset about.

"I'm going to find out what happened," she said. "No matter what I have to do."

"I hope like hell that you do, Lucy," I said. "I'll help in whatever way I can."

For the first time, she looked at me like I wasn't the enemy, but maybe an ally. "My mama doesn't have time to help. She hardly even has time to cry about it. Works over ten hours a day at the animal hospital in Winston, just to keep our rent paid. I'm doing this for her more than anybody."

"She sounds like a good lady."

Lucy wedged her phone back in her pocket. "My lunch period is about over. I better get to school before they try and call her at work again."

"You need a lift?" I asked. "Might be quicker than that bike."

"I don't need a ride," she said with a tough bravado.

"Thought I'd offer. And remember what I said about helping you. You know where to find me. I'm sure Charlie would be glad to help too."

"Help me, huh?" she said, the tone of someone who'd been burned by empty promise after empty promise. She slid a piece of folded-up, bright orange paper from her jeans pocket, then handed it to me. "If you want to help, you can start by learning something."

CHAPTER TWENTY-FOUR

She'd left me a flyer.

I smoothed it out on the counter when I got inside.

The top read "Justice for Marco" in bold letters. Below the heading was a picture of Marco Reyes and some information about when he'd gone missing. It mentioned his mysterious death and the fact that his body had been found at a junkyard, though it didn't mention Miller's Pull-a-Part by name.

Near the bottom of the flyer there was a local number for people to call or text if they had any information. Below that: *Follow @Justice4Marco on Instagram for more details and updates.*

I'd never had an Instagram account, but I was curious about what Lucy had created; I downloaded the app and made a generic profile. I found the Justice4Marco account and tapped "Follow," making me the forty-second person to do so.

At first, it had struck me as odd that Lucy was using Instagram as a platform, but when I brought up the account, it made sense. She'd uploaded a dozen or so pictures of her brother. Pictures of birthdays, goofy faces, and Marco doing things like skateboarding and fishing and playing baseball. In one, a teenage Marco was sitting on a plastic bucket, baiting a fish hook with a rubber worm. The caption read: *Mo loved fishing ever since he was little. This was the day he caught a bass and brought it home for Mama to cook and she got mad. Mama said it was gross and too small and made him take it to the dumpster. LOL*

All the pictures had captions like that, little tidbits that humanized him, made him more than a skimpy news blurb and a mugshot.

He was a regular guy. He was a brother and a son.

And the account wasn't just pictures of Marco. There were videos of Lucy giving details about her brother's case, starting with his disappearance.

Charlie came in the door as I was watching one of the videos. I paused it.

"What was that all about?" he asked, tossing his gloves on the loveseat. "You piss that girl off or something?"

I shook my head and held up the flyer. "The Reyes boy . . . that was his little sister."

"Reyes . . ." Charlie muttered, and then it hit him. "Lordy," he said. "Poor little gal. You tell her we don't know nothing?"

"Wish I could've told her differently," I said, sliding him the flyer when he reached the counter. "Seems like the cops haven't been much help."

"Color me shocked." Charlie's voice trailed off as he read.

"That little flyer isn't the half of it. She made an account online so she could tell people about the case. Seems pretty determined to get to the bottom of it." I turned my phone so it faced him. "Check this out."

Charlie came around the counter and stood next to me. I propped my phone against the cash register and resumed the video I'd been watching.

Lucy, standing in front of the police station, spoke fearlessly:

If we'd had help early on, maybe we would have some answers, but nobody around here wants to help a poor brown girl and her mother.

And do you want to hear some real bull crap?

We put up missing posters downtown on a Wednesday, and by Friday they were gone. I called the city enough until finally some lady who sounded like a mouse told us there was an ordinance about putting posters up. Something about solicitation. I'm like, we are out here trying to find my brother, not sell bathroom cleaner.

Man, whatever. That's Flint Creek for you.

"She's got some guts," Charlie said when the video ended. "Big time."

Charlie slid a stool up to the counter and sat. "What else she got on there?"

I scrolled down and started back at the first video.

We must've spent fifteen minutes watching them all. By the time we'd finished the last one, her page had been updated with the picture she'd taken out behind the shop less than an hour before.

RIP Mo. I'll find out who put you there. Love you. #justice4marco

Lucy was working harder on finding the truth than the whole police department combined. She'd taken it upon herself to interview her brother's friends and neighbors, even Marco's former parole officer. She'd been to the police station every week since October. Never an answer or any assurance that she'd ever get one. Now that Marco was her *dead* brother, not just her missing one, the lack of help had to be even more infuriating. I understood more than before why she didn't trust me.

"No wonder she was so pissed off," Charlie said.

"It's like the cops could give two shits. Imagine if that was Coble's daughter missing or dead."

"They'd have the guy from *America's Most Wanted* out here. Every newspaper in the state."

"No doubt about it."

"But like she said on that one video, ain't nobody breaking their necks for some Mexican boy." There was more conviction in his voice than I'd ever heard.

"They aren't even breaking a sweat."

"If I was that girl, I'd be raising a fuss too. She's dealing with Flint Creek bullshit at its finest."

"Ass-backwards town."

"Back-asswards, I call it."

I tapped my phone. "You know . . . those videos are kind of a gut check."

"What do you mean?"

"I know I wasn't close with Dad and all that, but I still feel like I should be doing something to find out what happened to him. A robbery sounded like a good guess early on, with some of those guns missing, the register empty. Seemed to make sense. Not so sure about that now."

"Reckon I'm in the same boat," he said. "Ain't much we can do, though."

"Maybe not, but just look at Lucy Reyes. She's what . . . fourteen? Fifteen? And she's beating down the damn doors at the PD. Meanwhile, I'm over here with a thumb up my ass, cashing in on Dad's death."

Charlie raised an eyebrow. "If it makes you feel any better, you ain't cashing in much."

"Thanks for reminding me," I said. "Anyways, before Lucy left, I told her I'd help her. That you'd help too."

"Me?"

"Yes, you. Besides, she'll probably be paying us more visits anyway. We might as well help. Might be the only help she's got."

Charlie didn't look enthused, but he didn't shoot down the idea either.

Before we got to work on the CRV, I looked on the Instagram page, found the tip-line number Lucy had put in the profile description.

I sent a text:

This is Hudson Miller. I watched your videos. Showed Charlie. We'd like to help.

A few minutes later, she responded:

If I find out either of you knew anything, I'm taking you down.

Then she sent another: *I'll be in touch soon.*

CHAPTER TWENTY-FIVE

Soon was very soon. Ten minutes before we closed up, Lucy came through the door, her backpack slung around her shoulder.

"Where's that one dude?"

"He's right back—"

Charlie poked his head in from the garage.

"You found my brother?" Lucy asked.

Charlie tucked a shop rag in his waistband and came into the shop. "Yes, ma'am. I'm the one."

"And you didn't kill him?"

He looked at me for a cue, but I had nothing. Charlie's voice was gentle: "No. I didn't kill your brother."

"And you swear you don't know who did?"

Charlie shook his head. "To be fair, I wouldn't have dug something up that I didn't want anyone to know about."

Lucy seemed to weigh Charlie's logic. "Maybe. Maybe not. I read this story in eighth grade about a guy who killed this old man, then he buried him underneath the floor in his house. One night, the guy dug that body up because all that guilt was driving him insane. So maybe you're like him."

"No, ma'am. I've done things in this world I might feel guilty about, but that ain't one of them. Hand to God."

"The truth always finds a way out. Just know that."

Charlie said, "I believe you. I saw your um . . . the thing on the—"

"Your Instagram videos," I told her.

"And?"

"I think you know more about your brother's case than anybody," I said.

Charlie nodded in agreement.

"If y'all say you'll help me, you better mean it. I don't have time to waste."

"We'll do anything we can. Won't we, Charlie?"

"Sure," he said. "Do what we can."

She walked a little closer, eyes on Charlie. "I'm Lucy Reyes, by the way."

"Charlie Shoaf," he said. He repeated her name back quietly, clunkily rolling the *R* sound.

"Y'all about to close up?"

"Just a few minutes." Charlie tapped his watch.

"Do you get many visitors this late?"

I said, "Not unless they want an earful from Charlie here."

"Good," she said. "I have something y'all need to see, so long as you promise you won't say anything. Not to the cops. Nobody."

"Got my word," I said.

Charlie said the same.

"Before you show us whatever it is you're going to show us, Lucy, there's just one thing," I said.

"Yeah?"

"Does your mom know about you coming down here? About us trying to help you out?"

"Yeah. We could be a couple psychopaths," Charlie added.

"Of course she knows," she said, "and for all you know, I could be down here just to collect evidence and catch you in a lie. You think about that?"

I looked at her, unsure if she was being straight with me.

She must've sensed my doubt; she scrolled through her phone and held it toward me. It was a text thread with *Mama Bear*. She pointed out her last message: *I'm going to talk to them at the junkyard. They said they can help. I promise I'll be safe. ILY.*

"Just so you know," she said, "I always document where I go, one way or another. If something ever happens to me, there won't be any mystery about it."

"Smart lady," Charlie said.

I said, "And just so *you* know, Lucy, I've been punched in the head a lot, and Charlie's got a few screws loose, but we aren't psychopaths. You can tell your mom that."

Lucy didn't laugh.

Just in case somebody might pop in, I locked the front door, turned off the outside lights.

Lucy walked to the waiting area. She slid some magazines out of the way and laid her backpack on the table. Charlie and I gathered around the table as she pulled a file folder from the bag. One by one, she began laying notecards with names on them on the table, then she matched each name with a drawing, which I quickly realized were comic book versions of myself, my dad, and some police officers, a couple of guys I'd never heard of. A drawing of her brother too. It looked like a professional had done them.

"You drew all of these?" I asked.

She tapped the note card with me on it. "That's why I took your pic today. So I could get it right. Wasn't being a creep."

"Did a hell of a job."

She looked back and forth between the real me and cartoon me like she was critiquing her work. Then to Charlie: "Guess I have to do yours next."

Charlie asked if she could make his muscles a little bigger. She looked at me as if to ask. *"What the hell is wrong with this guy?"*

I studied the pictures of the cops.

Chief Coble was even fatter in his cartoon depiction, a stupid-looking grin on his face, a string of drool trickling out. Detective Holden looked normal, questions marks above his head. Beside an officer named John Russell, who was most definitely Cooler Arms who I'd seen at the station, there was a drawing of a short, rail-thin man I didn't recognize. Lee Markham was the name below the drawing.

"These are the cops you've talked to?"

She nodded.

I tapped on Markham's notecard. "What about this guy?"

"Just another waste of a badge," she said. "Those are all the cops I used to harass when Mo went missing. Two of them had arrested him before. Marijuana charges. That Russell guy was one of them, and that jerk Markham."

"Markham," I repeated. "I've never seen him. You, Charlie?"

Charlie said he didn't know the guy, but he may have seen him before.

"That's because he don't work there anymore," Lucy said. "He quit at the end of last year."

"Quit?"

"I don't know. Quit or got fired. But he doesn't work there anymore."

"I take it he wasn't helpful?"

"Helpful? He told Mama right to her face that druggies like my brother just disappear. Said sometimes they come back, and sometimes they don't. Acted like Mo was a dog that got off his leash or something."

"That's pretty fucked up," Charlie said. "Pardon my language, young lady."

"It's super fucked up," Lucy said. "Pardon *my* language, Mr. Charlie." She reached into her bag and withdrew a small notebook that had a cat riding a unicorn on the front. "Everything that's said. Everything I found out. I write it down. Even if I don't think it's important. I didn't just draw those pictures because I was bored. It helps me process things."

"Right on," Charlie said. "Like a little detective."

"I'm not little, and I'm not a detective. Detectives get paid. I'm just the last girl you want to piss off."

"The hood of my Jeep can attest to that," I said.

Lucy unsuccessfully stifled a snicker.

"So what can we do to help?" Charlie said.

She slid a pen from the front pouch of her bag and clicked it. She sat on the sofa and opened her notebook. "First off, if you're going to help me, I need to know who y'all are, how y'all got here."

"Got here?" Charlie asked.

"*Here,*" she said. "As in this salvage yard. Seems like this is where all the bad stuff happens."

"Ground Zero," Charlie said.

"Something like that." Lucy leaned forward. "So let's start with you. How'd you get this job? You grow up around here?"

Charlie shook his head. "I've lived all around. Before I come here, I was living over in Eden. Wasn't there two years before I lost my second wife, Linda, to this window sales-man named George Jones—kid you not, just like the damn country singer. Not a month after that, the furniture outfit I was doing upholstery for moved about fifteen minutes up the road from here. Near downtown High Point. I bought a place down this way because it was a shit ton cheaper. Wasn't because I had romantic ideas about small-town living."

"So you got fired from that furniture job?" she asked.

"No, ma'am. My luck just kept humming right along after Linda: that furniture place went belly-up in less than a year. I spent about two months trying to find steady work after that, then I saw this job in the classifieds. Remember it like yester-day: *'Need an honest, hard-working man that's good with his hands.'*" He chuckled. "I was at least two of those things."

"And you've been here ever since?"

"Ever since."

Lucy wrote in her notebook and then shifted her attention to me. "You told me today you inherited all this, right?"

"Just weeks ago."

"But you grew up here . . ."

"Until I was ten. Once my parents split, I lived with my mom in Greensboro. Only stayed here some weekends until I was eighteen. Haven't been back much since."

She wrote some more and closed her notebook. "Kind of funny."

"What is?" Charlie asked.

"The three of us," she said. "Basically a bunch of outsiders."

I had a different thought, but didn't voice it: the names, Charlie and Lucy. I was teaming up with the *Peanuts* gang.

"Outsider? I'll wear that title with pride," Charlie said. "So, Ms. Lucy, I take it you're from—"

"This *Mexican* girl isn't from Mexico," she said, as if she'd had the same conversation a thousand times before. "My parents lived in Reynosa, but they moved to Texas when Mama got pregnant with me. This place called Three Rivers. My parents weren't good together, guess they thought another baby and a move could fix that, but . . . I don't know." For a moment, there was a vulnerability in her face I hadn't seen before, and I think she knew that I noticed. It was gone as quickly as it came. "Anyway, I don't remember him. Don't want to."

"Sorry to hear that, young lady," Charlie said with genuine empathy.

"Don't be. My mama is enough."

"How about Flint Creek?" I asked. "When did y'all move here?"

"About four years ago. We moved around a lot before that. I think Mama thinks the grass will be greener every time we move, but that's not always the case."

"Does she know about all of this?" I indicated the drawings.

"She knows I spend most of my time trying to figure all this out, but she hasn't seen my notebook. My Instagram either. At least I don't think she has. I just don't want to upset her any more than she already is."

"So you've been carrying all of this stuff around in that bag?"

"Uh-huh."

Charlie said, "Why don't we just stick it up on the wall like they do in those cop movies?"

"That's called an investigation board," Lucy said. "I'd be down with that. But like I said, I can't do that at home, my mama—"

"I got just the spot, Ms. Lucy." Charlie asked us to follow him, so we did. Past the front counter, down the hall to the break room. He pointed to the corkboard on the back wall that was covered in my dad's collection of random shit.

Charlie paid it no reverence. He began tearing down and untacking every single thing on the board, tossing it onto the table, topless centerfold included. Out of embarrassment, I quickly covered it with a Captain Tim's menu. Lucy didn't seem to notice.

Charlie turned to her once the board was cleared. "Voilà!"

Lucy didn't look so sure. "Does the door to this room lock?"

I said, "We don't ever lock it, but yeah, it locks."

"Then you better start."

"Yes, ma'am," Charlie said.

Satisfied, Lucy began arranging her drawings and note-cards on the board. She did so slowly and deliberately. She put up a newspaper clipping: *Body of Missing Local Man Found.* She tacked up a printed photo of herself, her mom, and her brother next to a Christmas tree. The final item she added was a small, handwritten note dated October 27, the last day she'd seen her brother.

I stood closer so I could read it.

Some of the events were as follows:

Approx. 10:30—Mo got up late. Mama wanted him to rake leaves behind trailer.

Afternoon: Mo got lunch from the McDonald's in Thomasville. Fell asleep on couch. Washed car after.

The last items piqued my curiosity. Text messages that Lucy had transcribed. They were listed at 6:50 and 7:33 PM.

The first message: *To Jackson Kimbrough—U getting into anything tonight?*

The second: *To Eryk Lawson—Bored AF. Trying to do something later? HMU*

Lucy noticed me reading them.

"Mo sent those to his buddies. Neither responded until the next day. Jax and Eryk were busy that night. One was working. One wasn't even in town."

"Cops find those?" I asked.

Lucy said, "*I* did. They've never recovered his phone. Mo's friends showed me those about a week after he went missing." She tapped the 7:33 message. "That's the last time anyone talked to him as far as I know. Nobody knows where he went that night."

"Well, *somebody* does," Charlie said.

"That's right, Mr. Charlie. And I'm going to find out who. My brother deserves that much. Despite what anyone around here says or thinks, he wasn't a piece of trash."

"Ain't nobody perfect," Charlie said.

"You ever done any time?" Lucy asked him.

Charlie said he hadn't.

"Ever smoke any weed?"

"Well, I did live through the seventies . . ."

"Mo smoked weed too. Not every day, but sometimes he did. Got charged a couple times for it." She pointed at the corkboard. "One of those times, that Markham guy had pulled him over for window tint. *Factory* window tint. Wasn't even close to being illegal. Markham said Mo was acting suspicious, searched his car and found a roach in a Wendy's cup in the floorboard."

"That's some bad luck," Charlie said.

"I said the same thing when it happened. Then like seven or eight months later, Mo and this White dude called Big Grant were smoking up near that muddy pond off Oakview Road. Somebody must've called the cops because Officer Russell showed up out of nowhere. Didn't find any weed in the car but found Grant's joint in the grass."

"Should've flicked it into the pond," Charlie suggested.

"He wasn't that smart," Lucy said. "And you want to know who took the fall for his stupidity?"

"I guess it wasn't the Grant guy," I said.

"Grant denied it was his, and Russell decided to believe him. No more questions asked. Mo got a little agitated because of it, yanked his arm away when Russell grabbed him, got booked for resisting."

"Ain't that some bullshit," Charlie said.

"I know Mo wasn't totally innocent," Lucy said, "and Mo knew it too. But I can name fifty kids at my school that come in five days a week, high as kites, and I've never once read their name in the paper. It's like those cops *wanted* my brother to be guilty. He got pulled a few other times for bull crap too.

They just couldn't always pin anything on him." Lucy picked her phone up and checked it. "Anyways, I better go before I get all worked up. Mama gets home around eight. I have to get dinner started."

After she zipped up her backpack, we walked out of the break room. "Anything we can do in the meantime?" I asked her.

"Just promise me this: if you hear anything or see anything, you'll let me know."

"I definitely will," I said.

Charlie added, "Me too, Ms. Lucy."

She nodded and looked between us. "Y'all are in this thing now. You best buckle up."

CHAPTER TWENTY-SIX

I expected I might see Lucy over those next few days, but she didn't stop by, and there hadn't been any updates on the Justice4Marco Instagram. As for the salvage yard, business was hit or miss. Not the gradual increase I'd been hoping for. I did snag a quality shift at Red Door Monday evening. A group of soon-to-be time-share victims who were staying at a downtown hotel stopped in. Turned out to be a three-hour dick-showing contest of *"Next round is on me, fellas"* and cash tips. I was all for it.

When I got to the salvage yard on Tuesday, luck again reared its ugly side. I got out of my Jeep to unlock the front gate, and I saw the padlock lying in the gravel in front of me; someone had taken a bolt cutter to it. I pushed the gate open, leaving my Jeep where it was. I scanned the yard for any intruders or vehicles that didn't belong, and that's when I noticed Buster pacing near the garage bay. The night before had been chilly, but tolerable, so we'd left him outside. When I got to the shop door, he greeted me with a nervous whimper, and it became clear as to why: the front door had been pried open. I walked inside and flipped on the lights, Buster right behind me.

The place had been ransacked. The tables in the waiting room had been flipped over, the magazines strewn about the floor. Some of the signs and license plates that had covered the front counter and walls had joined them in disarray. Even the pot from the coffee maker lay shattered.

I stepped over and through the debris and went behind the counter where the register had been opened. It was empty, but that's exactly how I'd left it, so I turned my attention to the computer. The CPU itself was intact, but the cables that connected it to the wall and monitor had been cleanly severed, a more methodical approach than the hurricane that had torn through the rest of the shop.

Buster roamed aimlessly as I checked the other rooms down the hallway; they appeared normal. The break room was still locked and undisturbed. The same couldn't be said for the garage. While the shelves looked untouched, the guts of the big Craftsman tool chest lay in a metal apocalypse on the ground: wrenches, screwdrivers, and the like.

A sound came from the office. My chest tightened like I was caught in a bear hug. I leaned down and grabbed a hefty socket wrench, and I peeked into the main room.

It was Charlie, eyes wide. Buster was by his side, wagging his tail.

I dropped the wrench. "You scared the shit out of me."

He slid off his toboggan, held it over his heart, which I'm sure was pounding. "We got robbed," he said, but it was more of a question.

I shook my head. "I don't see a damn thing missing."

*　*　*

The cop who showed up was wearing a badge that said "T. Watson." He was a few years younger than me, tanned and blond. A smooth-looking fellow that I imagined as a deep-sea fishing type. It wasn't until he spoke that his name rang a bell. *Travis Watson.* He'd called me the morning of Dad's murder. Neither of us acknowledged that fact when I shook his hand and introduced myself.

I briefed him on the situation, and he asked a few generic questions: What time did I get there? Was anything missing? Then he spent a few minutes walking around, assessing the scene, snapping a few pictures with his phone.

Charlie and I were seated on the big couch, one of the only undisturbed items in the room, when Watson slid a notepad into his pocket and came over. "I noticed y'all don't run any security cameras around here."

Charlie said, "They reminded us of that fact when Leland got killed. Those sumbitches are expensive. If you've got any extra money laying around, like maybe some y'all got in a drug bust, be my guest."

Irritated as Charlie was, I couldn't fault the cop for bringing it up. If it had been my place all those years, and I'd had the money Dad did, I would've made sure every last inch of the lot was under surveillance. In hindsight, with all that had happened, maybe it was less of Dad being a cheapskate and more of him trying to keep his own goings-on obscured.

"How about y'all's dog?"

"Buster," I said. "He was out in the yard last night. Guess somebody outsmarted him."

Watson said, "Perpetrator could've pulled up to the front door real close, avoided him altogether. Or hell, maybe they tossed him a slab of meat like they do in cartoons."

"Hope Buster sunk his teeth into whoever-did-it's ass," Charlie said.

Watson said he hoped so too. "Dogs can sure help, but a nice camera makes situations like these easier on all of us."

"Situations like these?" I asked.

"Ones with no clear motive in mind. Shit just happens, then you're just left to pick up the mess."

"So that's it, huh?" Charlie said. "Y'all aren't going to investigate things? Look for fingerprints? Call in one of those psychics?"

From Watson's dumbfounded gaze, I could tell he didn't know if Charlie was serious or not about the psychic. "Sir, there's no telling how many fingerprints you could lift in a business like this. Say we found twenty. What can we do at that point? Haul in a bunch of folks, ask them if they trashed this place for kicks?"

"So y'all just file it under 'fuck it' and move on, huh?" Charlie said.

The cop moved an antique North Carolina license plate across the floor with his shiny shoe. "Over Christmas break, somebody tore the field house and the concessions booth at the high school all to pieces," he said. "Thousands of dollars in damages. Even took themselves a shit in the popcorn machine. That sort of thing really makes me sick, so *hell yeah*,

I'd love nothing better than to catch every criminal that does cowardly stuff like this. Truth is, no small-town department in the world has the time and resources for that. An eyewitness or some security footage is really our only hope, and we have neither of those."

Charlie scoffed and got up, sat the hefty table top on the tires that supported it, then started picking up some of the magazines, tossing them onto the table.

Watson asked if we needed help cleaning up, but Charlie not so politely declined.

The cop took his glasses that were hooked on his shirt pocket and put them on. "I really am sorry, guys. Wish I could do more."

I said, "You don't think this has anything to do with everything else that has happened here? We've had two dead bodies turn up in a matter of weeks."

"Place wasn't quite torn to pieces like this after your daddy was shot. I think whoever did that would be crazy to come back here. This is all too messy."

"Maybe," I said, not entirely confident he was right.

"Either of you piss anybody off recently that would want to pay you back? Do something like this?"

I shook my head.

Watson said, "It could be that someone was mad they couldn't find any cash, threw themselves a temper tantrum."

"There's other valuable stuff in here," I said.

"If money and a quick fix was the motive, some strung-out druggie probably wouldn't waste their time trying to sell a box of drill bits for diddly-squat at a pawn shop. Too much effort required. A more experienced criminal would've just sawed off some catalytic converters. Them things have been going missing all over the place."

"They've got rhodium and platinum in them," I said, proud of my recently acquired knowledge.

The cop nodded, said to call if we needed anything.

* * *

I helped Charlie pick up the aftermath, which took a chunk of the morning, and then I called around and found what computer cords I needed, for dirt cheap, at a used electronics store right outside of town. When I got back, I got the computer up and running just in time to make the day's single, measly sale: a steering wheel for a Tacoma.

I convinced a locksmith to come out before we closed, paid him cash for fixing the front door, an unplanned expense that irritated the shit out of me. As I was locking up, Charlie hesitated before following me out the door.

"Maybe we'll just stay here tonight. Buster and me."

"You serious?"

"As the taxman," he said. "Just want to keep an eye on things. Got my KelTec. I'll have it ready if anybody decides to poke their head in again."

"They'd pick this place clean before your geriatric ass woke up," I said.

"I'm for real, Hudson. I'm staying," he said. "Hell, your old man did it all the time. That couch yonder sleeps like a cloud."

He wasn't going to budge.

"May want to slide a couple more heaters over there," I said. "Gets pretty chilly in here at night."

He pulled the door open and waved me on. "I used to walk to school in the snow, young buck. Uphill in a T-shirt and short pants. Didn't have no shoes."

"You'd be dumb enough to try something like that," I said, putting a hand on his shoulder. "What about *Matlock*, or whatever the hell it is old folks watch? Think you can survive without it?"

"That computer's fast enough to bring up some nudes, ain't it?"

With that mental image, I called it a day.

CHAPTER TWENTY-SEVEN

While I scarfed down an all-the-way hot dog in the Cross Tie Meat Co. parking lot after work, I searched the online White Pages and found the sole listing in Flint Creek for the last name Reyes: Maria J. Reyes, 24 Hyde Park Lane, #12. I hadn't told Lucy about what happened at the shop, and I'd yet to meet her mom. Figured I could check both things off my list with a quick visit.

I followed my GPS just over three miles to a place called Hyde's Mobile Home Park. I remembered my bus stopping at its entrance in elementary school. I had wondered why most of the kids that got off there didn't have nice clothes, and why some of them always seemed to need a haircut. I didn't understand why their parents couldn't just go find good jobs and buy nicer houses and nicer things. I was ignorant to a lot back then.

I pulled into a long row of single-wides, many of which flickered flashes of evening television in their small windows. I coasted slowly through the park, keeping my eyes peeled for the address numbers that were hard to read now that it was dark out. When I reached the fifth or sixth trailer on the left, I saw two teenage boys, one White, one Black, playing basketball, evening chill be damned. They didn't have a paved court, just a flat patch of dirt; their goal was a square piece of plywood attached to a light pole, a rim with no net. They stopped as I passed and watched me, the White kid cradling the ball against his hip.

Two trailers up, on the opposite side of the drive, I spotted what looked like Lucy's bike propped next to a set of front steps. The GPS said I'd arrived. I parked next to a white Celica, my headlights illuminating the trailer. I could see a woman's silhouette behind a set of blinds that spread apart as I shut my engine off. I got out of my Jeep, the sound of a basketball bouncing on the dirt some twenty yards away. I neared the cinder-block steps. The porch light came on, and the front door cracked open.

"Ms. Reyes?"

A tired voice: "Can I help you?"

"Ms. Reyes, my name is Hudson Miller. I work down at the salvage yard."

"Miller?" she asked, nudging the door open.

"That's right. I've met your daughter, Lucy."

She grabbed a coat from a nearby hook and slid it on, zipped it to the top. She stepped outside onto the tiny wooden porch. It was, in fact, the woman I'd seen outside the police station. She was at least six inches shorter than Lucy, but her widow's peak and tiny pug nose she'd surely passed on to her daughter.

"I guess you know that Lucy asked me to help her out. Me and my friend Charlie, the guy who works for me."

"She told me," she said in a tone I couldn't gauge. She stepped closer. Looked into my eyes in a way that made it feel like everything I'd ever done or said lay exposed before her. "Are you a good person, Hudson?"

"I try to be. I think I do a pretty good job of it most of the time."

"And what about this friend of yours? Charlie?"

"I haven't known him long, but I trust him. I can say that much."

One of the basketball players shouted, *"Foul!"* I jumped a little; Ms. Reyes didn't flinch. "My Lucy is a good girl," she said. "She's a special girl, strong willed. Very passionate."

"That she is. I guess she's got a reason to be."

"She's always been that way," she said. "When she was a little girl, she wanted nothing more than to go to Disney World. Not to see the beautiful princesses and the rides like other girls her age. She wanted to learn to draw like they did in all the Disney cartoons. She thought if she went there, they could teach her."

"Did she get to go?"

"I wanted to take her and Marco, but we didn't have the money," Ms. Reyes said.

The door opened behind her. It was Lucy, holding a glass bowl of what looked like SpaghettiOs. "What are you doing here?" she asked me. "I didn't say you—"

"Go back inside, Lucy," her mother said sternly, yet calmly.

"But, Mama, I—"

"Now, Lucy. I'm talking to Mr. Miller."

Lucy snarled at me and shut the door. I could hear her stomp away.

"Did I mention she was passionate?" Ms. Reyes said.

"I hope I didn't upset her."

"That wasn't upset. You've seen her upset. At the police station. She's going to pay for those dents in your hood."

"No need for all that," I said. "It needed some dents up front to match all the ones on the back and sides."

She grinned, and I switched the topic back to Disney World.

"Yes, Disney World," she went on. "One afternoon, when she was maybe seven or eight, I had just made her and Marco lunch. When I went to get Lucy from her room, she wasn't there, but her window was open. She'd left a note on her bed: *I'll be back soon, Mama. Love, Lucy.* Around the words she put these big Mickey Mouse ears. Thank goodness it only took me about ten minutes to find her walking down the road toward the highway."

"Did she have her bags packed?"

"Full of snacks and her favorite stuffed animal," Ms. Reyes said. "It's a funny story, but sometimes I still wonder how far she would've gone. And I wonder the same thing now. Do you understand?"

"I think I do."

"It scares me, Hudson. It scares me that she's going to throw every bit of heart she has into this and come up empty. She's just a kid, but she's already been let down too many times in her life. I don't want to see it happen again."

"It might not mean much, Ms. Reyes, but I'll help Lucy in whatever way I can. If that's okay with you."

She closed her eyes for a moment. "I can't be here all the time. My job doesn't allow it. I don't always know where Lucy is or what she's getting herself into, but I do trust my girl. If she says you're okay, and that Charlie is okay, I believe her.

She's a good judge of character. Better than I was when I was her age. I just need you to promise me one thing."

I didn't hesitate. "Sure. Name it."

"Promise me you'll watch out for her. This world is a cruel one. Not the world I ever wanted my kids to grow up in. It's already taken one of them. Lucy's all I have left."

"I promise, Ms. Reyes. I'll watch out for her the best I can. If Charlie was here, he'd say the same."

"It's no easy job," she said, and that same soul-boring gaze returned. "Do you mind if I pray for you?"

The request was so genuine that I would've granted it even if I didn't think there was a God out there somewhere. I didn't say anything; I just closed my eyes. There was only the sound of a basketball dribbling, then clanging off a backboard, until Ms. Reyes began praying in Spanish. She kept her words brief—none of which I understood—but there was a quiet intimacy to them. Not like Dean Peterson's thundering words that used to shake the walls of Hope of God Baptist and singe my soul with hellfire.

When Ms. Reyes finished, I thanked her and asked if I could have a word with Lucy.

She nodded. "Remember your promise, Hudson," she said, and she walked inside.

Soon, Lucy came out. She set her bowl on a rickety porch rail that was constructed of a splintered two-by-four. "You shouldn't have come," she said.

"You would've done the same if you were in my shoes."

"What all did you tell my mama?"

"Just that I wanted to help. That's it. Honest."

"Uh-huh," she said.

"I felt like I needed her blessing."

"That the only reason you came down here? For her blessing?"

I shook my head. "A police officer stopped by the salvage yard today. Officer Watson."

"About my brother?"

"Actually, I was the one who called the cops. We had an unwanted visitor or visitors last night. Messed the shop and garage up pretty good. Like a wrecking ball. Thought you might want to know."

"Y'all don't know who did it?'

"No. Watson said it could've been somebody I pissed off."

"Did you piss somebody off?"

"Can't really think of anyone. Not anyone recent anyway."

"How about our investigation wall?"

"They didn't get in there. Thank God."

The basketballers started bickering loudly, something about a charge and somebody being a whiny bitch. We both looked in their direction, but the argument died quickly when the one boy yelled, *"Check!"* and threw a firm chest pass to the other.

"You could've just called," Lucy said. She grabbed her bowl from the railing, the spoon falling to the porch, then to the yard. "Cocina del Hyde isn't a place to hang out after dark."

"Cocina?"

"Co-ci-na," she reiterated. *"Kitchen.* As in a place you cook." She held out an arm, slapped it a couple times like she was searching for a vein. She gave a disgusted look around the park. "I'm getting a job as soon as I get my license."

"That happening soon?"

"My sixteenth birthday's in December. A week before Christmas," she said. "Maybe I'll actually feel like celebrating it this year."

"I hope so too."

"Once I get a job, I can help Mama a little. Maybe we can get out of this dump for good. Find a new town and a new school. Start fresh."

I said, "Been down that road. New towns and new schools aren't always easy."

"You think going to Flint Creek Middle was easy for the Bigfoot beaner girl?"

I blinked. "Someone called you that?"

"A few kids did. The principal even knew. He gave them a warning, at most. That crap didn't stop until the day I used one of my big feet to kick one of those punks on my way to the pencil sharpener."

"Hope it was a good kick."

"Knocked him right out of his chair." A satisfied smile. "Nobody really messed with me anymore after that. I made some friends, found my tribe. But still, the schools around here are a flipping joke."

"You at North Payne now?"

"North Payne in the Ass."

"Haven't heard that one in a while."

"I hate it," she said. "And it's not really even the kids that make it bad. That school dumps all their extra money into the stupid football team over there. Got new jerseys and a new weight room last year, and they still suck."

"They've always sucked."

"I guess they think they should look good while they're getting their butts kicked," she said. "The poor marching band has to do those stupid chocolate bar fundraisers all year just to afford uniforms."

"'*World's Finest Chocolate*,'" I said with air quotes. "Damn things get smaller every year. I swear they—"

"Know what else pisses me off? Those PTA jerks banned one of my favorite books last year—freaking mid-semester—because some rich kid complained about it. You ever read *Invisible Man*?"

I nodded. "Not in school, but my boxing coach gave me a copy."

"Oh yeah?" She eyed me with skepticism. "What was the name of the main character?"

"He didn't have a name," I said. "He was the invisible man."

Impressed, Lucy said, "Sounds like your coach was a Mr. Miyagi type. Unlike the North Payne PTA that said that book was 'inappropriate' because of some bad words. I went to the board meeting with my teacher, Ms. Reynolds, when she tried to get it reinstated or whatever. Big waste of time." She sighed. "I just can't with these people."

"I feel you on that," I said, "but I guess everybody around here isn't so bad."

"Maybe not," she said. She pointed to the two boys who were now sitting under the goal, sharing a Gatorade. "The Black kid over there? That's Dytrice. His big sister Kia's my best friend. She's in my grade. It's like me and her have to prove ourselves all the time because we look different. I think it's even harder for her than it is me. I'm just tired of it."

I wanted to tell her that I was sorry and that I understood, but I didn't understand. Our struggles weren't the same. "You're a good kid, Lucy. Smart too."

She rolled her eyes.

I took my car keys out. "I'll let you get out of the cold, and just so you know, the cops think that what happened at the salvage yard this morning has nothing to do with everything else that's happened."

"Psh. Typical."

"So I assume you don't agree?"

"I don't," she said. "Whoever messed up your place was probably trying to tell you something. Send you a message."

"Yeah? And what's that?"

She regarded me like I was naive, as if she'd become the adult, and I the teenager. "That they don't want you around here."

CHAPTER TWENTY-EIGHT

Charlie was outside walking Buster when I got to work. Apparently, his sleepover in the shop had been uneventful. Said he slept well and that our computer was good enough to bring up some nude pics. He made a couple of Linda Lovelace references I hoped he was joking about.

That afternoon, we found ourselves busy in the garage. I'd bought Charlie a sixer of Keystone as an early week bonus for all the shit we'd endured of late, but that wasn't the only reason: I wasn't sure I could pay him on time, at least not in full. Thought I'd let him get a good buzz before I broke the news.

He drank his fourth beer while we drained the liquids and stripped parts from a Chevy Suburban. It made me wish to God we never had that make and model towed in again, because Charlie kept serenading the damn thing. He'd reduced the Rolling Stone's line "I'll never be your beast of burden" to his rendition: "I'll never be your big Suburban." It was funny the first time he sang it. Five minutes later I had to drown him out with the radio.

I'd just removed a couple of the wheels from the big Suburban, and I was holding some bolts for Charlie when I worked up some courage.

"How fast you think you can strip some cars before the weekend, Charlie?"

"Shit, it's already Wednesday. How many we talking?"

"I don't know . . . four or five."

Charlie stopped working. "Can't run a damn yard if you just sell everything off. This is a parts yard. Not a scrapyard."

"I know that," I said, "but we haven't exactly sold a lot of parts this week. Need to stop the bleeding a little. Got bills to pay . . . got *you* to pay."

"If you're telling me I'm doing this work for nothing, I'll carry my ass—"

"I'll have the money. Jesus Christ."

Charlie didn't look convinced. He started to say something, but a voice interrupted: "You fellows have a minute?"

We ducked out from behind the Chevy to see that it was Detective Holden.

Charlie silenced Pete Townshend on the radio.

I dropped some bolts in an empty oil pan. "Got something good for us, Detective?"

"Used to have an older model one of these." Holden eyed the Chevy. "Gunmetal blue. Gas guzzler if I ever saw one, but I loved that thing. Gave my liberal aunt a heart attack every time I cranked it." After another moment of lusty admiration, he looked at us. "The chief said I should stop by, share what news we have."

"I hope that news includes a murder suspect," I said, not sure of which murder I meant.

"It may just lead to that," Holden said. "For now, we have a strong idea who your father's gun supplier was."

"How'd you figure that one out?" Charlie said with obvious cynicism.

"Dumb luck," Holden said, a certain humility in his voice I couldn't imagine Coble mustering. "Got a call from a sheriff over in Colfax, a buddy of the chief's. They hauled in a big kahuna up there named Dalton Tucker. Fellow is suspected of running guns all over the state, maybe even up in Virginia. That name sound familiar to you, Shoaf? Dalton Tucker?"

"Only Dalton I know played in that movie *Road House*."

"This fellow don't exactly look like Patrick Swayze," Holden said, "but maybe a picture will jar something loose." I thought he was reaching for his phone, but he pulled out a printed picture and unfolded it.

Charlie took it with his grimy hands, and I peered over his shoulder. The man in the picture looked around fifty, an angular face and icy blue eyes, silver hair pulled back into a ponytail. Charlie studied the picture a moment before saying he'd never seen the guy.

Holden took the paper and tucked it in his pocket. "Needless to say, if Mr. Tucker is who they think he is, he's had some help in his business dealings. Retailers, if you will." He looked at me. "We think your father was one of them."

"You think or you *know*?"

"As confident as we can be without the suspect actually saying it. We do know the models of the guns we found hidden in that storage room were the same types this guy was running. Serial numbers ground down just as clean. Just don't know when or where the two crossed paths."

"Colfax, you say?" Charlie said.

"Yes, sir."

"Leland used to go to car auctions out that way once a month."

"You know the name of that auction, Mr. Shoaf?" Holden was typing a note into his phone.

"Nope. Never got an invite."

"We'll definitely look into it," Holden said when he finished typing.

"How'd they catch the guy?' I asked.

"Random traffic stop of one of the delivery vehicles near the Carolina–Virginia border. Close to Danville. Driver started acting all anxious. Crazy part, the guy was a *tow truck* driver. He was hauling a mini-van that had about fifteen guns hidden in it. Jammed up in the innards of the thing. Like I said. A stroke of dumb luck. The driver's phone showed a suspicious address in a recent GPS search, and the cops traced it to a warehouse on some land that Tucker owns. Issue is, Tucker owns a ton of land, and lots of it is leased to other names, so I'm sure he'll use his resources to try and weasel out of this."

"Let's say my dad and the Tucker guy were in business together," I said. "You think he was sending tow trucks out here?"

"Hoping we can figure that part out," he said. "But, hell, could it be any more perfect? Think about it. A damn tow truck showing up to a salvage yard."

"Pretty fucking genius," Charlie mumbled.

Holden nodded. "Unless you get caught."

I said, "So that Tucker guy could've had Dad killed . . ."

"Maybe if a business deal went south, sure. I wouldn't bet on Mr. Tucker owning up to that. Gunrunning is one charge. Murder is something else."

"Anybody bring it up?"

"The murder? Don't think so. Not yet anyways. That department has their own problems to sort out for the time being. There's just no telling what all this thing is connected to."

"What you're really telling us is that y'all have next to nothing," Charlie said.

"A warehouse with over six hundred guns in it sounds like a little more than nothing, Mr. Shoaf. The key now is if they can get Tucker to confess and squeal for a plea deal. Maybe we'd have something bigger then. At the very least, maybe prove the guns we recovered are from the same batch, then work from there."

"Honor among thieves," Charlie said, changing the head out on a socket wrench. "Types like that won't offer you shit unless you beat it out of them. But Lord knows, can't do that these days. Everybody's always waving lawsuits around." He muttered something about *snowflakes* as he walked over to the radio and turned it back on.

Holden and I traded glances. "Guess that means we're back on the clock," I said. "Hope y'all figure that shit out, Detective."

He gave me the okay sign with his hand. "Like my old man always told me, *'Sometimes it's better to be lucky than good.'*"

* * *

After Holden left, Charlie and I finished stripping the Chevy, and there was barely a word between us about the detective's visit. In fact, Charlie didn't say much of anything the rest of the day. When I locked up the shop right at six and told him I'd see him in the morning, he didn't so much as nod. He just sort of lingered next to his car, this bothered look on his face.

"About what I said earlier, Charlie—the whole money thing. Don't worry about it. I'll have it tomorrow."

His mind was stuck on something else: "Been doing some thinking. You know that auto auction I was telling Holden about?"

"Yeah. The one over in Colfax."

"Mm-hmm. I remembered something. I don't know if it amounts to a hill of beans, but somebody else around here used to go the auction pretty regular."

"I thought you never went."

"Not a once, but your dad told me some stories," Charlie said. "Leland would go out there to plug the business, make sure people knew where some cheap parts were. Reckon he liked the social occasion a good deal too—shooting the shit about cars and whatnot. Every once in a while, he'd even bid low on a vehicle. Sometimes he'd get lucky."

"Fix it up and sell it?"

"That's right," he said. "Other times he'd bid just to bust somebody's ass, force them to pay more. He thought that shit was hilarious. And it wasn't just any-old-body. Usually it was that match made in God-knows-where couple who runs Platinum Auto: Flash and Ash Rainey."

"The billboard people?"

"Yup."

"They might know something about Tucker if that's where Dad met him. *If* he met him."

Charlie shrugged. "If they do, I don't think they'd waste one second throwing your daddy under the bus."

"So you're saying you want to drive down to the car lot?"

"Don't go putting words in my mouth," he said. "I probably should've just kept this to myself."

"You wouldn't have brought it up if you weren't a little curious to see if your theory has legs. So let's do it. We'll go down to the lot, ask a couple questions. Simple as that."

"I'm already getting the feeling you ain't going to drop this."

"So you're in?"

"Don't get all eager beaver," he said. "We ain't driving down to that damn car lot. I don't much care to fuck with folks at their place of business."

"Have you got a better plan?"

He thought for a moment, checked his watch, then his mouth twisted into a wry grin. "If I swing by your place around seven-ish can you be dressed and ready?"

"Dressed and ready for—"

"Yes or no?"

I didn't know where the hell this was going. "Fine," I said, "but what should we tell Lucy?"

"I'm afraid she'll need to sit this one out. For a couple of reasons."

"I'm not sure I like the sound of this, Charlie."

"I'll see you at seven," he said, and he got into his car. Before pulling away, he rolled down his window. "There's one more thing."

"Yeah?"

"Wear something nice."

CHAPTER TWENTY-NINE

A car horn was blaring out front at a quarter after seven. I slid on a jacket and walked outside, where Charlie was leaning against the hood of his Buick, blazing a cigarette. And damn if he wasn't a Marlboro ad on two feet. Had on a pair of too-tight jeans and a Western-style button-up, brown and yellow plaid with pearl snaps. His snakeskin boots and tightly slicked hair rounded out the getup nicely.

He kicked some gravel over his cigarette as I walked up. "You smell something funny?"

"It's either you or the shit plant down the road."

He wafted the air and looked me up and down. "Thought I said to wear something nice."

I had on my current version of "nice": a clean pair of jeans and a black polo shirt. "This is as fancy as it gets for me. I'm sure as hell not borrowing anything from you, Slick."

He straightened his collar. "You just don't know class," he said, jangling his keys. "You driving or me?"

"This is your rodeo. I don't know where the shit we're going."

"Copperheads," he said, like it was something I should've known. "The Raineys' home away from home."

Copperheads. I'd never been there before, but I knew the place. A former country cooking buffet turned bar at the corner of Baker Road. Charlie said Flash Rainey's white Escalade with a Platinum Auto Sales decal wrap was parked out there nearly every night. When we showed up, there was no sign of it; the parking lot was almost empty. Despite that, Charlie claimed a spot closest to the road, hoping his pride and joy Buick could avoid any drunken door dings.

I got out of the car and took a long look at the bar. The building was painted charcoal gray. A big sign next to the front door had "Copperheads" airbrushed on it, above a coiled-up snake crushing a beer can. At the very bottom: "Come tie one on!"

"Mae Bee's," I said, recalling its former glory. "Last time I was here, I was probably six years old, trying to get Mom to sneak some yeast rolls home in her purse. Those sons of bitches were good."

"Laugh now, city boy, but this place'll be booming in no time." The confidence in his voice made me even more nervous for what might be in store.

"You've been here?"

"I get a wild hair now and then," Charlie said.

"You're just full of surprises, huh, Mr. Saturday Night Fever?"

After reminding me it was Wednesday and popping his collar, Charlie pointed down the road. "Looks like we ain't the only ones partying tonight."

He was indicating the Boars Club building, also known as The Lodge. There were probably a dozen cars parked in its lot.

"Sure you don't want to crash it?" I asked.

He threw a middle finger in the air, and then we walked into the bar.

For as low-budget-haunted-house as Copperheads looked on the outside, the inside was surprisingly decent. A long bar dominated the left side, a mechanical bull and a couple of pool tables stood on the right. The far end of the building was reserved for a dance floor that stopped at a tiny stage, an American flag and a Johnny Cash mugshot on the wall behind it. A hipster-looking dude wearing a deep V-neck was sitting on the end of the stage, tuning a guitar. A kick drum beside him said "Kiser and the Kemists."

"First round is on you," Charlie said, a hard clap on my back.

"Thought we were here to talk to the Raineys."

Charlie gave the bar a cursory glance. "They'll get here when they get here. Trust me. You can't miss them. Loud motherfuckers."

Based on general pessimism alone, I had a feeling the Raineys would be a no-show, but I played along for the time being. I sidled up to the bar where a guy around my age with a fauxhawk was pouring a too frothy Blue Motorcycle from a shaker. After he gave the drink to a man in an Atlanta Hawks jersey, he asked what he could get me.

I deferred to Charlie who needed no time to consider: "Tequila and soda water."

I was expecting something cheaper. Maybe a PBR that a chalkboard touted as the dollar-fifty daily special. For myself,

I ordered the closest thing to water on the menu: Michelob Ultra.

I drank that beer and nursed the next one while Charlie drained a couple tequila sodas. We talked nonsense and watched sports highlights on the TV for a while, both of us keeping an occasional eye on the entrance. There was no sign of the Raineys.

By eight o'clock, there were probably thirty people in the bar. Not exactly the types I'd imagined. I figured there'd be a bunch of blue-collar country folks wearing Wrangler jeans with tucked-in T-shirts that supported their favorite fishing or hunting retailer. Of course there were a few of those, but mixed into the Copperheads cocktail was a group of college-aged girls, some office-job types still in their work attire, and a collection of ratty band groupies wearing shirts for bands they'd probably never listened to: the Ramones, the Sex Pistols, Zeppelin.

Kiser and the Kemists soon took the stage, opening with AC/DC's "Shoot to Thrill," which kicked up a buzz in the place. Even Charlie, without a doubt the oldest dude in the bar, slid off his stool and strode toward the dance floor, so I followed. We propped ourselves up against the wall and listened to the band for a while, and when they fired up "Hold on Loosely," the universe delivered me the best laugh I'd had in months. Charlie's geriatric ass went from foot tapping to some unholy union of line dancing meets shag on the dance floor. It wasn't just me that got a kick out of it; a couple of the college-aged girls decided to join him near the stage. Charlie twirled one around a few times. Another rubbed her ass against his leg as she waved her hands in the air. A third girl took pictures and egged her friends on. I couldn't be sure which would kill Charlie first—the thrill of female attention or his overexertion.

I humored his antics for a while, but then I started to doubt why he'd dragged me to Copperheads. I fought through a lively crowd and pulled him away from his harem when the band announced their first break of the evening.

"So what's the catch, Tiny Dancer?"

"What are you talking about?"

"You just wanted a night on the town, huh? Which I'm fine with. You've earned it. But I thought this Flash guy was—"

"They're already here," Charlie said. He nodded toward the end of the bar, where a man and woman were sitting elbow to elbow. The man wore a blue sport coat and had on one of those visors with the built-in, bleached blond hair that made him look like Guy Fieri's slimmer brother. The woman looked like a brunette, late-model Dolly Parton. I'd been expecting the bald guy and the blonde from the billboards, but I guess those attributes are pretty easily altered.

"Why the hell didn't you say something?"

"Because I'm having a damn good time," he said. "Plus, I was waiting until they got good and tipsy before we made our move. He's on drink number three, by my count, and I think she probably just did a line in the restroom. I figure just a couple more drinks and—"

"I don't want to stand around here all night, Charlie. If we're going to do this, let's do it. They could be out that door in two minutes, and you'd still be out on that dance floor, wishing you'd remembered your Viagra."

Charlie looked at the college girls. "Can't I at least ask one of these gals if they have a hot mama or a crazy aunt that might stoop to my level?"

The "fuck off" look I gave him did its job.

"All right," he said. "But I need you to sort of just hang nearby while I move in. Act like you aren't a party pooper. Got it?"

This time I verbalized the "fuck off," and Charlie made his way to the bar and ordered another tequila soda. I ordered a beer, just to keep myself occupied. We inched closer and closer to Flash and Ash Rainey, to the point I could smell his cologne and her hairspray, either of which could ignite a wildfire. Charlie waited until Ash headed—high heels in hand—to the restroom, then sat on her vacant stool. I stayed a few feet back, pretended to care about the TV.

Flash's head swiveled a little when he talked, his voice hoarse like that of a veteran football coach: "Sorry, mister. My wife is sitting there. She's gone to the pisser."

Charlie put on like he was genuinely sorry and slid off the stool. "Wait a sec. Ain't you the Platinum Auto guy?"

A certain pride washed over Rainey. "Hell, everybody knows that."

"Thought that was you," Charlie said. "And it's a damn funny thing; I'm in the market for a car as we speak, but seeing as you are off the clock, I'll leave you be. Besides, I saw a nice ride over at Automart last night that I'm—"

"I didn't catch your name, mister . . ."

Hook. Line. Sinker.

"Shoaf. Charlie Shoaf."

"You look awful familiar, Mr. Shoaf."

"Call me Charlie."

"All right then, Charlie. Flash Rainey." A handshake. "You come up here much?"

"I stick my head in now and then. You?"

"Only on days ending in *Y*," Flash said with a wink.

Charlie had a laugh. "Flash, I'd like you to meet my friend." He waved me over. "This here is Hudson Miller. Guess you could say we're in the car business too, except ours ain't all nice and shiny. Me and him run his daddy's old salvage yard."

Flash, who was mid-sip on what looked like straight vodka, lowered his glass. "Miller, you say? As in Leland's boy?"

"Guilty as charged," I said.

Another sip emptied Flash's highball glass. He whistled and motioned to the bartender for another. "It's a crying-damn-shame what happened to your dad. Didn't think stuff like that happened around here. And then that shit with the Mexican kid. Sheesh. Saw that on the news."

"I reckon evil don't have no area code," Charlie said.

Flash asked Charlie to sit, and Charlie returned to Ash Rainey's seat.

I asked Flash if he knew my dad.

"I did," he said. "I won't blow smoke up your ass and say we were buddies, but I knew him. He was a salesman, like I am. We were cut from the same cloth. That's something I can respect. You got that salesman blood too, Hudson?"

"Not exactly," I said. "I was a pro fighter, a boxer. Still do some bartending and bouncing part-time when I'm not at the salvage yard."

"A bouncer. Kind of like on *Road House*," Charlie said.

"What is it with you and that movie, Charlie?" I asked.

"What's not like to like? It's got fistfights, beer, and women. And it comes on basic cable."

"Cheers to that!" Flash said, and he and Charlie clanked glasses so hard I thought they might shatter. After a heavy gulp, Flash looked beyond us and threw a hand up. "Ash! Come over here, sugar. I'd like you to meet Mr. Charlie Shoaf and Hudson Miller—Leland Miller's kid."

Ash squeezed between Charlie and me and set her high heels on the bar. Her black, low-cut dress was so tight it looked like she put it on with a paint roller. She draped an arm around her husband and frisked me with her eyes. "Ash Rainey," she said. She held her hand toward me, palm down, as if presenting it for a kiss. I wasn't going down that road, so I shook it like a dead fish. Charlie took her hand right up, kissed it with an audible smack.

Flash didn't seem to mind one bit. "Ash, they were just telling me that Hudson here is a boxer."

If her eyes had undressed me before, they'd now checked us into a cheap motel room. She said, "We *love* boxing. Don't we, babe? Remember that match we went up to in Atlantic City? The one we bet five large on the underdog, then got thrown out before the last round because we got shit-canned on champagne?"

"I don't know who felt worse the next day," Flash said, "us or the fighters."

Ash asked, "You got a fight coming up, Hudson? We'd love to come."

"Hell, yeah," Flash said. "We'll bet the house, you take a fall in the third, we can split the profits, then hit up the strip club after."

The Raineys laughed their asses off until I told them I wasn't fighting anymore on account of other affairs. It sort of killed the mood until Flash resumed his salesman role: "Honey, Charlie here is in the market for a vehicle. Ain't that right, Charlie?"

"Mixing business and booze," Ash said. "My kind of man."

Charlie blushed. "Yeah, but I may as well be pissing in the wind. Can't nobody find what I'm looking for."

"Try us," Flash said.

"All righty then," Charlie said. "What I'm looking for is a Chrysler LeBaron, convertible. You ask me, it's the most underrated sports car of all time. Had one back in '94, a real cream puff, but I lost that and half my good years to my second wife. Lordy, I think about that beauty every day of my life. The ex too."

"A LeBaron, huh?" Flash's expression did a shit job at hiding his indifference to Charlie's dream machine. "That's not typically the kind of car we keep down at the lot. Don't really sell anything made before 2000."

"What about that big auto auction?" Charlie asked.

After stealing a swig of Flash's drink, Ash asked if he was talking about Kepley's.

"Yeah, Kepley's. Over in Colfax." Charlie leaned a little closer. "I'm sure y'all been out there."

"We might as well pay rent," Flash said, "but I don't think we've ever seen a LeBaron for sale. Tell you what, you leave me your contact information, and I can surely holler if we do. I love a good challenge."

Ash grabbed her purse from the bar, scrambled through it, and pulled out a pen. She slowly slid the pen around the curve of her breast before handing it to Charlie.

Charlie didn't miss an inch of the show. I wouldn't have been shocked if he'd tried to leave his number on Ash's breast, but he snatched a bar napkin from under his drink. "There's just one more thing, Mr. and Mrs. Rainey. Seeing this is just the wildest coincidence, you two being here and all, I'd like to ask you something about that auction."

Flash: "Shoot."

Charlie nudged my ribs with his elbow. I took out my phone and brought up a picture of Dalton Tucker I'd found on a website for a construction company he owned; I showed the Raineys.

Charlie said, "That man look familiar? Name's Dalton Turner."

"Tucker," I corrected.

"Car dealer?" Flash asked.

I shook my head. "He's from Colfax, and I think my dad knew him. I also think this guy might be connected to what happened to Dad."

Flash shifted in his stool. "Is this some sort of interrogation?"

"No sir," I said. "Not at all. I'm not accusing you of anything, but let's cut the shit about one thing: my dad could be a real dickhead. I know it and you know it. I think we can all agree that a bullet through his head was a fucked-up way for him to go out. Me and Charlie here are just trying to get to the bottom of it."

The Raineys' spunk vanished. It was like they lived a twelve-step program in a millisecond. Flash sat up straighter and reached for my phone, and he and Ash gave it a long look. I couldn't read their expressions, nor could I interpret their eye contact with each other before they looked at me.

Flash spoke: "There's a lot of folks at those auctions, Hudson. Hundreds sometimes."

"I don't need a head count. I just want to know if you recognize him or not."

"Can't rightly say one way or the other," Flash said.

"You can't or you won't?" Charlie asked.

"We can't," Ash said. "I can tell you this: most of the crowd out at Kepley's are salt of the earth, but there are seedy characters out there too. Cockroaches is what I call them."

Flash nodded and handed me my phone. "Anywhere with that much money changing hands is going to bring out a few cockroaches."

I said, "Y'all have Charlie's number, and you know where we work. I hope you'll reach out if you remember something."

Charlie handed Flash the bar napkin. "Sorry we pissed on y'all's lovely evening, folks," he said. "Turns out y'all ain't hiding anything from us, I'd love to do it again. Hudson here's a lightweight when it comes to drinking. Ain't all that fun."

Flash tucked the napkin into Ash's bra. "You weren't serious about the LeBaron were you, Charlie?"

"You find me a '94, convertible, I'll give you the damn deed to my house."

CHAPTER THIRTY

Charlie said he was liable to blow a .09 on a breathalyzer if a cop pulled us, so I drove when we left Copperheads. He was buzzed and hungry—I was just hungry—and since there were no fast-food joints between Copperheads and the rental house, I stopped at the Marathon station. I got us a couple of premade ham and cheese sandwiches that we ate in the car.

"Your daddy always said that those Raineys were a couple freaks," Charlie said through a mouthful of food. "I believe it now. That Ash was a real sex kitten. You think they were trying to take us home?"

"Wouldn't have surprised me, but I'm sure they would've checked our credit first," I said. "Do you think they were bullshitting us about Tucker?"

Charlie picked at his teeth with a fingernail, then said, "I don't think they know the guy, but I have a feeling they've seen him at that auction. After what we told them, they probably just don't want to get involved. Can't really blame them."

"Seedy characters. Ash said there were some seedy characters."

"You can find those about anywhere, Hud."

I took the last bite of my sandwich and stuffed the wrapper into a bag. "You know, in a span of ten seconds, they showed more interest in my boxing career than my dad did in a decade. Pretty messed up, huh?"

"Reckon it is. But I guess I've never asked you about it."

"You aren't my dad."

"You'd be a shade better looking if I were."

"And two shades dumber."

"Ain't sure that's even possible," he said. "So what's the deal? Were you some scrawny little nerd that got your ass whipped a bunch in grade school? Signed up for boxing lessons?"

"Believe it or not, wiseass, the refined gentleman that's sitting next to you used to get in some trouble in his teenage years."

"Like when you busted up your daddy's Mustang with a ball bat? Kind of wish I'd have been there to see his face."

"I actually used a rock, and that was just one instance. Couple months after all that, me and these dipshits that lived next to Mom, the Pruitt twins, got caught trespassing at this abandoned factory in Greensboro. Cop caught us out there with a bag of Wild Irish Rose we'd stolen from a package store and some M-80s—the juvenile delinquent starter kit. Got fifty hours community service for it."

Charlie chuckled. "Boys will be boys."

"Well, part of that detail had us *boys* picking weeds and cleaning up graffiti next to this city-owned rec center," I said. "Had a gym in there with a boxing ring, a bunch of bags along the wall. Couldn't hardly do my work because I couldn't take my eyes off that gym. Even after my required hours were over, I used to ride my bike out there, stand outside, and watch all these people train. One day, I finally found the guts to walk inside."

"And that's that?"

I nodded. "I stopped getting myself in trouble. Coach would've kicked my ass. Probably why Mom let me do it. She knew I needed the discipline."

"You're right about your old man. He never said much about it."

"Probably because it wasn't *his* idea. That asshole only came to one fight of mine when I was an amateur. One fucking fight."

Charlie finished his sandwich and I pulled out of the parking lot.

"Hell, I love a good brawl," he said, adjusting the radio dial until an Eagles song played quietly.

"I was just an amateur then, but it was a damn good win," I said. "I didn't realize Dad was there until I came out of the locker room afterward." I looked over. "Want to know what he told me?"

"Something tells me it wasn't 'congrats.'"

"Not a chance. Bastard looked around the gym, said 'Damn, Hud. Looks like a jungle in here.'"

"A jungle?"

"Mm-hmm. I was one of two *White* fighters in the whole place."

Charlie made a whistling sound. "Anybody else hear that shit?"

I took a sharp left turn onto Old Mountain Road. "Nah, but he was at the fight. He'd seen my coach and my cornermen. Didn't stop him from saying it."

"They were Black . . ."

"Yes sirree."

"You slap him for it?"

"Should've," I said. "Sometimes I just wish we'd had it out one good time. Made a clean break, like him and my mom, instead of pussy-footing around the fact that—"

"The hell?" Charlie said, clicking the radio off, his eyes on the rearview.

I'd been so lost in my reminiscing, I hadn't noticed a car behind us. For a second, I worried it was a cop when the lights got closer and closer. I checked the speedometer; I was only going eight over. I sure as hell wasn't drunk. But there were no blue lights, only high beams that I could hardly see as the car inched even closer.

"Brake check that motherfucker," Charlie said; he turned in his seat to flip off the driver.

"Hell, no," I said. "They can pass if they're in that big of a hurry."

Old Mountain is one of the curviest roads in Flint Creek. With every glance I stole in the rearview, I risked running a tire off the low-shouldered pavement, finding myself in a ditch. I sped up just a little, and so did the car that could've been any car with LED headlights. I rolled down my window, held my arm into the icy air to wave the prick around, and that's when the car rammed us. Charlie unloaded some expletives and I death-gripped the wheel as we headed for a tight curve in the road.

The car nudged us again, sending the Buick over the white line. I held steady, and as soon as the road straightened, my mind went from survival mode to anger, to images of bent metal and glass and blood and me dragging somebody from that car and beating them to a pulp.

"Slam the goddamn brakes!" Charlie shouted.

And I did, hard. The car hit us solid; we broke traction into a tailspin. I nearly pulled a one-eighty until we straddled the centerline. I threw the shifter into park, ripped off my seat belt, and jumped out to get a look at the car. Its lights went dark. I couldn't distinguish the car in the soft glow of the moon and Charlie's parking lights, but it looked dark blue or black. The guttural sound from its tailpipes grew fainter and fainter. It sounded like an aftermarket kit on a four-cylinder.

I looked over to see Charlie on the opposite side of the Buick; he was holding his KelTec he must've pulled from his glove box. He chambered a bullet and aimed into the blackness.

"They're gone," I told him with what breath I had. "Put that shit away."

"Fuckers come back, I'll blow their goddamn heads off!" he yelled, like his words might reach hundreds of yards down that road. He slid the pistol into his waistband. "What in God's name was that all about?"

"You get a good look at the car?"

"Couldn't see a damn thing," he said, kicking some loose rocks to the roadside. "You?"

"Not really," I said. My heart was working like a speed bag.

Charlie was hunched over, grumbling *fucks* and *damns* as he inspected the Buick's damage in the moonlight. He looked up. "Think it was just some crazy-ass pill popper? Hopped on PCP or some shit?"

I shook my head. An idea crossed my mind, one that frightened the hell out of me, but I wasn't ready to say it out loud just yet.

CHAPTER THIRTY-ONE

We didn't call the cops that night. Charlie and I were in agreement: waiting by that death wish of a roadside while some half-interested deputy scribbled half-assed notes about a car we could barely describe wasn't something we were in the mood for.

In the morning, I got a better look at Charlie's car. The bumper was sagging and there were a few dents, a couple of small paint smears that were undoubtedly black. Charlie held vigil with a cigarette, almost misty-eyed. He talked about the '91 Park Avenue like it was his first love, how it was built like a tank, or otherwise we'd both be dead or close to it. He said the Buick's name was Regina, but he never explained why.

Once we were inside the shop, he started speculating again about who could've done it and what he'd do if he found out. His first theory was that one of his dance partners had a pissed-off husband or boyfriend that followed us from the bar. His other theory? A gang initiation. He'd seen something about it on the news a few years back.

After he spoke his piece, I finally said the words that had haunted me all through the night. Something that

Lucy Reyes had suggested days before, that I now believed. "I think somebody's trying to send us a message, Charlie. Spook us."

"The hell you talking about?"

"Think about it. First we had a break-in, then the demolition derby last night."

"Yeah, but *spook* us? I don't know, Hud," he said.

"I *do* know. Something about all this doesn't add up. There have been two dead bodies not twenty yards from each other on this property. *Two.* And we're stupid enough to still be hanging around here like nothing ever happened. Now somebody's fucking with us."

He slouched; the life-of-the-party Charlie from the night before was light years away. "That's a bit of a stretch, though. Don't you think?"

"Bullshit *it's a stretch.*" I slammed my palm against the Coke machine. "You just don't want to believe it because it's scary as hell to think about. Especially if it all has to do with a murderer or that slick-haired, gunrunning fucker."

"That just wouldn't make no sense. Why would—"

"I don't know why, Charlie. Or who. But it's a little too weird to just ignore it and move on."

He dragged his feet aimlessly around the room, his hand tapping a nervous rhythm on his hip. He halted at the front counter. "I just ain't sure I can do this anymore."

"Do what?"

After a long look around the shop: "Be here," he said flatly. "I told you that first day it was hard for me to come back to this place. I should've listened to myself, left this salvage yard in my past. I let you talk me into playing Johnny Detective last night, and look what happened half an hour later. If that shit ain't a sign to call it quits, I don't know what is."

"Then what the hell am I supposed to do, Charlie?"

"Get rid of this place. You can barely pay me as it is. You gave it a try, and it ain't working out. No shame in it."

"You say it like it's easy. This isn't a lawn mower I can just stick out in the yard with a 'For Sale' sign attached to it."

"Never said it was easy, but there's no reason to be here if we ain't making money, especially if you really believe the crazy shit you're telling me. I'm sure you can find other ways to make a buck with those fists of yours."

I walked over to Charlie, stood face to face with him. "This isn't even about the money."

"Then what's the issue?"

"If I just disappear, leave this place in the dust, then who-ever is trying to run me—run *us*—out of here got exactly what they wanted."

"If that means I get to wake up tomorrow, then so be it. Let this place burn. I'll strike the goddamn match."

"Fuck that, Charlie. There's something going on, and I want to know what that something is. Maybe you're right about last night being a sign. I think it's a sign we're getting close."

"And I think I've humored all this shit long enough, Columbo. I'm too old to be checking my closet for monsters every night, but that's exactly what I'm going to do if I stick around for any more of this." He tried to step around me to leave, but I blocked his way.

"I'm scared too," I said. "Honest to God. I've barely slept since we found that guy's body, but—"

"Since *I* found it."

"I'm sorry. Since *you* found it. I'm sorry it was you, but I'm not sorry it happened. Somebody needed to find that boy, awful as that was. Call me crazy, but I think we can figure it out. Same with Dad's murder."

"What's it to you anyway, Hud? You didn't even like your old man, and you didn't know that Reyes kid. So what's in this for you? You enjoy having somebody fucking with your life? That give you a thrill? Make your pecker tingle?"

I moved out of his way, presented his path to the door. "I don't even know why I'm having this conversation with you," I said. "Your mind's made up, and I'm not changing it. And you're right, maybe I wasn't tight with my dad, but I never wished harm on the bastard. I sure as hell don't want whoever killed him to get away with it. If that costs us a car bumper, or worse, then so be it. I'm not a chickenshit."

Charlie clenched his jaw, the cords in his neck taut. "You think I'm some sort of coward?"

I didn't. And I didn't blame him for wanting out of our spiraling shit show. I shook my head.

"After I got out of Nam, I swore I'd never again get tied up in some bullshit that could get me killed," Charlie said with some rancor. "That's been over fifty years and three wives ago, and I'm still ticking. If I can help it, I'd like to see another decade. So forgive me if I ain't keen on being your deputy anymore."

"You know where the door is," I said. "It's in the same place it's always been. So make up your mind what you want to do. I'll keep going down this road whether you tag along or not."

"You don't even know which road you're going down," he said, "and I don't either. Neither of us know shit. Then you got the Raineys, who are just trying to fuck and sell cars. And the cops? They don't know their ass from a hole in the ground."

"There's somebody you're leaving out, Charlie. The reason you and me are still here." As those words hung in the air between us, I realized something. It wasn't just Lucy's persistence in finding justice for her brother that made me stick by her as long as I had. It wasn't the fact that my dad had possibly been involved in Marco Reyes's murder—and the twinge of guilt that possibility burdened me with. It was this: Lucy, who the world had given no reason for hope, who had been told 'no' at every turn of her life, was still waking up every day, fighting with the same ferocity as the day before. She was firmly clinging to a youthful idealism that I'd lost years ago and that some part of me desperately wanted back.

Maybe that realization settled on Charlie too. The anger and uncertainty left his face, and he slowly nodded.

CHAPTER THIRTY-TWO

Lucy stopped by after school let out. She was wearing a shirt I thought suited her personality: long sleeved and black, the words "Not Today" in a sparkling rose gold.

"So what's the news?" she asked when she came in.

Charlie and I led her outside and showed her the Buick.

"Looks like a pile of crap, Mr. Charlie," she said. "No offense. I'm just saying . . . y'all do work at a junkyard. Maybe you should replace that bumper."

I said, "That bumper didn't look like that twenty-four hours ago. Somebody ran us off the road last night. Lucky we aren't dead."

"Last night?" Lucy ran a hand across the bumper that Charlie had secured with a coat hanger and a length of Gorilla Tape.

"Remember what you told me the other night?" I said. "That maybe somebody is trying to send me a message?"

"Yeah."

"I think you were right."

"Of course I was right."

"It's got me thinking: What if that person last night is connected to my dad and your brother?"

"Could be."

"Maybe even connected to that gunrunner," Charlie said. "You see, Hudson and me went and did a little investigation ourselves last night, talked to a couple folks down at Copperheads."

"What are you talking about?" Lucy asked.

"The Tucker guy in Colfax," I said. "The one Holden told us about."

"Hold up." She placed a hand on her hip, her other hand articulating her words. "You talked to the cops and didn't tell me? Then you went on some little mission?"

"I thought all that gun stuff had more to do with my dad than your brother. It hasn't even been confirmed yet. I'm sorry, Lucy, I should've—"

"Rewind. What hasn't been confirmed?"

"Maybe we should go inside," I told her, ashamed that we'd kept her out of the loop. "You'll probably want to write this down."

Disgusted with the both of us, she went into the shop. Charlie unlocked the break room, and we all sat around the plastic table. Lucy pulled her notebook and a pen from her bag: "Start talking," she said. "And don't leave anything out."

"Detective Holden came by yesterday," I said. "He told us that last week the cops arrested a guy up near Virginia who was driving a delivery vehicle with a bunch of guns in it. Some info on the dude's phone connected him to a man named Dalton Tucker from Colfax who they think is running an illegal weapons operation. They think my dad's guns could be from the same batch, like maybe Dad was one of his middlemen."

She repeated Tucker's name as she wrote. "Anything else?"

"Charlie said Dad used to go up to Colfax to this auto auction once a month. That detail might just be a coincidence, but Charlie mentioned it to Holden."

"What about last night?"

"I'll take this one," Charlie said. He gave Lucy the rundown on our little trip to the bar, our convo with the Raineys. Even specified what he'd had to drink and how much. "Sorry, Lucy," he said when he was finished. "They check IDs, being a bar and all. That's why you couldn't tag along."

Lucy closed the notebook and leaned back in her chair. She chewed on her lower lip and tapped her pen against the table. She whispered the word *guns* a few times until her look of concentration turned to one of realization. She dug her phone from her pocket and rapidly swiped her finger across the screen. She stopped and laid the phone on the table.

"This belonged to Mo."

The picture she'd brought up was a black pistol. A Glock .9 mm.

"After I came by here the other day, I had this crazy thought," she said. "I spend half my time playing out all kinds of situations in my head, trying to find out which ones are possible about what happened to my brother. Mo wasn't perfect. Everybody knows that. But he was doing better. He'd even got himself a job at this bowling alley. Swore to me and Mama he wasn't smoking and partying anymore."

"Think he was telling the truth?" I asked.

"I think so, but sometimes I have to play devil's advocate. Think about things I don't like. One of them is this: What if Mo had gotten himself into trouble with somebody, a drug dealer or something like that, maybe owed them some money? Then, what if he got desperate, got that gun of his, and drove out here one evening? Let's say that maybe Charlie had already left for the day and—"

"Your brother tried to rob Leland?" Charlie asked.

"Uh-huh," she said. "And that's not something I think he'd do in a million years. Especially at a random place like this. I want y'all to know that. But *if* he did, and maybe things went wrong . . ."

I felt terrible she had to even consider that. "Maybe my dad killed him," I said. "Covered it up."

"Yeah. Something like that."

"I'm sure there are crazier theories . . ."

"Probably so," she said. "But I don't think that theory's true." She pointed at the phone. "I found his gun under his bed, took that picture just the other night. It was right where he always left it. He only had that one. Wasn't something he tried to hide from me, or even Mama. He kept it at home because he wanted to protect us. He didn't carry it around either; it would've violated his probation big time if he got caught with it. Plus, that's just not the kind of guy he was, carrying guns around to look tough or whatever."

"What was he protecting y'all from?" I asked.

"You've seen where we live. Break-ins and crazy stuff happens all the time. Can never be too careful."

"Can't blame your brother," Charlie said. "I keep a piece on me twenty-four seven." He picked up the phone and squinted.

After a moment: "This one's got a serial number." He showed me, then handed Lucy the phone.

"Exactly," she said. "I don't know where Mo got that gun. It wasn't from Hudson's dad. I'm ninety-nine percent sure they didn't even know each other, but still . . ." she sighed. "They're connected somehow. Got to be."

"Maybe Mo saw something he wasn't supposed to," I said.

"You never know," Lucy said. "That's why y'all can't keep *anything* from me. We're in this together. We figure one of these murders out, bet we figure out the other."

"No coincidences," I pondered aloud.

She nodded. "This isn't just y'all helping me with Mo. I'm trying to help you guys, too. I'm mad y'all left me out last night, but I'm kind of proud."

"Speaking of last night," I said, "I guess we need to find that car, for starters. Sounds about impossible since we don't exactly know what we're looking for."

"Or it means we need to go ask some questions."

"Questions?"

"Yeah," she said. "That one guy . . . Tucker."

"If anything is a job for the cops, that's it," I said. "Last night—talking to a couple drunks at a bar—is one thing. This is bigger. Much, much bigger. The guy is probably in jail anyways."

"You said the cops *think* he did it. That's not enough to lock him up. Even if they've already pressed charges, a dude like that's got to have serious money."

"Meaning what?"

"That somebody would've bailed him out," Charlie said.

"Right on, Mr. Charlie," Lucy said. "Bet the guy's sitting at home right now. Probably lawyered up or laughing because the cops haven't got enough evidence."

I said, "He can stay his ass there, and we'll stay our asses here, Lucy. This is an FBI-level crime we're talking about."

"I'm with Hudson on this one," Charlie said.

Lucy shoved her notebook into her backpack and slid away from the table. She stood up. "I can't believe you two," she said with sharp disappointment.

"All we're saying is that this isn't safe," I told her. "If this Tucker guy is who is behind all this, or even some of it, that makes him bad news. The type we don't need to get tangled up with."

"Oh, so you're going to tell me what's safe? You said it yourself: y'all could be dead right now. You call that safe?"

Charlie and I didn't respond.

"Unbelievable," Lucy said. She stomped out of the break room toward the front door.

I followed her. "Where are you going?"

Before she reached the door, she said, "Dalton Tucker's house. Where else?"

"And just how do you think you're going to get there?" Charlie asked. "That's a hell of a bike ride."

"I know you're old and all, Charlie," Lucy said, "but haven't you ever heard of Uber?"

"Heard of who?"

"*Uber*. It's like a taxi."

I butted in: "Nobody is biking, Ubering, driving, or taking a damn spaceship to Dalton Tucker's. It's ridiculous. You think this guy is going to admit something right to your face?

I'm sorry, Lucy, but that's not going to happen in a million years. This isn't some mouth-breathing, Payne County dipshit we're talking about."

"Never know until you try," she said. "And it's not even about him confessing. He needs to know that we are here, and that we aren't going anywhere. If you want to sit around until something else happens, fine. I can't live that way. What if someone starts messing with me or Mama?"

"Nobody is going to mess with you or your mom," I said, hoping those words would never come back to haunt me.

"You don't know that. I bet you never expected your dad to get shot either."

She was right; I couldn't counter that point. "I do know that it's my job to watch out for you, and that's exactly what I'm trying to do."

"I don't need a stupid babysitter."

"Oh, so now I'm stupid because I give a crap about what happens to you? I gave your mom my word. I plan on keeping it."

"My mama thinks there are angels flying around and that God will magically solve all of this when He feels like it," she said, fluttering her hands mockingly. "You don't give a crap what happens to me. You're just trying to protect your own neck."

"Think what you want about me, call me whatever you want, but I need you to promise me you won't do anything crazy," I said.

Finally, after a long silence, then a huff, she said, "Fine then." And she was out the door.

"Chrissakes," I said, watching her pedal out of sight. "Here I was thinking you were the stubborn one, Charlie."

"Me? I ain't got shit on Ms. Lucy. Think she's all right?"

"She's a kid. Just needs to cool down. She isn't thinking straight."

Charlie shrugged. "I wouldn't be either if I were in her shoes."

* * *

Not thirty minutes later, I was in the waiting area, dumping an obscene amount of Ol' Roy into Buster's bowl, when my phone vibrated in my coat pocket. I set the dog food down and checked my cell—it was a push notification from Instagram: *Justice4Marco is live.* I swiped right to open the app. Lucy's face was on the screen.

She was riding in a car, mid-sentence when I turned up my volume: "—people always doubting. Always. But you know what they say? If you want something done, you have to do it yourself. So that's what I'm doing. Stay tuned for updates. Peace, y'all!"

The screen went black and my mind went into *oh fuck* mode.

"Charlie!" I shouted, loud enough for him to hear me from the bathroom.

"You good out there?" He appeared from the hallway, wiping his wet hands on his pants.

"Get your keys. Lucy's headed to Tucker's."

CHAPTER THIRTY-THREE

I tried Lucy's cell over and over as Charlie drove like white hell down I-85 North. He weaved in and out of highway traffic, giving the Buick all she had. It felt like we were in that *Grand Theft Auto* game that my ex-roommate Danny would play all hours of the night, except we wouldn't get a reset if things went to shit.

"Should've known she'd do this," I said. I stomped my foot on the floorboard. "I'm a fucking moron."

"Nothing you can do about it now, Hud. Just hope to heavens she ain't got herself into a jam by the time we show up."

"But what if—"

"Ain't no time to play the what-ifs game. If I have anything to say about it, we might just beat her there," he said. He pretended to change gears, though the Buick was an automatic, and he whipped around a big rig at the last second. The engine roared past ninety miles an hour.

"You're a little *too* good at this," I said when my breath allowed. "There something you're not telling me?"

Charlie just smiled and flirted with death half a dozen more times before we exited toward Colfax. Several miles and turns later, my GPS commanded a right turn into an immaculate neighborhood. Charlie barely eased off the gas as we zipped by beautiful brick houses, expertly manicured yards, mailboxes with personalized name plaques on the sides. We were about a quarter mile from Tucker's street when I spotted a Nissan Altima just ahead of us. There was a familiar square decal on its back glass.

"That's an Uber," I said. "Might be her."

As we closed in on the Altima, the silhouette of Lucy's hair became distinct in the car's backseat.

"Sweet mother of Pearl," Charlie said. "Goddamn, I'm good."

"*Good* and crazy," I said. "Ease up on the damn gas."

Charlie slowed down and we tailed the car from a distance, and sure enough, it took a left onto Tucker's street. A hundred yards or so later, just before the road ended in a cul-de-sac, the Altima stopped. Lucy got out and quickly spotted us, showing no hint of emotion. She said something to the Uber driver, slung her backpack over her shoulder, and turned to walk down an immense driveway.

"She's lost her ever-loving mind," Charlie said.

I took my wallet from my back pocket and laid it on the center console. "Pay the driver," I said. "Should be enough cash in there. I'll see if I can stop Ms. Vigilante."

"Why do I have—"

"Just do it, Charlie."

He stopped beside the Altima to pay the driver, a light-skinned woman in a beanie, and I hopped out of the car. Lucy was already halfway down the descending driveway that boasted a black G-Wagon and a red F-250 but still had room for ten more vehicles.

I picked up my pace, made up some ground, then whisper-shouted: "Lucy!"

No response.

As she neared the sprawling house's white-washed brick porch, I got louder: "Can you stop?"

She spun in my direction.

I caught up to her, undeterred by her seething scowl. I said, "You promised me you wouldn't do anything stupid, Lucy."

"I don't find this stupid," she said. "I find it necessary. If you think I'm turning back now, you don't know me too well."

"If I have to drag you back to the car, I will," I told her. "Now let's get of here. This isn't some kind of game."

"You're right about that part, Hudson. It isn't a game."

The Buick came racing down the drive and screeched to a halt behind me. Charlie got out of the car.

"That was my freaking ride." Lucy threw her arms up as the Uber pulled away.

"It *was* your ride," Charlie said. "A thirty-two dollar one at that. Now you're stuck with us."

"I don't care how the crap I get home. I made it here, and I'm not leaving until I talk to Tucker. Period."

Charlie said, "You'll leave when we tell you to leave, young lady."

Lucy wasn't moved.

I tried a different approach: "Listen, me and Charlie will talk to the guy, but you're going back to the car. If something happens to you, it's my ass that's in trouble. Charlie's too. Don't you understand that?"

"Like I care," she said.

"You should care. Charlie just broke every rule in the driver's handbook to get here on time. We're lucky we made it here in one piece."

"You made that choice."

"You didn't *leave* us a choice."

"Then I'll give you one now," she said. "Take your freaking phone out."

"Do what?"

"Your *phone*." She stood there, cross-armed, until I gave in. She went on: "Go to your home screen . . . bring up your voice memo . . . then hit 'Record.' If you're going to talk to Tucker, you need to document any evidence. If you do that, then I'll go to the car."

I followed her instructions, hoping she'd keep her end of the bargain. "Done." I held my phone toward her. "Are you happy?"

She walked past me and toward the car. "Y'all better not screw things up."

Charlie closed his car door and we exchanged looks like *are we really about to do this?* I'm not sure if it was Lucy's iron will or our morbid curiosity that propelled us, but we followed a cobblestone walkway to the porch, which was occupied by heavily lacquered wooden rockers. I just hoped the fact that we were in an upper-class neighborhood and it was still light out would mean that nothing crazy would go down.

I thought we might strategize how we'd handle things, but Charlie, without so much as a countdown, walked to the door and rang the bell. I listened for footsteps, watched for movement beyond the frosted privacy window next to the door, but detected nothing. Charlie rang again. We waited, and still, there was no answer. I looked back at the Buick where Lucy was leaning against the rear driver's-side door.

"After all this hoopla, the sumbitch probably ain't even here," Charlie said.

"I'm kind of hoping he's not."

He rang again, held a hand up for silence, then pressed his ear to the door.

Still nothing.

I said, "I really hate to disappoint Lucy, but she just wasted a trip and cleared out half my wallet in the process."

"At least we didn't die on the way up."

I told him it was time to roll, and he followed me back to the car. I told Lucy, "Don't look like we'll be talking to anybody today."

Her eyes were straight ahead. "Bullcrap, we won't. The lights are on upstairs."

"People leave lights on all the—" before I could finish, Lucy made a beeline toward the front door.

I yelled for her to stop and Charlie did too, both of us at full decibel level.

Lucy reached the porch, then looked back at us, all giddy. "They've got one of those fancy doorbells with the video camera. Saw one on TV."

I said, "Whoop-de-frickin-do. Charlie rang the damn thing three times. Nobody's home. It's time to go."

She loudly beat on the door, followed by some hoots and hollers and a wild waving of her arms, like those inflatable wacky dancers in front of Platinum Auto Sales.

"Lucy!" I shouted during her charade.

I started for the porch when I heard an unmistakable, mechanical sound.

The garage door ahead of us began to rise. Lucy heard the sound and ran to the driveway. The rising door slowly revealed a gray-haired man and a much younger woman in a garage that housed an impressive fitness room, complete with treadmills and a bench press. The man was wearing a sweat-dampened Under Armour shirt, and the brunette woman, in a sports bra and yoga pants, looked like one of those car magazine models, aftermarket boobs and all.

The man spoke: "What the hell is wrong with you people?"

It took me a second to realize it was Dalton Tucker. His hair wasn't long like in the mugshot Holden had showed me; it was short and neatly gelled into a side part.

Lucy looked at me and winked. "People don't like it when you get their neighbors riled up."

Charlie and I walked up, positioned ourselves in front of her, some ten feet from the garage.

"Dalton Tucker?" I said.

"Who's asking?"

"My friends here are Charlie and Lucy," I said. "And my name's Hudson Miller. That last name sound familiar to you?"

"Should it?" He looked past me, at Charlie's Buick, almost fearfully, like the rattletrap was leaking oil on his exquisite driveway. Chances are, it was.

"My dad was Leland Miller," I said.

Tucker was either confused or playing stupid. "I don't know any Lelands."

"You sure about that?"

"Positive."

"If you want to give that name a quick google, you can read up about his murder that happened last month."

"Over in Flint Creek," Charlie added. "Not that you didn't know that already."

Tucker studied the three of us, then looked at the woman. "Go on inside, honey."

She asked if she should call the cops, and he shook his head.

Once she was inside, Charlie said, "No need to run your wife . . . or your girlfriend off. Just here to have a friendly conversation."

"That's my daughter, you asshole." Tucker took a small, white towel from the side rail of a treadmill and wiped his forehead. "Now, why the hell are you people here?"

"I already told you," I said. "I'm Leland Miller's son."

"Are you hard of hearing? I don't know anyone by that name."

"That's funny. I'm pretty sure he knew yours. Or maybe it's just a wild coincidence that y'all share a similar taste in black-market firearms."

A knowing look crossed his face, however fleeting.

"I've got some pictures if you want to compare," I told him.

"I'll tell you like I told the cops. I'm a hard-working, tax-paying citizen who's just about tired of being harassed. A man will only hear his good name trashed so much before he does something about it."

"Nice flex, dude," Lucy chimed in. "Why don't you just come right out and threaten us? No need to be subtle about it."

"Pardon?"

"I know your type. You think you can say and do what you want because you've gotten away with it your whole life. You throw enough money at things and they just go away."

"Sounds to me like you watch too many movies."

"Movies?" Lucy stood between Charlie and me. She rolled up her shirtsleeve and held her arm toward Tucker. There was a skull with devil horns inked on her forearm that I'd never seen before. She quickly pulled her sleeve back over it. "My dad worked for the Mexican cartel. I grew up in the streets, *pendejo*. I've seen the baddest of the bad. So yeah, I know your type. And you don't scare me."

Charlie looked as if his mind had just exploded, but Tucker was unfazed. "Sounds like you've got your own issues to work out, kid," he said. "Now, y'all have about five seconds to get in your vehicle and leave my premises."

I said, "How about I give you a heads-up before we go?"

Tucker crossed his vascular arms.

"Pretty soon, Mr. Tucker, the cops will probably be asking you about more than those guns they found on your land. There's a murder, maybe two, that could be caught up in all this. And that's why we're here."

"Murders . . ."

"My dad and Lucy's brother were both murdered. You know any reason why that might be?"

"I don't, but you sound pretty sold on your accusations. So let's hear this one, Mr. . . . Miller, was it?"

Charlie said, "You know his fucking name."

"I see this one of two ways, Tucker," I said. "Both of which should be of interest to you. Either (A) you or someone that

242

works for you had my dad killed over a bad business deal, or (B) someone else killed my dad and stole a bunch of the guns he was selling for *you*. Makes you connected one way or the other. So which one is it?"

He pressed his palms together like a praying saint. "I'm going to answer this like a general contractor, because that's what I am."

"Get your popcorn ready," Charlie muttered.

Tucker went on: "Let's say I've got a lucrative job underway, a strip mall or a big apartment complex. What sense would it make for me to up and fire a productive member of my own work crew? That's shooting myself in the foot. It costs me time, and it costs me money. Do I look like a man who likes to lose money?"

I said, "Maybe if that worker was cheating you, compromising your business somehow. I'm sure a man in your position could find a way to keep things rolling."

"You folks sure do operate on a lot of *maybes*. I deal in reality." He removed the workout gloves from each of his hands and tossed them to a weight bench. "I think you've wasted enough of my time."

"Wasted your time?" Charlie said. "This convo is a hell of a lot more interesting than the ones you'll have with your future cellmate."

Tucker stepped forward and jabbed a finger in Charlie's direction. "If you don't get—"

"We're leaving," I said, "but there's one last thing. If you have anything to do with this, I'm sure the feds will figure it out. Meantime, I'd appreciate if you'd tell whoever you have following me, trying to hurt me and my partner Charlie, to leave us the hell alone. We don't have shit to do with any of this. I'm trying to run a business. I think you can appreciate that." I motioned for Charlie and Lucy to follow me to the car.

"Would you care to elaborate on 'hurt you'?" Tucker asked.

Charlie said, "Some motherfucker took his car and tried to put us in a ditch last night. Goddamn *Dukes of Hazzard* style."

"That so?" he said. "You mind describing that car?"

"Shit, I don't know. A little black one."

Tucker laughed. "I have unlimited access to duallies and dump trucks. If I was going to hire someone to put you into a ditch, doubt they'd be using a *little black car*. Sounds to me like you're dealing with some small-time, amateur job. So that should put your little theories to rest pretty easy. This has nothing to do with me. If I wanted a job done, it'd be done right. Now you all scurry on back to fantasyland. Trust me when I say this is your last warning."

"Let's go," I said, tugging Charlie by his shirt.

"Could y'all do me a favor while you're at it?" Tucker asked, cockily grinning.

We all looked but nobody answered.

"That nice gray SUV parked at the end of the cul-de-sac has two cops in it. Officer Graeser and Officer Ferguson. Can you tell them I ordered them a large pizza from Papa John's for their little stakeout party?" He sneered as he clicked a key fob that closed the garage.

I looked across the street. A gray Tahoe with tinted windows was parked near a neighbor's mailbox. Charlie suggested it could be any old Tahoe, but it looked like an unmarked cop car to me.

We all got in the Buick.

Charlie slammed his door. "I'd like to kick the shit out of Tucker. Give me about five minutes alone with him, and I—"

"He isn't the one," Lucy said. "It doesn't matter."

Charlie cranked the car and backed out of the driveway. I gave a glance at the Tahoe; there were two men inside, watching us intently. I was surprised they didn't pursue us when we drove away.

"How can you be so sure Tucker isn't our guy, Lucy?" I asked. "He got awfully squirmy when we brought up the guns."

"That's not what I'm talking about. Of course he's into gunrunning, and I'm sure your dad was working for him. But I don't think he killed your dad or my brother. He isn't the one messing with you." She punched the roof of the car in frustration. "That guy's too rich and too smart to mess around with some nobodies from Flint Creek. I should've known."

"I'd still like to whoop his ass," Charlie said before making a left at a stop sign. "By the way, you never told us anything about that cartel stuff."

A sigh. "I was lying, Charlie. The tattoo is fake. I drew it on my arm on the way up here."

"Had me fooled," I said. "Thought it was a nice touch."

"What's a *bendejo*?"

I could hear a bag unzip, a pen clicking. "*Pen-dejo*," Lucy said. "Doesn't matter what it means. He's not the one. That's another off the list."

I looked back. "Anyone else in that notebook you haven't crossed off?"

She handed the notebook over the seat. "Look for yourself. That's everyone I can think of that might know something or might have seen something."

I checked the list. The name of every person we'd added to the evidence board was crossed off, now including Dalton Tucker's. Other names were on there too. All crossed off. "I don't know some of these . . ."

"Neighbors. Some old friends of Mo's. They were the first I cleared."

"There'll be more people, Lucy. Everyone that you eliminate just puts us closer."

"Bet the cops ain't talked to half as many people as you have," Charlie said. "Wouldn't doubt if they've talked to me more than everybody else put together."

"Because you found both the bodies," Lucy said.

"Thanks for reminding me."

"Sorry, Charlie. I'm just saying. It's probably—"

"You've got to be shitting me," Charlie said, slowing the Buick. "Tucker wasn't lying."

I looked over, then followed his eyes to our left. A Papa John's delivery car was turning into the neighborhood.

CHAPTER THIRTY-FOUR

We'd barely crossed the town line in Flint Creek when blue lights lit up the Buick's rearview.

"This day just keeps getting better, folks," I said.

Then Charlie: "Jesus God. Bet you my right kidney that's Coble's car."

It was already too dark out to tell.

Lucy laughed sarcastically and said, "I knew it. I freaking knew this would happen."

I pulled into an empty parking lot next to a former appliance repair shop, and then I watched until a cop appeared in my side-view.

I said, "About that right kidney . . ."

Coble, backlit by flashing lights, his head shaking, approached my door. He seared Charlie and me with his eyes, then ducked his head, clicked his flashlight on, and looked into the backseat.

"Unbelievable." He clicked off the light, and then he dropped a heavy hand on the roof of the car. "All three of you. Out. *Now*."

We all shared a similar look, as humorous as it was "hand in the cookie jar." Fifth-graders on their way to the principal's office. We filed out of the car, and Coble directed us to stand next to one another on the driver's side of the Buick.

He paced in front of us, roughly stroked at his goatee before stopping. "Y'all know why I've got you pulled over, don't you?"

Lucy said, "Window tint?"

I wanted to laugh.

"That's cute," Coble said. "I got a call from the Guilford County Sheriff's Department. You see, they ran Charlie's tags while y'all were out on your little 'adventure,' saw his address was in Flint Creek. My good buddy, Chief Walker, called me up half an hour ago and asked if I knew of a Charlie Shoaf, and why he and a younger man and some girl would be paying a visit to Dalton Tucker. I had the 'young man' part figured out pretty quick, but for the life of me, I couldn't figure out—"

"These are my friends now," Lucy said.

"Your *friends* . . ."

"Yeah," she said. "I guess you could say we have a common interest."

"The only thing y'all have in common right now is downright stupidity. Especially the so-called adults, Mr. Miller and Mr. Shoaf here. Do you have any earthly idea how stupid and dangerous the stunt y'all just pulled is? Any at all?"

"It needed to be done," Lucy said.

"Lucy, I've told you before, the wheels of justice don't always turn at the speed you might want, but that don't mean they aren't turning."

Lucy persisted: "Could've had me fooled."

"This is my fault, Frank," I said. "I shouldn't have—"

"No it's not," Lucy interjected. "This was all me."

"I don't doubt that one bit given your track record," Coble told her. "Did you get the answers you were looking for?"

Lucy grinned and shrugged.

"How about you, Shoaf?" Coble said. "This give you any peace of mind?"

"The young lady needed help. I helped her."

Coble laughed obnoxiously loud. "In all my years, I've never heard of something so damn foolish. Just so y'all know, this little 'let's play cops' charade is over. Done. You're interfering with an investigation, and I won't tolerate it." Coble stood in front of me. "I knew Tammy would be a thorn in my side during all of this, and I can understand that, given her situation, but you?"

"We all just want answers," I said.

"Then let the professionals do their jobs. You got it?"

I nodded so he'd get out of my face.

"Good," he said. "Now, you and Charlie get in the car and get out of here. I'll be taking Ms. Reyes home. Don't believe her mother is going to be real happy about all this."

Lucy said, "She doesn't need—"

"Save it," Coble said. "Get in the car."

"Can I at least get my bag?" Lucy asked.

Coble told her to make it snappy.

While Charlie and I got into the Buick, Lucy took her time gathering her backpack from the rear floorboard. She stuffed her notebook inside and zipped it up. She looked toward the rear of the car, where Coble was talking to someone on a walkie.

"Who the crap is Tammy?" Lucy whispered.

Charlie turned. "Huh?"

Lucy looked at me. "Coble said something about a Tammy."

"She's my stepmother," I said quietly.

"Sounds like another name for my list," Lucy said, a quick glance back at Coble, who was still in convo.

"Waste of time, Lucy," I told her. "She won't be much help."

"You don't know that. When's the last time you talked to her?"

"I don't know. A few weeks?"

"I think things have changed since then. Don't you?"

A tap on the back of the car. Coble motioned for Lucy to hurry up.

"Promise me you'll talk to her. We're the only voice Mo has left." She slid toward the open door.

"Fine," I said.

"Make sure you record it. Okay?"

I promised her I would. "You let us know if Chief Numb-nuts gives you any grief."

Lucy nodded and shut the door, and Charlie gave me a stern look akin to the one Coble had given us all moments before. "You heard what the chief just said, Hud. It's time we get out of their way so they can do their job."

"Damn, Charlie. Of all people, I can't believe—"

"I'm fucking with you," he said, winking.

We shared a laugh as I pulled away.

CHAPTER THIRTY-FIVE

I wasn't sure if I'd woken her or she was heavily medicated, or both, but Tammy looked like death warmed over when I stopped by Dad's house that night. A tornado of a messy bun; no trace of makeup; an ill-fitting crushed velvet sweat suit.

Through the screen door, she said groggily, "If you came to gloat, you can go ahead and leave."

"That's not why I'm here, Tammy. Not sure what I'd be gloating about anyway."

"The cops told me about that Tucker fellow. I guess you might be right about your daddy being tied up in all that gun nonsense. Congratulations."

"I stopped by to ask you something."

"About that boy they found?"

I shook my head.

Instead of inviting me in from the cold, Tammy opened the screen door and brushed past me. She picked up a pack of cigarettes from the armrest of an Adirondack chair that seemed to swallow her whole when she slid into it. She cupped her hands against a slight breeze. While she struggled to spark a flame from a lighter, I slid my phone out of my jacket pocket just enough to give it a quick glance. My voice memo app was still recording.

Tammy's cigarette wouldn't light. She flicked it to the porch and slammed her lighter on the armrest. She tucked her fuzzy-slippered feet into the chair, arms around her legs. "You got something to ask, then ask."

"I was wondering if anything strange has happened to you over the last week or so. Anything out of the ordinary, maybe."

"*Out of the ordinary?* I haven't left this house but a couple times since your daddy passed. I'm not fit to be in public like I am. Ain't really had no visitors either."

"I guess that's a no?"

"That's an *I don't know what the hell you're even talking about.*"

"This might sound crazy, but I think somebody's trying to hurt me. Scare me, at least."

"I ain't following."

"Somebody broke into the shop at the salvage yard, messed the place up pretty good over the weekend. Then last night, a car tried to run me and Charlie into a ditch on Old Mountain Road. A black one."

"Old Mountain? You know how many people have died on that road? Probably been three crosses on the roadside in the past ten years or so."

"I didn't know that."

"'Cause you ain't been around," she said. "Sounds to me like the person driving that car wanted to do more than hurt you."

"All of it started happening after the Reyes boy's body turned up. Starting to think that whoever is messing with me and whoever shot Dad or hurt that boy might be connected."

She dropped her feet to the ground, pushed out of the chair. "Awfully convenient that you give a shit now that it's *your* life in danger."

"I've given a shit since the first day, but what the hell could I do? I only knew what the cops told me. Same goes for you."

"*Same goes for me,*" she said mockingly. She made for the door, where her dogs awaited in sphinxlike stances. She stepped inside and spoke through the screen. "You know what Coble said to me about a week ago? Said I probably gained an awful lot when Leland died."

"Like you had something to do with it?"

"He didn't have the balls to say that, but the suggestion was enough." She brought her face close to the screen. "Let me ask you something: Do I look like a woman that's gained a damn thing?"

"No," I said, "and for the record, I never thought you knew a thing about it."

"Bullshit. Probably thought you'd drive down here, find me at the kitchen table counting a stack of money, having myself a celebration drink, huh?"

"Honest to God, I didn't."

"I barely want to wake up in the morning anymore, Hudson. Leland could've left me a billion dollars and a two-story house in North Myrtle, and that wouldn't have made a damn bit of difference." She bent down to scoop up Cody, her Pomeranian, while Stormin' Norman whimpered. "If it wasn't for these dogs, I wish somebody'd run me off the god-dang road."

"Things are going to get better, Tammy," I told her. "Once all this stuff is figured out."

"Better? Leland will still be dead, won't he? And say we find out that Leland killed that boy? You think that'll make things better?"

"I don't. But we don't know that's what happened."

"You do realize that whoever killed that kid used the car crusher," she said. "That don't leave many possibilities, now does it? It's like a real-life version of that board game—Clue, or whatever—except there's only a couple characters to choose from. Your dad and—"

"Charlie had nothing to do with it."

"You don't know who did what."

"Maybe I don't, but I'm trying to find out. I'm not exactly one to throw in the towel."

Tammy shook her head and lowered Cody to the ground. "You have fun with that." She started pushing the wooden door to.

"Put yourself in my shoes, Tammy."

The door stopped.

"I could be dead right now," I said.

"There's nothing that I can tell you. Like I said a minute ago: I ain't seen or heard nothing strange."

I nodded. "That's all I wanted to know."

"You want to know something else?"

I raised an eyebrow.

"If your daddy had listened to me years ago, we wouldn't even be having this conversation."

"What are you talking about?"

"If I told Leland once, I told him a thousand times to put some cameras down at the yard, but he was too stubborn. He was skeptical of the whole outside world, but acted like Flint Creek was damn Mayberry. You see where that got him?"

"Cameras or not, it still could've happened."

"You sound as hard-headed as he did," she said. "You're more alike than you'll ever know." A slamming door punctuated the sentiment.

* * *

I stopped the recording when I got in my Jeep. Other than Tammy's parting words, only one remark replayed in my head as I drove away. The single detail that Tammy's hindsight was snagged on: the cameras. It's something I'd brought up the day of Dad's murder; it's something the cops had mentioned more than once.

Thing is, there'd never been a single camera at Miller's Pull-a-Part, or anywhere close by for that matter. The salvage yard was as remote as any business in the whole town. Offered a privacy that probably served Dad well until the one day it didn't.

But what had happened to Charlie and me, the almost-crash, hadn't been far from the civilized world. We'd come from one of the busiest streets in town, which meant whoever it was gunning for us was getting more daring, maybe even desperate.

It gave me an idea.

CHAPTER THIRTY-SIX

I made my way out to the Marathon station, hoping to God they'd had security cameras running the night before. When I got there, my optimism kicked up a notch. The gas station had cameras; there was one at each end of the building.

I walked inside, where a young woman was standing behind the counter. She had dyed black hair and a nose ring, a joyless face. It wasn't the same girl that had rung me up the night before.

"Help you?" she said.

"Is Mr. Fields in?"

"You got some sort of complaint?"

"No, ma'am, just needed to ask him about some security footage from out front."

"Security?"

Knowing the truth would sound bonkers, I toned it down a bit: "I was involved in a hit-and-run when I left here last night." I pointed outside. "Not twenty feet down the road. Cops couldn't do anything about it because I didn't get a good look at the car. Thought maybe those cameras could help."

"I don't know how to work all that. Got to have a password. And sometimes them things don't even work right."

"Could you at least tell your boss?"

Her expression didn't change. "I'll let him know."

"It'd be really helpful," I told her. "My um . . . my uncle got whiplash pretty bad from the wreck. Poor guy's in a lot of pain. Probably can't get shit from the insurance company. You know, it's a shame how they treat our veterans these days."

To my surprise, she tore off a blank piece of register receipt and found a pen. "What time you say this happened?"

"Somewhere between nine fifteen and nine thirty. It was a car that hit us. A small two-door, I think. Black."

She scribbled the info down. "And you said your name was . . . ?"

"Hudson Miller," I said. "Mr. Fields knows my family. Please make sure he gets this."

After she jotted down my name, she looked up. "Miller? Wait, don't you own that uh . . ."

"Junkyard?" I said. "That'd be me."

Big eyes.

I relayed my phone number, and she slid the slip of paper under the register.

I read her name tag. "I really appreciate it, Paula."

An inkling of a grin softened her face. "Hope your uncle's okay."

"He made it through Vietnam. Sure he'll be just fine."

A full smile. "Anything else I can help you with, sir?"

"As long as y'all have a sixer of Keystone, I'm good to go."

* * *

When I got to the rental house, I sent Lucy a message about my visit to the gas station, and I sent her the voice recording I'd made at Tammy's.

Minutes later, I got a phone call, but it wasn't from Lucy. It was a local landline; I picked up.

"Hudson?" a woman's voice, faintly familiar. "This is Maria Reyes."

My heart hit the ground. "Ms. Reyes . . ."

"I know what Lucy did this afternoon," she said. "Frank Coble was waiting in front of the trailer when I got home from work."

"Ms. Reyes, I'm really sorry. I tried to—"

"I called to thank you, Hudson," she said. "Lucy told me that you and Charlie went after her. That you drove her back."

"You don't need to thank me. We were worried about her. I probably should've tried to reach you at work. I apologize for that—but I just—well, we didn't have any time to waste. I'm glad we got there when we did and that nothing happened."

Ms. Reyes said, "She told me everything. She showed me her videos, her notebook. All of it. She said she was trying to protect me, keeping those things from me."

"I'm sorry you had to find out like that. I know it's a lot to take in."

"It is, but I can handle it. Nothing's worse than what I've already been through. What I can't handle is how Frank Coble spoke to me tonight."

"And how's that?"

"Like I'm a terrible mother," she said. "Like I should be doing a better job of keeping an eye on my daughter."

"You're a great mother, Ms. Reyes."

"He talked to me like I didn't just lay a child to rest. He even made a—" her voice broke up a little. "He made a threat, Hudson. He said if they confirm that man, Tucker, was involved with your dad, they might search our trailer, and he'd even get a warrant if needed."

"So he can connect Marco?"

"Why else would he do it?"

"There's a lot I don't know, but I don't think your son was involved in all that gun business. I do know that Coble is an insensitive asshole."

"I haven't touched Marco's room since he went missing. His bed is still unmade. His socks are on the floor. If they come in here and tear up his room, looking for whatever they're looking for, I don't know what I'll do. I don't know what Lucy will do."

The thought of Coble pulling a stunt like that, or even making that threat, made my blood boil. "I'm surprised Lucy didn't slug him."

A quiet laugh. "She knows the law pretty well. I think that's a felony."

"You mad about what she did?"

"I'm a lot of things right now," she said. "I'm mad, frustrated, sad . . . I think I'm even a little proud. But mostly, I feel helpless. It's just me here. I don't have family nearby. When I'm gone for hours, I just hope Lucy is taking care of herself. I felt the same when Marco was alive. Maybe if I had been here more, he would still be—"

"Please don't think of it that way. You do what you do to make a better life for your family."

"And look where it's gotten me."

"It's hard not to have hindsight when bad stuff happens, but it'll eat you up if you let it. My dad tried to call me the night before he got killed—twice, actually—and I didn't even answer. Would it have changed the outcome? I don't know. And maybe that's not even the same type of thing. You losing your son and me losing my dad are . . . it's just different."

"Loss is loss, Hudson. I hope you find the answers you're looking for. I hope we both do. That's my prayer every day."

"Does your faith ever get shaken, Ms. Reyes?"

"All the time," she said. "I don't think faith can be strong if it isn't tested. It's sort of like boxing, no?"

"Yeah. I guess it is."

"My father used to say that all we can do in life is to try and meet God halfway, then hope for the best. When I was a little girl, my father and my uncles worked on a big sugar cane farm. They would spend weeks preparing the fields and planting, but once that work was done, they could only hope God would send the rain clouds. If that rain was too little or too much, my father could rest knowing he did his part. If the crops never came, he always found a way to keep us fed. God provided a way."

"I think Lucy is a lot like your father."

"I think so too," Ms. Reyes said. "I don't know if Lucy prays anymore. That's not my business. God knows her heart, and I think she's met Him halfway, and then some."

CHAPTER THIRTY-SEVEN

Lucy messaged me back in the morning, just as I was leaving the house. She was embarrassed that her mom had called, but she was also relieved she didn't have to keep her in the dark any longer. When it came to my attempt at detective work, Lucy agreed there wasn't much to glean from my convo with Tammy, but my impromptu visit to the Marathon station impressed her. She seemed hopeful something good would come from it. Told me I was the second best PI in town.

I caught Charlie up to speed when I got to work. In lieu of our broken coffee maker, he was in the break room pouring near-boiling water over a filter and coffee grounds, funneling it into his thermos. He was making a hell of a mess doing it.

"Chief Shitstain told her mama all that?"

"You can't be that surprised."

"More surprised he didn't do it sooner," he said, tossing the coffee filter into the trash. He wiped some grounds on his pants and took a seat. "You know he threatened to search my house the night the body turned up?"

"You never mentioned that."

"Wasn't nothing to tell. It was just a stupid threat. I told him to search my house right then and there. Fuck a warrant. He didn't even need one."

"I'm shocked he didn't turn your house upside down, give you a cavity search just to piss you off."

"That'd require actual effort on his part." He took a sip of his grainy coffee. "It's the same deal as last night. He could've searched Lucy's place, but he knows he won't find a damn thing. It's a crime that my tax dollars pay his salary."

"If my trip to the Marathon turns something up, think you can slide a few of those tax dollars my way?"

"Keep dreaming," he said. "With our luck, the security video will have magically erased itself. That's if the thing worked in the first place. I've always said that technology is like a fart. Can't never trust it."

"You ever thought about being a motivational speaker, Charlie? If not, you've damn sure missed your calling. You could go on tour, give old geezers like yourself the hope they've been looking for."

He sipped his coffee, chewed it a little. "I'm a realist," he said. "Sue me."

"Well, if the Marathon doesn't have footage, maybe there's somewhere nearby that does."

"I wouldn't hold my breath, bucko. You know what they say about wishing in one hand and shitting—"

"All right," I said. "I get it. The world sucks. Life's a bitch. We're in over our heads. Anything else you'd like to add?"

"The value of the dollar's gone to shit. Other than that, you've pretty much got it covered."

"Don't you have some work to do?"

"Can't I at least finish my coffee?"

"Coffee? I'm pretty sure they could pave a highway with that shit, but go right ahead, old man. Caffeine up. That piece of junk waiting in the garage isn't going to dismantle itself."

Charlie took his sweet time finishing his coffee, then busied himself draining the brake fluid from a PT Cruiser. I should've been helping, but I sat at the computer for a while, purposelessly clicking and scrolling, too anxious to be productive.

Late morning brought a couple of customers: a teenage boy who found a rearview for his Dodge Ram, and some Hawaiian shirt–wearing bro with a man bun who thought he could find a lift kit for an old CJ-7 Jeep. Charlie literally laughed out loud, said he'd have better luck pissing on a light socket.

I'd been checking my phone obsessively; it was a few minutes after my lunch on a dime—chicken flavored Cup O' Noodles—when I got a text from a private number:

Hey Hudson. This is Jim Fields. Paula told me what happened. Didn't know u had an uncle. Anyway, hope this pic helps. Not sure if it's the car u r looking for.

A picture came through, a snapshot from a small security monitor. The image on the monitor wasn't exactly high resolution, but clear enough to spring me from my stool. Just beyond the parking lot, a black coupe was heading in the direction of Old Mountain Road. I could tell by its shape it was an Acura, though I couldn't recall which model. The time on the security screen was the most convincing evidence: 9:22.

As far as a driver, I could only see a thin arm reaching toward the steering wheel. The guy, assuming it was a guy, was White or really light-skinned.

I saved the picture and sent it to Lucy.

Look familiar?

She responded almost immediately.

IDK. Let me post this on Insta.

And she did. Not even a minute later, the picture I sent was at the top of her feed. A caption below it: *Anyone recognize this car?! DM me ASAP please!!*

I hurried to the garage and pulled the plug on Charlie's radio that was blasting Toto's "Hold the Line." He looked like he was about to cuss me until I held my phone up.

"Ever seen this car before?"

He squinted as he came closer. "Jim send that?"

I nodded.

"I'll be dipped." He studied the picture. "That's an Integra," he said. "Reckon I've seen plenty of those in my life, but nah, can't say that one rings a bell."

"It's definitely the car from last night. Has to be. It was headed toward Old Mountain around 9:20."

"Well, hot damn. You might want to shoot that to—"

"Lucy? Already did."

Still pessimistic: "Maybe she'll figure it out by the time I'm eighty. Meantime, you can help me finish tearing this PT-P.O.S. apart." He tapped the roof of the purple car with a wrench. "Ugliest damn vehicle since the Gremlin."

As much as my divided attention allowed, I assisted Charlie for the next fifteen minutes or so until my ringing phone perked me up. Charlie too.

It was Lucy: "I know whose car it is. Come pick me up!"

"Your mom will literally kill me, Lucy. Especially after yesterday."

"Mama's at work. If I get in trouble, then whatever. It'll be worth it. Trust me. This is big, Hudson. Huge. I freaking know that car! I'll go over there without you. You know I will."

I put my good sense on hold. I told her we'd be there soon.

* * *

Lucy was waiting outside of her trailer when we got there; she hopped in the back seat.

"Poole Road," she said. "Step on it. This dude gets word I'm looking for him, he'll probably skip town."

"What dude are you talking about?" I asked her.

"This wannabe gangster they call Forty."

"Forty? You know the guy?" I made a U-turn out of her lot.

"He went to school with Mo, but they weren't friends. He was a grade or two ahead. Total chump from what I know." She tapped my headrest. "Let's get moving."

A couple tire-squealing miles later, I turned onto Poole. I drove, eyes peeled, passing double-wides and modular homes similar to those at The Ponderosa.

"A little farther up," Lucy said.

More houses came into view as I crested a hill. Then, up on the left, I spotted a black Acura. It was sitting under an aluminum garage shelter next to a small house with mud-caked siding. "Jackpot," I said.

Everyone sat forward.

"I knew it was his car," Lucy said.

"Looks like the same one to me," Charlie added. "If the front of that car's busted, Mr. Forty's going to have some explaining to do."

I parked near the road and turned to Lucy. "This time you're staying put."

Surprisingly, she didn't fight me on it.

Charlie and I got out of the Jeep. We walked closer to the house that looked dark inside, and when I rounded the front of the Acura, my remaining doubt was cleared up. The bumper was banged up and hanging loose, streaks of champagne paint across it.

Charlie saw what I saw. "That son of a bitch."

The side door of the house flung open; a man as tall as I was but even skinnier stepped out in nothing but baggy blue jeans. "Hey! What the hell y'all think you're—" His words faded when our eyes locked, but his mouth hung open.

Before anyone could say anything, he bolted toward his backyard.

Thought I'd be in for a hell of a foot race, but when he reached the back of his property the guy's plans changed from flight to fight. He made for a firepit, grabbed a half-charred two-by-four that hung over its edge. By the time he spun around, gripping the board like a Louisville Slugger, I was spearing him at the waist. The board went flying as we came crashing down beside the firepit. We clawed and scrambled for dominant position until finally I grabbed one of his wrists and secured it into a tight lock—something I'd learned from bouncing. I pulled the wrist close to my chest and got into a squatting position.

"Chill, bro!" he yelled from his back, squirming in the dirt. "You're breaking my fucking wrist!"

I tightened the wrist lock. "Calm your ass down, Slim Shady. The more you flop around, the more it's going to hurt. Got it?"

Charlie was beside me now; he'd snatched up the two-by-four. "Damn, I didn't know string beans could tackle like that, Hud!"

"I don't know who y'all are or why the fuck you're on my property," Forty said, grimacing.

Charlie leaned down close to him. "That why you ran, *Forty*?"

"Fuck no. I ran because y'all were—"

"You know exactly who we are." It was Lucy, right over my shoulder.

Before I could tell her to go back to the Jeep, Forty said, "Ah man, this little shit. Need to mind your own goddamn business."

I was already charged from the chase and tussle, never mind his having tried to run us off the road a couple days before, and what he said to Lucy was one step too fucking far. I twisted his wrist tighter with my left; I cocked my right and was on the verge of crossing a line that ended with Forty's face rearranged and his wrist bent in a way that God hadn't intended. But when I glanced at Lucy, her eyes were on me—frightened by what they saw. What she saw in me, not Forty.

A breath steadied me. A different Hudson took over. "That girl you just insulted?" I told Forty calmly. "You better be glad she showed up when she did."

"Maybe you should do a little homework on people before you screw with them," Lucy said. "Hudson's a pro fighter. He's the last guy you want to tangle with."

Forty looked at her, then me, and then he rested his head in the dirt.

I said, "Now, I'm going to ease up, and you're going to sit up and tell me why you tried to run me and my friend Charlie here off the road the other night."

I let go of his wrist and stood. He cradled the wrist with his other hand. As he sat up, dirt and leaves clung to the back of his head.

"I didn't run nobody off—"

Charlie kicked a clump of dirt toward him and said, "Are you deaf? Or do I—"

"That's enough," I told Charlie. "He's going to talk. His ass isn't leaving that dirt until he does."

Forty rotated his sore wrist a few times, seemingly mesmerized it still worked. "I wasn't trying to kill y'all," he said. "Just scare y'all. Goddamn."

"Scare us from what?"

His eyes left mine. He opened and closed his hand a few times, then spread his fingers. "I don't know, man. Just scare y'all. It was like a . . . it was a fucking prank. That's it."

"You can't even look at me when you're lying, huh?" I said. "There isn't a soul here stupid enough to believe you nearly killed a couple of guys you don't even know as a prank. You realize it took us no time at all to find out who that Acura belonged to and where you lived?"

"And we'll figure out the rest too," Lucy said. "Look at me," she commanded, and begrudgingly, he did. "We know what this is connected to," she told him. "I've done my home-work on you. I know who you hang around with. I know who your family is."

"Don't you bring up my family," he muttered.

"Imagine if you were in my shoes. You have two older brothers. Imagine if you lost one of them like I lost Mo. You'd be doing the same thing I'm doing now."

He shifted uneasily. "I swear to God I don't know shit about that. The other thing with the car? The mess at y'all's garage? Yeah, I did that. You fucking caught me."

"We've already figured that part out," I said. "We want to know, why us?"

"I was doing somebody a favor, okay?"

"A favor?"

"Yeah, dude said he had a beef with y'all or something, that if I could run y'all off, he'd pay me. I was just doing a job, that's it. I don't even know y'all."

"Clearly somebody does," I said. "Who put you up to this?"

It took Forty a moment to answer. "Don't matter if I tell you or not, you're just going to beat my ass."

"I should, after you tried to split my head like a water-melon with that damn board. But all I want is answers."

Then Charlie: "Yeah, Hudson, he owes me pretty big for my Buick too. Don't think we can let him go that easy."

"He's not the person we're looking for," I told Charlie.

"Fine," Charlie said. "But I know where the bastard lives now."

During our scrum, Forty's phone must've slid from his pocket. I tapped it with my foot. "Call the guy up," I said. "Don't need you sending us on a wild goose chase."

"You think he's stupid enough to come out here with y'all here threatening me?"

I said, "I advise you to get creative. We aren't leaving until Mystery Man gets here."

Forty thought for a while. He looked up at Lucy, who was steadily staring at him. Then he picked up his phone with a trembling hand. He spit into the dirt, took a few labored breaths, and brought up a number.

"Hey, man," he said into the phone, an assumed calmness. "Got some news about those guys at the junkyard . . . nah, man, ain't nothing like that. Something we need to talk about in person. Trust me . . . uh-huh. Down at the house . . . make it quick."

He ended the call and looked up at me. "I'm so fucked. You happy now?"

I handed Charlie my keys. "Move my Jeep around back here. Out of sight of the road. Don't want to scare off the man of the hour when he shows up."

"Ten-four, bossman," Charlie said, tossing the two-by-four aside.

Forty didn't even react to that, just mumbled, "I'm so fucked." Then he wrapped his arms around his knees. "It's cold as shit out here, man. Can we at least go into the damn house?"

I grabbed him under an armpit and helped him to his feet. "You're lucky I didn't break that wrist," I said. "Now, don't bullshit me. Is there anyone in that house we need to know about?"

He shook his head and led the way back to the house, his gait unsteady. The side door opened to a kitchen that reeked of reefer and mildew. There were dishes piled in the sink, beer bottles and some rolling papers on a round table. We followed Forty through the kitchen toward a living room that had clothes strewn about, a TV on mute, and some breed of lizard chilling in a terrarium next to the window on the far wall.

"Park it," I told Forty when we reached a futon. I scanned for any guns or weapons he might make a move for. A neon-green bong was his only hope.

Forty sat. He grabbed a white T-shirt that was draped over an armrest and pulled it on.

While he was doing that, Lucy hit "Record" on her voice memo app. Forty didn't even notice.

When Charlie came in, I said, "Get Forty here something out of the freezer for his boo-boo."

Charlie gave me a salute and went to the fridge. "You mind if I grab one of these Milwaukee's Best, Mr. Gangster Man? A little below my social status, but it'll do."

Forty said he didn't give a damn. A moment later Charlie strolled into the room, sipping a beer. He tossed a bag of Pizza Rolls onto Forty's lap.

"The hell is this?"

"All you had," Charlie said. "It's cold enough. Stick it on there and shut up. Ain't like those are good ones anyway. Fucking *supreme*."

"Charlie," I said. I motioned my hand for him to tone down the bullshit.

He raised his beer and nodded. "You reckon I should call the cops?"

"I don't know, Charlie," Lucy said. "Say the cops beat him here. Dude won't come close to this place if he sees blue lights. Not like the cops will believe a word we say anyways."

"That's a good point, Ms. Lucy," Charlie said.

"Sure you don't want to tell us who we're expecting?" I asked Forty.

He didn't answer.

Other than heavy breathing and the occasional groan from Forty, we were all silent for the next several minutes until we heard the sound of an engine outside.

Forty sat up. "Guess you're about to get your answer."

CHAPTER THIRTY-EIGHT

I moved to a window, eased the curtain aside; a Ford Ranger was parked in the road. The driver, a White man I didn't recognize, got out. He had his hat pulled so low I could barely see his face.

"Charlie," I said, pointing to a hallway between the living room and kitchen. "Y'all stay back there for a minute. Keep Lucy close." To Forty: "Go let your boy in."

Forty adjusted his pants and moseyed to the kitchen. I stayed in the living room, just out of view of the side door. Forty creaked it open.

A voice: "What you got for me, Shane?"

Shane. Never would've guessed. *Forty* was more fitting. The door clicked shut. Footsteps through the kitchen.

"You look spooked as hell," the guy said.

"Nah, I'm straight," Forty said, lifelessly.

"You sounded a little—" The man saw me as they entered the living room; my face must have registered because his eyes shot wide. "What the fuck is this, Shane? This some sort of setup?" He was in jeans and a Carhartt jacket. A snapback hat. Clean cut.

"A setup?" I said. "I think we are the ones who've been set up for something."

The guy backed toward the kitchen, like he was about to hightail it out of there.

"If you walk out that door, mister, I'm calling the law. You and your partner in crime here can sort it out with them. So you might wanna think about—"

"Oh my God," Lucy said, appearing from the hallway.

The man, startled again, looked toward her and Charlie.

Lucy said, "Oh my God," again, her face pale. "Hudson, he *is* the law. Or . . . he was."

Charlie looked perplexed.

"You know this guy?" I asked Lucy.

"He's . . . that's Lee Markham."

Lee Markham?

"*Officer* Markham," she said.

Lee Markham. One of Lucy's sketches on our evidence wall. It came back to me: the cop who'd quit Flint Creek PD a couple months ago.

I thought Charlie might drop his beer.

"The fuck?" Forty mumbled.

"This isn't what it looks like," Markham told me. He glared at Forty.

"They saw my car," Forty said, dejected. "I fucked up."

I told Markham, "Homeboy here told us you put him up to all this. Piece of shit nearly killed us."

"This isn't wh—" Markham started. A breath. "Y'all don't know what you're stepping into."

"I can't wait to hear this BS," Lucy said. "You do remember me, don't you?"

He could barely look at her. "I do, Lucy."

"The first thing you ever asked me at the police station is if I was a legal U.S. citizen. Do you remember that? Freaking prick. And you didn't do anything to find my brother."

"You've got no way out of this now," I told him. "Whatever *this is*, it's over, so you best spill it. Or we can just wait until some of your ex-coworkers show up."

"Just . . . fuck, man," his voice quavered. "Just don't call the cops."

"And why the hell not?"

"You don't get it," he said, as if he envied our ignorance to whatever it was he was hiding.

"Either take a seat and explain what we don't get, or you can take your chances on the run. I don't think you'll get too far."

Markham looked back at the door, and I could tell he'd reached a crossroads. Had he made a run for it, I would've let him. I could only hope the cops would catch him and do the right thing, if so. To my relief, he walked to the futon, each step timid and measured. He sat and rested his elbows on his knees and covered his face; his cheeks were wet when he pulled his hands away. "This isn't over," he whispered. His eyes darted around the room, like the last frantic passengers on a sinking ship. "No matter what I say. It's not over. I'm just—"

"What's not over?" Charlie said, frustrated. "Christ Almighty. You beat around the bush worse than a damn politician."

"You know what happened to Mo," Lucy said. "Don't you?"

Markham's chest heaved and trembled with every heavy breath. The look on his face seemed to beg, to plead with Lucy not to make him say whatever truth was haunting him.

Lucy said, "You know."

Whatever spell Markham had been under was now broken. He nodded and removed his hat, almost reverently.

"Tell us," Lucy said. Her voice was quiet.

He exhaled long and slow. He rubbed his palms on his jeans and finally settled his eyes on Lucy. "You know where the old train tracks are? The caboose?"

Lucy nodded. Even I knew where that was. Deep in the woods off Randolph Street, there was an old train caboose on a set of abandoned tracks. I'd ridden my bike out there a bunch as a kid. Teenagers used to hang out on the back of the caboose, drinking and smoking, doing things teens do when parents aren't around.

"I was off duty that night back in October . . ."

"When Mo went missing," Lucy said.

A nod. "Saw your brother's car parked near those woods out there, thought I should walk down to the tracks to see what was going on. We'd been working a case on some drug deals—prescription pills and whatnot—and I had a suspicion that's where a lot of them were going down."

"He wasn't a dealer," Lucy said.

"No," Markham said. "No, he wasn't. He was just down there that night. Walking along the tracks."

"Mo liked to go down there sometimes."

"He was out there drinking. I told him I wasn't going to let him drive home, that I was going to call it in if he tried to.

Ended up having words with him. As you know, I'd brought him in before."

"He hated you."

"I grabbed a hold of his arm, tried to escort him back to his car. Since I wasn't in uniform, he didn't take too kindly to that. We had some words. Ended up in a bit of a scuffle."

Lucy stepped closer. "You killed him." Her words were not so much angry, but more of a beckoning for Markham to keep going.

After Markham took a shuddering breath, he said: "I tried to wrestle him to the ground, and I sort've picked him up. Lost my balance, dropped him right there on the tracks. He landed . . ." He brought his hand to the back of his head. "Landed on his neck."

"Then what?" I thought Lucy would be crying by this point, but she wasn't. She was calm and her voice was level, almost soothing.

Markham went on: "He was unconscious, but he was breathing. I tried not to panic, tried to wake him up, but . . . nothing. I couldn't get a response. So I called for help. Thought maybe everything would be all right."

"Everything wasn't all right," Lucy said. "It wasn't an ambulance you called."

"I was promised everything would be okay, to just leave, that everything would be fixed. For a day or so I didn't ask about it, didn't sleep much either. But then you came up to the station, said your brother was missing. That's when I knew something was bad, bad wrong."

"That's why you wouldn't help me," Lucy said. "It's the same reason you quit."

Markham nodded. "A week or so ago I found out what really happened when I left the tracks that night." He looked at me. "That's when I freaked out. Heard y'all started asking questions when that body showed up. Didn't want y'all poking around and figuring it out. Wanted that junkyard to be shut down and forgot about for good."

Charlie spoke up. "Trying to save your own sorry ass."

"It'd be a lie if I said I wasn't," Markham said. "I was a cop in this town long enough to know Shane here had plenty enough illegal shit going on that I could bribe him to scare y'all a little bit. Make y'all think twice about sticking around that yard. Thing is, Shane didn't know anything about any of this. Didn't even know I quit the force. He was just a warm body stupid enough to listen to me."

"That's fucked up, yo," Forty said quietly.

"So what did you have in store next?" I asked. "Have your errand boy here set my damn house on fire? Loosen the lug nuts on my Jeep?"

He shrugged. "For the record, I didn't tell him to ram your—"

"It doesn't matter anyways," Lucy said. "Hudson isn't scared of anything. He wasn't going to run away. Charlie either."

I said, "Assuming what you're saying is the truth, Markham, how did the salvage yard get involved?"

He answered without hesitation. "Marco's car was taken out there, crushed, buried. That's it. Your dad didn't know he was in the trunk. Didn't have a clue."

"But why my dad? Why the hell would he agree to do that?"

"Let's say somebody knew about his illegal firearms and let him by with it for over two years, and that same somebody knew your dad owed them big time for not exposing him. Called Leland up late that night in October, I suppose . . ."

Lucy said, "You keep saying *somebody*."

Markham closed his eyes and exhaled slowly. "He didn't want my mistake with your brother to tarnish the reputation of the whole police department."

"My Mexican 'criminal' brother," Lucy said.

Markham nodded. "That's why he covered it up. At least he thought he did."

Every moment since that early morning phone call, every word, thought, and theory hadn't prepared me for the reality that rang my bell like a sucker punch. "That's why he killed my dad," I said. Even to me, my voice didn't sound like my own.

The room fell into one of those rare, heavy silences, like those seconds after a bone-shaking roll of thunder. Not until I drew a deep breath did anyone speak.

"No fucking way," Charlie whispered.

"I want to hear you say it, Markham," Lucy said, and it was almost frightening how calm her voice was. "*I want you to say his name.*"

Markham slid his hat back on, and it felt like I lived a year in that long moment before the next words formed on his lips. Words that Lucy, Charlie, and myself already knew to be true.

CHAPTER THIRTY-NINE

Frank Coble wasn't on duty that evening. It was the third Saturday of the month, a big day for The Boars Club: member social night. Markham knew that Coble rarely worked on those nights, always boasting about his hangovers during Sunday shifts. We'd gone back and forth on it, and in the end, we agreed there'd be no better place to confront the chief than right there in front of his closest peers.

We'd left Forty at his house with his wrist swollen and his mind blown. Dude was probably headed for rehab after the story he'd heard and the realization of what he'd gotten himself mixed up in. As for Markham, he'd helped us formulate a game plan and was more than eager to come with us. A massive burden must've lifted when he came clean, and I'm certain whatever consequence might come paled in comparison to his inner torment of the last few months. He'd already quit the force, moved out of town into a single-bedroom apartment, was working night security for some tech company. Still, it was hard to spare any pity for him.

Tried as I might, I couldn't convince Lucy to stay home. It was her brother who was thrown into the trunk of a car and buried, and she was going to see her investigation to the very end. She deserved—maybe needed—to be there. Plus, her live streaming of the takedown, as she called it, was the final and crucial piece of the plan.

* * *

As if my nerves weren't already abuzz, there were around ten cars in the Boars Lodge lot when we showed up in my Jeep around seven. Member night had started at six thirty, no different from when Dad used to go when I was a kid. On those nights, Mom and I would always go out for pizza and stop by Blockbuster, wondering what time Dad would stumble through the door or call Mom for a ride home.

The Lodge was windowless, which gave us cover when we arrived. We did a quick rundown of our game plan and then quietly walked into the front lobby. A lobby that had a stuffed, massive boar guarding one corner of the room. Pictures of current and former members and leaders, or "Supreme Elders," as they were called, covered the side walls. Plaques and service awards were scattered among the photos. Next to the front desk, a small display case with various Boars club regalia: badges, insignias, rings, burgundy and gold rank collars. Just above that case was a plaque with the names of fallen members—Dad's had yet to be added.

"The social room is downstairs," Markham said, indicating a staircase, but those words had hardly left his mouth when a booming voice from a set of double doors to our left commanded our attention. A placard next to the doors read "Meeting Hall."

"I'm going in first," I told the others. "If Coble does anything crazy, I don't want y'all in there."

Lucy said, "He's too big of a coward. He only does his dirty deeds in secret."

Nobody could argue otherwise.

We moved closer to the double doors. The sound of chimes seemed to shake the whole building. I pressed my ear against one of the doors.

The same booming voice: "You have heard the tolling of eight strokes. The hour of eight is of utmost significance to all Boars. It is the hour of homecoming for Boars far and wide, and a reverence to Boars who roam no more. A Boar is never forgotten, never forsaken . . ."

I turned around. "What is this shit?"

"Member induction," Markham said. "Sat through one when Coble tried to recruit me. Weirded me out. Maybe we should come back when—"

"No," Lucy said. "This is perfect."

Charlie and I quietly echoed her. Markham faintly nodded; he could barely look at me.

"Just wait for y'all's cue," I said. I steadied myself with a few slow breaths, and I thought of my next steps like those when I would leave the locker room on fight night, my focus zeroing in as the ring got closer and closer. I could hear the words Coach Rob would say when he'd pat me on the back. *Just another day in the office, Champ. You were born for this.*

I opened the heavy door enough to peek inside before entering. The mayor, Roger Segers, was talking, standing at a podium in an airy, marble-floored room with four other podiums occupied by men, all wearing sport coats and Boars

Club collars. A younger man, I assumed the prospective new member, stood alone in the middle of the room, facing Segers—his son, Chip. His right hand was held up in some sort of pledge.

I slipped inside where I expected immediate eyes, but I was still a ghost.

Segers went on: "Morning and noon may come and go, the sun resting peacefully in the West, but none shall be—"

"Excuse me," I said.

Segers whipped his head in my direction. "Sir, this is a private meeting. I'm going to have to ask you to—"

"I'll handle this, Supreme Elder." It was Frank Coble, standing in front of a podium labeled "Valor."

"There something I can help you with, Mr. Miller?" he asked with feigned concern.

The other men at their respective podiums were eyeballing me now. A couple were familiar, the fire chief one of them. Several other men were sitting stiffly in wooden chairs.

"Just the man I was looking for, Frank."

He said, "If you've got an issue, Mr. Miller, please call somebody down at the station."

"That won't be necessary."

"Can I ask what this concerns? We're kind of in the middle of something important."

Something important didn't scratch the surface of what was in store. If our plan worked, the lives of every man in that room—and in a way, the whole town—were about to change forever, at least in some way.

"Gladly," I said. "Since my dad was a member here since God knows when, and he isn't here to speak for himself, I figured I'd take the podium on his behalf." I reached back, rapped my knuckles on the door behind me.

Charlie and Lucy stepped into the room. Mumbles and strange looks from the Boars.

Coble's jaw went slack.

I said, "My good friend, Lucy Reyes, here, will be videoing, so if anyone in here thinks of doing something idiotic, just remember: people all over the country will be watching."

Lucy held her screen up for all to see.

"Kids these days," Charlie said, standing next to her, arms crossed.

Coble moved around his podium and stepped heavily toward us. "Y'all have no right to be in here. Now, it's time y'all take this circus somewhere else. I've warned you three already, so if you don't leave now, I'm afraid I'll have to have you—"

"Have us what?" I smiled, and I knew it wasn't a pleasant smile. "Arrested? I'd love to hear the charges."

"Trespassing on private property, for starters."

"I'm not so sure you'll have the authority to do that here shortly."

"You're talking crazy, son. Just—"

"Can you ever shut up and listen?" Lucy's voice reverberated through the room. "Everything Mr. Hudson here has to say has already been documented by yours truly, so you might as well hear it in person. *Comprende?*"

"Thank you, Lucy," I said, approaching the podium. "Mayor, do you mind?"

The mayor, who looked like I'd just ruffled his perfectly coiffed hair, moved out of the way.

I stood behind the podium, Charlie and Lucy's presence strengthening my resolve. "As everyone here already knows, just over a month ago somebody murdered my dad, Leland. Shot him in the back of the head at his place of business. Left him in a puddle of blood. And I'm sure everyone has also heard the most recent news about Miller's Pull-a-Part." I pointed at Lucy. "Charlie found this young lady's older brother buried in the trunk of his own car. A death and cover-up that they were probably about to pin on my dead dad. Because, hell, why not? He can't exactly hire a lawyer at this point."

"This is ludicrous," Coble said angrily. "If anyone in here believes this nonsense, I'm mighty ashamed to call you a Boar."

The side door opened and Markham stepped in, ahead of schedule. "Drop the shit, *Chief.*"

Coble's face tightened. "The fuck are you—"

"I thought Lucy here told you to shut the hell up," Markham said. "You've already ruined my life, so you at least owe me the courtesy of speaking my mind."

"Ruined your life, huh? Just because you couldn't cut it on the force, you think that's—"

"It's my turn to speak," Markham said with quiet emphasis. "You've been telling me what to do and how things are going to be most of my adult life. Not anymore."

Lucy stood without moving, filming steadily.

"I was your superior," Coble told Markham. "The things I told you were for your own good."

"For my own good? Like you told me everything would be fine when Marco Reyes lay there unconscious that night at the railroad tracks? 'Don't worry about it, Lee,' you said. 'Go on home, Lee. I'll take care of everything.' Let me ask you something—when I left the scene that night, did you finish that boy off right then and there? Or did you just throw him in that trunk, let the car crusher do all the work?"

At that moment, there wasn't another sound in the room. All eyes were riveted on those two, the police chief and the former cop.

"You don't know what you're talking about," Coble said, and even he had to realize those words were weak.

"The hell he don't, Frank," I said. "Go ahead and tell your buddies here about Dad's gunrunning—wait a second, that's right—most of these people already knew about that. Y'all were probably his best customers, because a Boar would never give up a Boar. Isn't that part of your pledge?" I looked around the room. Almost all of the Boars were slack-jawed; the mayor's son seemed like he wanted to be anywhere but there. "Difference between you and the rest of the men in here is they aren't the law. Can't throw their weight around quite like you. Guess you thought because you didn't arrest my dad for all that shit, he owed you a favor. 'You scratch my back, I'll scratch yours.' Kind of worked out perfect for a while until somebody wised up, huh?"

Sweat was spreading around Coble's collar like a slow bleed-out.

"Go ahead and say what you got to say, Frank," I said. "All these Boars will probably believe whatever comes out of your mouth, but before you do, there's one thing you should know."

I looked over at Markham. This was his cue—we'd gone over this in detail, figuring out the best way to deliver a one-two punch.

"Remember when I called you late Tuesday night?" Markham asked Coble. "Told you how bad I hated living with this goddamn secret?"

"I don't know what you're talking about."

Markham, unflinching, delivered what our entire confrontation hinged on, a total lie. "I recorded the whole thing."

Seconds passed. A chair creaked somewhere in the room.

"You stinking coward," Coble said, his voice low, almost a growl. He scanned every face in attendance. "I've been in law enforcement for thirty-three years, ten of those as chief. I do whatever it takes to protect this town. To keep law and order. Every man in this room can vouch for that. Am I right, gentlemen?"

No one said anything. Even the mayor averted his eyes.

Coble glowered at Markham. "That Reyes boy was nothing but trouble, Lee. Would've been all over the news if they'd found out you'd put him in a coma, or worse. You know how the media is, how quick they are to throw law enforcement under the bus these days. Would've soiled the name of this whole town. Is that what you wanted?"

Markham didn't blink. "He was breathing when I left him," he said.

"He was *suffering*. Would've been a damn vegetable at best. And that's on you. *I did what you didn't have the fortitude to do.*"

"Don't act like you give a damn about my brother, you crooked-ass pig," Lucy said, still filming as tears flowed down her cheeks.

"Tell them what you did after Leland Miller started to put two and two together about that car you had him crush," Markham said.

Coble worked his jaw around.

"He shot him," I said. "Then he covered it up."

A voice from one of the seated Boars: *Oh my God.*

"I was closer to your father than you were, boy," Coble said. "Why in the world would I—"

"Kill him? I don't know, Frank. Why don't you tell us?"

He hesitated just long enough that something in my brain clicked, and the words came out as smoothly as if I'd rehearsed them for weeks. "I think it's because Dad was about to do what we're doing today. I think he figured out that wasn't just a car he buried that October night, and maybe he called you up. Like you did with Markham, you probably tried to smooth things over. Only Dad wasn't going to play your games anymore, so you decided to shoot your lifelong *friend* in the back of the head." I pushed back from the podium and looked at the man who had pulled the trigger on my father. "That pretty much sum things up?"

A snarky little laugh from Coble. If he had an inch of ground left to dig his heels in, I'm sure he would've. But he didn't. "You think this makes you some sort of hero? Ruining a town like you're about to do?" He waved his hand around the room. "Ruining a force that keeps one of the lowest crime levels in the state?"

"The force isn't ruined. *Just you.* Owning up to what happened to Marco Reyes from the get-go never even crossed your mind, did it?"

"And then what? Have the news make a big to-do about an off-duty White cop paralyzing a Mexican? Can you imagine the fallout from that?"

"That horseshit answer just summed up your entire career," I said. "And to answer your question: No, I'm not a hero, Frank. My dad sure as hell wasn't either."

"Your dad was a fine man," he said. "Just had poor judgment there at the end. I tried to show him the big picture, but he couldn't see it. He made his choice."

"He made the right choice. Doesn't mean he wasn't part of what's wrong with this town."

"You going to throw the whole town under the bus now?"

I shook my head. "There's some great people in this town." I thought of Lucy and her mom, Charlie, Mr. Fields at the Marathon station, the waitresses at Captain Tim's, even my tenants. "It's some of the people that run Flint Creek—some of the men in this very room—that keep it from being great. You're the only people around here that have a fucking say around here."

"A-fucking-men," Charlie said.

I went on: "There's no chance Mr. Segers here ever loses a mayoral race so long as he's in the good graces of the Boars Club. And who is it that appoints the Chief of Police?"

"The mayor," Lucy said. "I googled it."

I nodded. "Heaven forbid anybody that isn't in bed with y'all ever have any pull in this town or hold any sort of position." I looked at Chip Segers. "Is this the kind of 'brotherhood' you want to be part of?"

Surprisingly, the young man shook his head, his eyes on his dad.

"Such high and mighty words coming from a washed-up boxer who ain't even allowed in the ring anymore," Coble scoffed. "A man that managed to get arrested in front of Hope of God Baptist on his own daddy's wedding day."

"I own my mistakes, Frank. And God knows I'm my own special brand of fuck-up, but I'm nothing like you. I'm nothing like my grandpa or my dad. All that toxic, bellyaching bullshit that made them miserable pricks their whole lives . . . the idea that if someone doesn't look like you or talk, act, and vote like you, that makes them less of a person. That all dies with them. It dies with you too. I don't want any part of it."

Coble clapped slowly, sarcastically. "Congratulations, Mr. Miller. That was quite a speech. Are you done now?"

"Not yet, Frank." I looked over at Markham. "Did you send that message?"

Markham grinned with what pride he could muster, and nodded.

"Perfect," I said. "Mayor Segers, if you'd like to go ahead and relieve Mr. Coble here of his duties, my new friend, Detective Jeff Holden, will be here momentarily." I looked over at Lucy, who smiled at me through her tears. "I hope you got all that."

"Every word, Hudson," she said. "I got every word."

CHAPTER FORTY

I was 5–0 when I lost my first professional boxing match. It was the first time I'd ever been knocked out. I remember waking up near my opponent's corner, fluorescent gymnasium lights blinding my eyes, a referee standing over me waving his arms, saying, *"It's over. It's all over."*

It was one the loneliest feelings I'd ever experienced. I think that's the nature of a one-on-one sport like boxing. It wasn't my coach or sparring partners or the hundreds of people in the crowd that had to own that defeat. It was me. It was my fault. It was one fraction of a second of losing concentration, leaving my chin exposed, that put me on my back in the fourth round that night. All those years of training, conditioning my mind and body, only to come up short because of a single, perfectly placed uppercut.

But then something happened. Coach Rob came into the ring and sat me up, asked me if I was okay. He and my cornermen helped me up from the canvas when I said I was. They hugged me; they told me they were proud of me. Not two rows from the ring, my mom was standing with tears in her eyes, the look on her face assuring me that she was hurting too, but she was proud. Even people from the crowd stood and cheered as I made my way back to the locker room, bloody and bruised.

I wasn't alone at all that night, and I count myself lucky for that.

The same couldn't be said for Frank Coble after his arrest and conviction. His closest friends, his "brotherhood," weren't there to vouch for him any longer. Nobody was. The bullshit world he'd spent so long building was no match for his pride in the end. I can only hope that he felt a terrible loneliness when those cell doors clanged shut behind him for the first time, and I hope that feeling stays with him for the rest of his life.

Lee Markham suffered a lesser fate, and rightfully so. He was charged with assault inflicting serious bodily injury, and he didn't hesitate to plead guilty. The fact he'd helped us take down Coble surely earned him leniency in the judge's eyes. Markham will still have a life ahead of him when he gets out of prison, and if he's smart, he'll learn from his past mistakes, make something of his future.

Roger Segers ended up resigning as mayor. It's hard to say what he or some of the other guys in the Boars Club knew, what sort of things they may have concealed over the years in the name of a meaningless credo, but Detective Holden has been looking into it. He's a damn fine cop. It was him that eventually got a full written confession out of Coble. Really bolstered a case that had hinged mostly on Lucy's cell phone video to that point.

Like Lucy, Charlie, and myself, Tammy was at the trial every day. We spoke very little, but I sensed an unbearable guilt in her for not knowing the truth about my dad all along. Grief has already taken its toll on her. Guilt, if she carries it much longer, won't be any less merciful.

As big as solving that case was, it wasn't a knockout blow to the rotten underbelly of Flint Creek, but it was a hell of a start. A long fight looms for the tired and pissed-off souls who have the stomach for it—the ones wise to the reality that the worst people of all are often hiding in plain sight.

I know Lucy's up for the fight. Her voice is growing louder. Her videos have become a viral sensation worldwide. Today, she reminds me of her online fame when she walks into the shop.

"Three hundred thousand," she says, laying her phone on the counter.

"For real?"

"Three hundred thousand and *six* followers. Can you believe it?"

"Craziest thing I've ever seen," I tell her. "How many views is 'Crooked Cop Crumbles' up to?"

"Almost half a million."

"A sight more than 'Dumbass in Flannel Meets Pavement,'" Charlie says, entering the shop from the garage. "She got me set up on Instagram, didn't you, Ms. Lucy?"

Lucy beams.

"I still maintain that it was another dashingly handsome bouncer in that video," I tell them.

"Speaking of handsome." Charlie taps his phone. "Think I can meet me some women on here?"

Lucy brings a palm to her forehead. "I knew I'd regret this, Mr. Charlie."

She's become somewhat of a celeb. The story of Coble's arrest garnered attention from every major network. One reporter even tabbed Lucy "The Nancy Drew of Instagram," but Lucy reminded her that Nancy Drew wasn't Latina. She's still got that same fire that she had the first time I met her, and she's used her notoriety for good, raising awareness for missing person cases, cases of injustice. Anything that needs and deserves a voice.

"If you prima donnas are finished, we can close up," I say. "You got your gloves, Lucy?"

"In my backpack," she says. "Are you going to teach me that left hook today?"

"That depends," I tell her. "Still dropping your left when you throw that right cross?"

A shrug. "Guess you'll find out, huh?"

I laugh and follow her out beside the shop where Charlie and I cleared a space. We've been selling the vehicles for scrap, little by little, since late February. I think I'll put the place up for sale soon. This yard has a history to it, one I'm ready to leave behind. Figure I might hang on to the rental properties though, stick around Flint Creek a while longer and do something positive with whatever money I can pull together. Help Lucy get a nice headstone for her brother's grave, maybe send my mom a nice big check for all she's done for me over the years. And maybe, if things go well, I can open up a little gym of my own somewhere close by. Somewhere with kids that need it, like I did. That's the plan, anyways. Already have one client for sure. Even have a solid maintenance man lined up, so long as he understands pounding Keystone at a boxing gym is frowned upon.

Sometimes, I like to think that Dad's intentions were self-less when he wrote out his will. That some part of him, a part I'd rarely seen while he was alive, wanted to do one kind and final gesture for a son he hardly knew. The night before he died, he must've known the decision he was about to make. He must've sensed that his time was short. I think that's why he called me. I doubt it was to tell me he was sorry and that he loved me, whether he felt that way or not. I'll never know any of those things for sure, but it's something I've made peace with.

"You ready, champ?" I ask Lucy once she's wrapped her hands nice and tight. Around the wrists and hands, through the fingers like I taught her.

"Almost." She scrounges in her backpack until she pulls out her boxing gloves. A present Charlie and I got her in March on what would have been her brother's twenty-third birthday. That day was tough for Lucy, but she loved our gift. Of course, we got permission from her mom before we bought them.

Lucy slides on one glove, tightly straps the Velcro. I help her secure the other. The cuff of the glove has "Mo" written in silver Sharpie.

"Remember what I told you Tuesday?"

"About turning my punches over?"

"That was last week."

Her mind briefly searches. "About my feet?"

"Bingo," I say. "You're only as strong as your base. Got it?"

"I think so."

"You better know so."

She nods and lowers herself into a stance, holds her hands next to her face.

Charlie lets Buster off his leash, then cracks a beer and sits on the hood of the last Pontiac in the lot. "Give him the business, Ms. Lucy!"

"I'm ready, Coach," she says.

I slip on one focus mitt, then another. "Ready for what?"

"I'm ready for anything," she says as I brace myself.

She steps and fires a one-two. She keeps her chin down, her eyes up.

ACKNOWLEDGMENTS

Many thanks to the team at Crooked Lane Books for making my dream of becoming an author a reality. Matt Martz, an email you sent years ago made me believe my next book would be "the one." Ben Leroy, thanks for the vision and the chance. To my editor, Sara Henry, thanks for making my words sparkle and shine (and for your love of salvage yards). Melissa, Madeline, and Rebecca, you have made this process so enjoyable; I appreciate the work you put in daily. Thank you Nicole Lecht for such a badass cover.

To my agents, Ellen Levine and Martha Wydysh. Ellen, thank you for believing from the get-go. Martha, your vision for this novel challenged me and kicked my ass into shape. Thank you, Judi Farkas, for your appreciation of these characters and their big screen potential.

Thank you to my MFA folks. Dave Moloney, the Cape Cods and encouragement have been wicked awesome. John Vercher, mmm-hmm, I reckon you and Russell's Reserve have talked me off the writing ledge more than anyone. Mark, Nadia, Garrett, Lauren, Ted, and Laura: your friendships have meant so much.

Thanks to Wiley Cash, Katie Towler, and Ben Nugent. Wiley, you never let me by with mediocrity. The tough love changed everything for me. Katie, your grace and wisdom were such an inspiration. Ben, you taught me to truly appreciate the beauty of a sentence. To my other MFA instructors: thanks for shaping me as a writer.

Deskimo Brothers, I'm forever indebted to you. Eryk, Russ, Phil, John, and Grant, I truly value your input and friendship. To the other authors who have so graciously supported me, thank you so much.

Thanks to my local bookstores, Sunrise Books and Scuppernong Books. Keep doing the great work you do.

Thanks to my friends who have shown love and support. To my "boys" (you know who you are): our group texts alone could churn out another ten novels.

Thanks to my fellow teachers. You're fighting the greatest fight of all. To my students: No, you can't read this novel in class.

I'm grateful to all of my family. Mom and Dad, your support of your "dreamer" son has been constant since day one. Garett, thanks for keeping my wit sharp all these years, and for always being a rad brother. Debbie, your optimism hasn't gone unnoticed. Tim, thanks for the insight.

Tiffany, I promised to never let you read my words until they were good enough for the world to see. Nothing was going to stop me from reaching that goal. Thank you for the love, toleration, and always standing behind me. You're the best.

To Ruby and June, my beautiful children. You're my world. Everything is for you two.